'The Tale of the Urban Misfits'
Series

Out of Order
Book 1

II

'The Tale of the Urban Misfits'
Series

Out of Order
Book 1

Meita Kasim

Arung Wacana

'The Tale of the Urban Misfits'
Series
Out of Order
Book 1

Meita Kasim

Editor by Dr Margie Ellery
Cover Design by Anggito Rahman
Foreword by Wendi Putranto
Layout by Dany Rachman

Typeset in Arung Wacana
Printed and bound by Arung Wacana, Yogyakarta
Address: Bangunharjo, Sewon, Bantul, Yogyakarta 55188, Indonesia

ISBN: 978-3-200-08723-1
E-BOOK: 978-3-200-08724-8

First published in Indonesia 2022

To Dr Jan Achyar Kasim
May God and Angels be always by your side.

VI

Foreword:

The Years of (Female)
Living Dangerously

By Wendi Putranto
(Former Managing Editor of Rolling Stone, Indonesia)

For the young generation, either from Indonesia or the rest of the world that glorifies the lifestyle of the Nineties generation without ever experiencing it firsthand, then the fastest, most comfortable, and, of course, the safest way is to read through this 300-page novel through puberty.

Why is it safest? Simple. Outside the media spotlight, the decade of the Nineties in Indonesia was very dangerous, chaotic, and the deadliest. There are many of the most terrible life threats to being a young Jakartan, all of which boil down to that era. Maybe, you escaped the Metallica phenomenal concert riot at Lebak Bulus Stadium (1993), but most likely did not survive the July 14th, 1996 civil riots and the kidnapping of pro-democracy activists by second president Soeharto's soldiers or the SARA (ethnicity, religion, race, and between groups) riots of May 13th, 1998. If those weren't deadly enough, an overdose of crack cocaine or amphetamines would successfully end your life, just as it had taken the lives of many friends in my immediate environment at that time.

In short, the decade of the Nineties—to quote the first president Bung Karno in 1964—was Vivere Pericoloso, the years of grazing with danger. For women, the dangerous living level in the so-called New Order era multiplied to ten.

Imagine a life without the World Wide Web, let alone social media, with the mass traditional media controlled by the authorities.

VII

In an era where the patriarchal society rules, no justice for the ethnic minorities and the poor, the military penetrated various aspects of social life (down to remote villages), no gender justice, no Komnas Perempuan (women foundations and organisations), at least until post-reform in the year 2000.

Only a few women were sitting in the ruling ministry cabinet. For the women's affairs, a chosen lady minister whose roles were merely a cosmetic of the misogynistic system.

Sigi, the central female character of this novel, lives in that era. Born to an upper-middle-class Minangkabau family living in an elite area of Jakarta and always prioritising education, Sigi grew up against the noble ideals of her parents. She began to rebel against the family and often isolated herself with her friends by attending various underground music circuits of the capital as Pid Pub and Blackhole.

Her love for underground rock music from abroad led her to form Wanderlust, an all-girl band, which was rarely seen or heard of at the time. Sigi's adventures in the underground arena develop into a more complex and complicated one with typical teenage puberty problems.

Who still remembers metropolitan nihilist-fatalist characters like Andre, Aksan, Lina, Maya, Sofi in Kuldesak, an Indonesian film released 23 years ago? This film that broke the norm--and remains relevant today--quite vividly captures the spirit of the Nineties in the Capital City on the big screen. A novel version finally arrives.

Meita Kasim, an Indonesian author, released her debut novel, Out of Order. It is the first book of The Tale of the Urban Misfits series, which was highly anticipated.

"Here we are now; entertain us."
(Kurt Donald Cobain)

Acknowledgements

I am forever thankful for the love and support from my family and friends, who gave me the courage to begin this path as a writer. Without them, I would have never written this novel.

I would also like to thank a beautiful man, my dear friend Lloyd Hassencahl, who was guided into my life to tell this story; I will always be grateful to you.

My deepest gratitude goes to my Editor and colleague, Dr Margie Ellery, who'd been a tremendous help in organising my thoughts and converting the events of the past into a manuscript.

To everyone who believed in me and, without hesitation, pre-ordered the book, my deepest, everlasting gratitude to you all, especially to my generous boys; Graham Zink, Oliver Barg, Robert Marchio and Rudy Slow. My amazing girlfriends; Novita Loekmantoro, Indira Sahab-Zink, Carmen Chung, Dewi Nursanti, Maria Tsudon and Karen Ni Shea.

I want to give a special shout to my husband, Simon Karner, for all his love, support, and encouragement in understanding that this writing journey is essential to me.

And, to my daughter Sophia-Putri for her beautiful present and unconditional love.

I thank you all from the bottom of my heart.

Meita Kasim
October 2022

X

Contents

Overture
Part I

"Too Many Creeps"
Bush Tetras

April 1993

The area around the stadium was a swirling mass of metal fans from all over town that afternoon. And there were thousands of them coming in from the other islands. They came from places like Medan, Makassar, and Bali. They came in cars, buses, and trains; some even walked on foot for miles.

Outside the Lebak Bulus Sports Stadium in south Jakarta, journalist Iwan Sentosa watched intently. He was a thin, wiry man in his forties, with long black and silver hair that fell loosely around his shoulders. His media card hung on his chest, and his Nikon camera was aimed and ready.

Iwan smiled a little. He had never dared to dream that this day would come. He knew the situation of these fans in the crowd, living in a struggling third-world country that operated under Islamic rules and a hardline authoritarian leadership-not so accessible for world-class acts. And yet, there they all were, waiting in lines outside, in readiness for the Metallica concert.

As he took a few photos of the young guys streaming in, he contemplated further. Metallica, the thrash metal band from California, had put Indonesia on its Nowhere Else to Roam world tour-two concerts in Jakarta, followed by a third in Surabaya. Following the success of Sepultura, the Brazilian thrash metal band that had toured the previous year, the future of international rock concerts in Jakarta looked bright and promising.

Iwan took a few more shots, close-up and intimate. Most of the faces were excited and filled with energy, but there were anxious

1

faces as well. He couldn't help but wonder what might be the cause. Within a few seconds, he knew.

The cheapest ticket was 30.000 rupiah, the cost of a month's living for many in the crowd. Yet these guys were there, and they were Indonesians who couldn't afford to buy a ticket. The thought made Iwan nervous.

***

Kurniawan Budi, the legendary promoter of ROAR Productions, was sweating. He was inside the stadium, standing on the side of the giant stage. He held a walkie-talkie as he liaised with his production team, listening to reports from all over the premises. Outside several groups of brazen teenagers were clashing as they approached the stadium.

He considered it shouldn't be a problem because he had paid an enormous sum for professional security to manage the event. The police and his youth guardians were also on patrol. That last thought calmed him down.

Metallica would not arrive in the usual manner, an idea from one of his men. Shortly, a V.I.P. bus with dark tinted windows would come in with a police escort. Indeed, fans would pay attention to the bus instead of the ambulance following it, ensuring a stealthy entrance for Metallica into the venue.

Kurniawan turned his attention back to the stage. On an elevated circular platform, back and centre, sat Lars Ulrich's drum kit. The main stage was twenty-one metres wide and thirteen metres deep, with two nineteen-metre catwalks that reached out on both sides into the audience so that the band could interact with the fans. He couldn't wait to see Metallica's stage blocking. The way the band used the stage space was considered legendary.

He thought about his decision to hire Vortex as the opening act. It was a risky choice. The band hadn't been signed to a major label, and they played their brand of thrash metal faster and more complex than what these fans were used to. They had jammed with Sepultura at his home the year before when he had brought the

Brazilian band to Jakarta. He liked Vortex. In his opinion, they were brutal enough for this significant event.

He looked around the stage and admired the work of his team. 400.000 watts of lighting were perfectly placed, and the 200.000 watts sound system would shake this stadium to the core.

If only he could have got his hands on Senayan Stadium, the most famous sports stadium in the centre of Jakarta. It had double the capacity of Lebak Bulus. However, the Asia-Africa International Conference was scheduled, so there was no mess around that. Senayan would have to wait for future concerts.

He gave himself a pat on the back. This massive event was a long-held dream. A proper amount of his blood, sweat, and tears had been invested in lobbying the government and raising the big money needed to fund this brave venture. It seemed like a victory, but maybe that thought was premature. He felt the blood, sweat, and tears were about to get real.

***

A few young guys were sitting on the terrace outside a home in Setia Budi in south Jakarta. Others were milling around inside. There were about a dozen at first, and then, as the day wore on, more and more turned up. Like many teenagers in the city that day, they were there for just one reason. They were getting ready to go to the Metallica concert.

Most were in their late teens, and they didn't look like metal fans. They wore ripped t-shirts, leather jackets, and army boots with silver spikes and chains. Their hair was styled in colourful mohawks, their faces and bodies full of piercings. The sound of "Sick Boy" from the band GBH was on full blast. They were busy preparing their look and joking around.

'Nice,' said one, spraying his hair as he stood in front of the mirror. 'We've got five tickets. We can make about 150.000 rupiah with these.'

'You're too ambitious,' said the boy on the sofa. 'They're all poor. No one is going to buy them. Metallica sucks! I'd rather play football, Satria.'

'Come on, Aqila, we can play after we sell the tickets,' said Satria, the punk with the hairspray. He grabbed his backpack and threw it deftly at the guy on the sofa. 'Put the ball in this.'

'We're going to play there?'

'It's a sports stadium, isn't it?'

Aqila rolled his eyes as he crammed the ball into the bag.

'Let's go,' Galih decided. He was one of their unofficial leaders. 'We're taking the two cars, and the rest of you are on the bus. We'll meet in front of the stadium in about an hour. Everyone ready?'

With that, they left the house, about fifty of them dressed with an attitude.

***

The stadium finally opened the four gates, and a steady rush of the ten thousand strong crowds began filing in. Danu and I hurriedly ran to the front of the giant stage. But I wasn't happy. I was struggling to stop myself from sobbing. Tears were streaming down my face as my boyfriend Danu stood in front of me, wrapping his arms around me, hugging me.

'So they touched you,' he whispered as he wiped my face dry with the palm of his hand. 'So what, let it go. We made it, and we're here.'

'You don't understand,' I said, still weeping. 'Hands were coming from everywhere, touching my … you know, in between my legs. Thank goodness I'm wearing jeans. And my breasts too, so rough they hurt.'

'I know. I saw it.'

'And you did nothing,' I said accusingly. 'I yelled and struggled, and nobody did anything, including you. Thank god for that security guard.'

He tightened his hug, and, for a while, we stood there in silence as my tears continued.

We had been waiting in line for a few hours, so we could get in early and score a spot close to the stage. I was dressed in all black; black sneakers, black jeans, a black t-shirt, and an oversized sweater.

4

My hair was tucked up under a large cap. I supposed I failed; I still looked like a girl despite my best efforts to look like a boy.

'Do your parents know you're here?'

'No, Danu.' I broke away from his hug. 'They would never let me come if they knew, you know that.'

'And yet you're here,' he sighed. 'I'd tell you the same thing, but I know you. You won't listen to me either. I knew you'd get into trouble. This concert is no place for a high school girl like you.'

'I'm eighteen, not a baby, and I see a lot of boys my age and even younger. So you're saying those guys should be allowed to do want they want to me because I'm a girl?'

Danu didn't reply.

'I want to be here as much as these guys. It's not fair.'

Danu didn't answer that either. I turned back to face the stage.

'Oh, come on, Sigi, forget about it,' he whispered behind me as he put his arms around my waist. 'Look around. Here we are, the two of us with thousands of fans right in front of the stage. We're going to see Metallica! And Agam and Ray are playing. Vortex, I can't wait to see them too.'

I couldn't help but smile a little, although my body was still trembling.

'Do not leave my side!' I fiercely whispered back.

'I promise.'

I placed my arms over his as I swallowed my tears.

He was right. Nobody could stop us now.

***

Iwan Sentosa was outside the stadium, clicking away with his Nikon. Thousands of fans were still waiting to get in with only the four small gates between them and the anticipated excitement. The stadium had opened all its entrances, but those without tickets had become aggressive, booing and swearing at those who had them. They gave the middle finger to the police barricades without fear. That resulted in the closing of two entrances, leaving just the other two open. With or without tickets, the crowd struggled to gain access to the stadium.

Suddenly, a mini-bus rolled down the narrow street, guarded by a large police bike escort. Hearing the loud wail of the sirens, the crowd went ballistic. They saw guys with long hair sitting inside, dressed like rock stars. Iwan quickly aimed his camera at the scene, capturing the fans clamouring around the bus. The crowd soon realised that the passengers weren't Metallica. They were Vortex, the opening act from Indonesia. They gave the sides of the bus some friendly knocks as they cheered them on, and the vehicle moved forward into the stadium in peace.

Inside the bus, the Vortex boys, Agam, Ray, Farid, and Rizki, looked anxious as they gazed out the windows. It was a dream come true to open for Metallica. It was a privilege, yet at the same time, an intense pressure. Everyone who was anyone was going to be there: music executives, producers, musicians, local and international media, and thousands of metal fans from all over Indonesia.

The bus stopped in front of the backstage entrance, guarded by security. A few policemen checked around and inside. Satisfied, they opened the gate to let the vehicle through.

One by one, the Vortex boys got off the bus, followed by their roadies. Their faces were serious as Kurniawan Budi, and his crew led them into their air-conditioned V.I.P. tent.

***

The sun gradually disappeared over the smoggy horizon of Jakarta while concertgoers continued to pass through the gates and into the stadium. The show would start soon enough, but thousands of fans with tickets were still waiting in lengthy queues. With each passing minute, they were losing patience. Security searches were rigorous, and there wasn't enough staff to accommodate them.

'They're way too slow,' complained a young guy. 'I don't know if we'll get in on time. It's starting in ten minutes.'

'This is insane,' said another impatiently. 'I've been here for hours.'

'Hey, look!' said a third, pointing. 'Who are they?'

A group of teenagers dressed in a manner the metal boys had never seen before walked towards the crowd. The fans stared.

'They're punks, a new thing. I've seen a few of them, but never that many.'

One took a ball out of his backpack and kicked it to the others. All of a sudden, a game of football was on. The metal teenagers began to laugh and cheer as they watched the colourful crew passing and kicking the ball around right in front of the barricade.

***

'Alright guys, let's pray together,' said Kurniawan Budi as he looked into the eyes of those standing around him in a large circle.

The Vortex boys and their team, lighting and sound experts, stage workers, management crews, and the MC joined hands as Kurniawan began reciting an Islamic prayer. In Indonesia, it was customary to pray before an event, especially at one as big as this. He broke the circle with a cheer, and off they went in their respective directions, ready to blast that stadium.

The MC, Mi'ing, was a comedian from the famous trio Bagito. The crowd cheered as he grabbed a microphone, '*Salam metaaal*[1]!'

The fans roared the words back, pointing their three fingers in the air.

He joked and teased, making the crowd laugh. Finally, he took a deep breath. 'Are you ready for Metallica?' he yelled.

The audience thundered back in their collective excitement.

'I know you are, but first, we're going to get warmed up with Indonesia's best metal band. Our very own Vortex is opening tonight for Metallica! Let's show them our support!'

The crowd cheered in anticipation.

'Alright! Stay pumped, *salam metal semuanya*[2]!'

As Mi'ing walked off, the Vortex roadies raced onstage, plugging in cables and quickly running through their final checks. Rizki,

---

[1] *Salam Metal* loosely translates as 'Hail metal fans!'
[2] *Salam Metal Semuanya* loosely translates as 'Welcome to all you metal fans here tonight!'

the drummer, came on first. His kit is located in front of Metallica's drums. Next, Farid, the bassist, came into view with Agam, the lead guitarist. Dressed in black, they looked brutal and determined. All eyes were on Agam, standing behind the mic, ready with his guitar.

'Woiiii!'

His voice echoed across the stadium. Danu and I were breathless at the sight of him. The crowd screamed.

Their first song began with a crushing speed and energy like nothing anyone had seen or heard. The guttural screams of the man behind the mic mesmerised the audience with their opening number.

A few minutes later, the thunderous roar from the crowd escalated as Ray, the frontman and our friend took his place in the middle of the stage. He was tall and of mixed race, with fair skin and long black curly hair. His all-white outfit contrasted with the rest of the band. He took his mic and started to growl fiercely. The pounding sound of Vortex inside that stadium was hair-raising.

***

Overture
Part II

"Bombtrack"
Rage Against the Machine

Outside something else was stirring. Fans with tickets were furious and frustrated, and they shouted to the people in front to hurry up. Fans without tickets had begun joining hands and shouting obscenities as they pushed towards the long winding queues.

The punks were unfazed by the deafening music. They were still playing football. A few were moving around talking to people. Tickets in hand, they were trying to sell them.

Suddenly, wailing sirens could be heard coming down the road. The waiting crowd went crazy. Another sleek bus escorted by police officers on big bikes was moving slowly towards the stadium.

'Metallica, they're here!' A voice was screaming, followed by hysterical shouting that came from everywhere.

Fans were in a frenzy, banging against the tinted windows of the bus, desperately calling out the names of guys in the band.

As the crowd began shoving, the orderly lines broke in confusion and fell into disarray.

Tailing the bus was an ambulance, its siren blasting, but no one paid any attention. They were focused on the bus moving at a snail's pace amongst the crowd blocking its path. Amid the chaos, the ambulance overtook the bus and slipped unnoticed into the stadium. Kurniawan Budi's plan had worked.

***

Iwan was back inside, standing in front of the stage. Unfortunately for Vortex, the sound system wasn't working properly. It began glitching in the second song, and it didn't improve during their third. The crowd began booing, demanding they stop playing and leave the stage. My heart sank.

The sound engineers had the issue sorted before the opening of the fourth, but the damage was done. The audience resented the ongoing performance, and some even yelled *turun*, meaning 'get off the stage'. Nonetheless, Vortex kept going, and slowly, the crowd became silent as they watched the yet unsigned Indonesian band smash that stage.

With his head spinning, his long black hair swirling like a propeller following the crushing speed of the music, Ray's deep growls shook the entire stadium. Agam was brutal on guitar; his backup growls fierce. Farid, on Ray's right, was coolly playing bass. Behind them on drums, Rizki had taken off his shirt. He provided the high-speed, powerful beats with his double pedal.

The crowd merely tolerated them as they counted down the minutes until it was time for their idols, Metallica.

Iwan watched as Vortex finished its set of five songs. They bowed to the crowd, who gave them a rather average applause and left the stage. The lights dimmed, and heavy booming background music filled the dark silence.

Metallica's crew were preparing their gear. The audience eagerly watched as they, too, prepared themselves for the moment they had all been waiting for.

***

'Hey, I think Vortex is finished,' said Aqila loudly to the fans outside of the stadium.

He put his right hand up in the air to show the tickets, waving them around dramatically. 'You've got just one minute to buy these. Now down from 30.000 to 10.000 each. Five tickets! Who wants them?'

The crowd laughed.

'Hey dickhead, piss off!'

'Shove the tickets!'

'Alright then, if nobody wants them!'

The punk took a lighter out of his pocket. Theatrically, he slowly started to burn them.

As if on cue came a chilling sound, its majestic tone dominating the stadium, followed by the harmonies of an orchestra, playing the theme from the old 70s film *The Good, The Bad, and The Ugly*. It was the signature tune Metallica used to open all their concerts. The crowd inside the stadium roared and cheered.

Outside, a voice came screaming out of nowhere.

'Fire!'

'Burn, burn everything!' urged another from deep in the crowd.

Aqila panicked. He dropped the tickets to the ground and stomped on them, putting out the flicker of flames.

'Come on!' said Satria, and the two raced back to where the rest of the punks were gathered. They had stopped playing football and were looking at the crowd in awe as a wave of metal fans began thrusting in total confusion towards the barricaded gates. Bedlam was emerging against the backdrop of Metallica's opening tune. 'Boys,' he said with a worried look, 'Prepare yourselves for chaos.'

***

As the spine-tingling sounds of the orchestra resonated through the dark, the stage burst into view, brighter than daylight. Inside, the metal fans went mad as their idols began waving enthusiastically.

Iwan let out a deep sigh of admiration. James Hetfield, the buff vocalist and the rhythm guitarist, all two metres of him dressed in black, took centre stage in front of the mic, carrying his legendary black Kramer guitar. Jason Newsted, the handsome bassist, stood to Hetfield's right. He was tough with his bald head and goatee. Lead guitarist Kirk Hammett looked somewhat unassuming compared to the stature of the others with his slim frame and long dark hair that consisted of cute curls. Everyone knew that his melodic guitar was the soul of Metallica. Finally, Lars Ulrich, the Danish drummer, stood tall behind his large kit. He smiled and, without a word, raised his right hand in the air with a clenched fist. The crowd roared hysterically.

Metallica kickstarted the show with "Creeping Death". The fans instantly fell into a sea of movement, following the colossal beat. They sang, pushing, shoving, and headbanging in a collective mania.

Hetfield stood fixed in the middle stage while Hammett and Newsted ran down the wings, engaging with the crowd. 'Hello, Jakarta!' He pointed his finger to the masses, 'You're amazing. I believe you know the lyrics. Sing with me!' With that, they launched into "Welcome Home", followed by "Sad but True".

Abruptly, Iwan's instincts told him to retreat from the front of the stage and get out. The stadium's capacity was limited to twenty-five thousand, but it seemed to him that there were thousands more. Heading for the backstage gate, he quickened his pace.

Little did the audience know, but a raging fire had taken hold outside the stadium. Flames were visible from the VIP area, and the vantage point of the stage, high above the audience. The hearts of Metallica and their crew must have been racing. While the screams of sirens were heard closing in around the stadium, they kept playing.

***

Not wasting any time, the punks took off, scrambling to safety along the roofs of the cars that lined the verge. The fire was now vibrant red with thick black plumes of pungent, choking smoke. At the end of the street, they jumped down from the last vehicle and stopped to look back.

'Wow, they've started rioting!' Galih said breathlessly. 'They're burning cars, ransacking the mini-marts and the *warung*[3]. This is madness!'

'It's fucked up!' said Satria. 'And, it's going to escalate. Let's get out of here while we still can.'

---

[3] *Warung* are the street-side stalls that sell a range of goods from food and cigarettes to small household items.

'Meet you at the Pondok Indah roundabout,' said Galih as he and a few others disappeared in the darkness.

Satria took control and led the rest of the punks on the long trek towards Pondok Indah, about five kilometres north, away from the stadium and the raging crowd.

***

Despite seeing the fire, the four horsemen, the nickname fans had lovingly bestowed on the members of Metallica, continued to rock the stadium with their hits "Nothing Else Matters" and "Wherever I May Roam", for which Hetfield played a double-neck guitar.

Two giant screens on each side of the stage showed the band in close-ups, right down to the sweat that poured off them. Then came "Blackened", "Seek and Destroy", "Battery", and finally, the song that the fans were all waiting for, "Master of Puppets".

The stadium reverberated. It was thrilling! Danu and I held on to each other as we watched water bottles flying everywhere, landing on the head-banging crowd.

'I think there's a riot,' Danu hurriedly whispered in my ear.

'What?'

'Jump up,' he said as he bent down and signalled for me to climb onto his shoulders. He stood up and turned to face the entrance of the stadium.

My jaw dropped. Outside, beyond the low roof of the entrance building, vast luminous flames of red and yellow and billowing black smoke were rising into the night sky.

***

Onstage, Metallica kept their performance powerful and steady, showing the audience what the term 'world-class' meant. Their stamina was astonishing. They ran up and down that stage non-stop to keep their connection strong with the crowd. When they were performing the slow number "The Unforgiven", some fans

13

were in tears, holding each other, singing every line. Next came "And Justice for All". Hetfield and Hammett played their solos, leaning back-to-back, showcasing their guitar skills. It was a huge spectacle, and everyone was in awe.

At precisely 9:10pm, two hours after the concert had officially started, the organisers finally opened the stadium's four gates. It was in preparation for the audience to leave when the show ended. With that, thousands more fans came running into the stadium. They ran up to the second floor to the VIP seating, causing havoc among the guests who were used to the protection their money and status brought.

'Look at the gatecrashers,' exclaimed Danu.

The hair on the back of my neck stood on end as the freeloaders were shouting and hugging each other, celebrating their win. They were finally inside.

When Metallica finished their closing song, they disappeared off stage. Danu and I had been to a concert before, so we knew that there would be an encore, that Metallica would come back on stage and stun the audience with another song or two. But for those who crashed the concert, they assumed it was over, and they turned around and began pushing their way back towards the exits.

'This is our chance,' said Danu, 'Let's get out of here.'

He grabbed my hand and pulled me towards the gates. Halfway there, we were almost crushed when fans changed direction and began charging towards the stage again. Metallica were back on. Danu quickly drew me into his arms as a shield against the onslaught. Confusion reigned as the freeloaders pushed and elbowed their way through.

We had almost reached an exit when Metallica began to play "One", a slow melodic number.

The stadium was now well over capacity, all singing along with Hetfield. Lit cigarette lighters were raised high in the air. It was a spine-tingling moment.

'Thank you, Jakarta! Thank you for having us. Tonight has been amazing,' Hetfield shouted. 'This one is our last.'

As the crowd cheered, Hammett launched into the iconic intro to "Enter Sandman". It stopped me dead in my tracks. The sound of the solo guitar was so imposing that I wanted to run back to the stage.

'Come on, Sigi,' Danu insisted. 'We need to get out of here, now!'

I nodded heavily and followed him.

The crowd inside was going off, singing and headbanging on every beat. Hetfield was smiling from ear to ear. He let the crowd shout the whole song. He didn't sing a word, allowing his fans to express their love and adoration for the last time.

Then, they bowed. The concert of the century was over.

***

Outside, the riot was clearly still on. Hordes were panicking amongst the burning cars and tyres that illuminated the area with fire and filled the road with choking black smoke.

'Oh my god,' I gasped, my eyes watering. 'How are we going to get out of here?'

A public phone booth erupted in flames. The consuming fire seemed to reach the sky. It was an unnerving centrepiece to what was already a disturbing sight.

A rain of stones and beer bottles began pelting down. Teenagers behind me were screaming as the random projectiles hit them.

'Watch out!' yelled Danu as a beer bottle flew past and crashed as it hit the front of a car. 'Come with me!' He grabbed my hand, leading the way as we ducked and weaved through the nightmarish scene.

An electricity pole near the entrance had caught fire from the burning cars. causing widespread fear, and fans were desperately trying to move further away from the gates.

'Come on,' urged Danu. 'We have to get to the end of the street now!' He cut a path, aggressively jostling people out the way. We stopped for a brief moment at the edge of a small side street while we tried to comprehend what was happening further behind us.

The wires burst into rapid fireworks, ending with an enormous flash that lit up the neighbourhood, coupled with a *boom*! A loud explosion rocketed around the front of the stadium. The ensuing blackout was stifling.

'What are we going to go now?' I shrieked in horror.

'Dirga's house,' he shouted back. 'It's around the next corner. This way, Sigi, now, don't look back.'

The smoke-filled haze cast an eerie moonlight mood as he led us through a series of shadowy alleyways and into an expansive housing complex. We ran, and we ran. After what seemed like a lifetime, we came to a small home tucked away in a cul-de-sac.

'We should be safe here,' he said as he pounded on the door.

An older lady with a worried expression peeked out into the darkness.

'Dirga, is that you?'

'No, *Tante*[4], it's Danu. Is Dirga here yet?'

'No, he's still at the concert. What happened? I heard sirens, and I could smell the smoke.'

Danu and I were shaken and scared, and I was trembling.

Her face fell in horror. '*Ya Allah*[5]! Come in, quickly.'

***

The chaos was escalating. It was like an urban warzone. The PMI, the Indonesian Red Cross, arrived in ambulances. They jumped into the riot zone to assist the bloodied and broken bodies of fans who were scattered on the street. There were too many victims for the resources of the Red Cross teams to handle. It was going to be a long night.

The concert may have been over, but the riot continued unabated until way past midnight. More cars and shops were burned to the ground, including a Suzuki showroom that suffered the most significant loss.

As the night turned into morning, most of the crowd had left the area on foot. Many were helping the injured, and they marched

---

[4]*Tante* is a polite form of address for a woman older than herself.
[5]*Ya Allah* loosely translates as 'Oh my god!' A phrase used in moments of surprise or distress.

slowly together, thousands of them in long lines moving towards the Blok M bus terminal ten kilometres to the north. It was the only place where public transport was still running.

Led by Satria, the punks kept up their pace, heading towards Pondok Indah. Out of nowhere, two cars approached one driven by Galih. A couple of punks who had been injured were placed in his car and driven away to safety. The rest crossed the main road and disappeared on foot into the night.

***

Reports of the casualties were all over the news. About forty thousand people had been at the concert, and over a hundred had been injured. Surprisingly, no one lost their lives that day. One multi-story building, fifty-three cars, twelve shops, and forty-five *warung* were razed by the fires. Eighty-eight people were thrown in jail.

The unexpected riot also caused a dramatic setback to Indonesia's concert scene. International acts from all genres were, from that night, banned for eighteen months.

***

Chapter One

"Been A Son"
Nirvana

June 1993

I stormed out of the house and onto the street, quickening my stride as I headed for the bus stop. A series of impatient honks blared from a truck idling in the heavy traffic. As the lights changed, smoke from its broken exhaust flooded the narrow artery leading north from Cipete. Behind it, the crowded bus that was heading to Blok M bus station, the hub of life in south Jakarta, screeched to a brief stop and I scrambled on.

Thirty minutes later at the terminal, I quickly jumped off and pushed my way onto the next, destined for central Jakarta. This time I was lucky to get a seat at the back by the window. My jaw was clenched as I stared aimlessly at the urban sprawl and the choked streets.

Life was pouring out of the skyscrapers in Sudirman Street, signifying that the workday was over. The madness of trying to get home in a city famous for some of the world's worst traffic had begun.

I sought to distract myself by people-watching as the old bus overflowed with office workers. A few high school girls were going home late, like me, still in uniform. I smiled cynically, knowing they'd tell their parents they had been with a trusted friend when they had actually been with their boyfriend. The very thought of it made me shudder.

After a long hot forty minutes, the bus turned into my street.

***

In the living room, my parents were watching *MacGyver*, a television series from the west that they loved.

'Hi,' I called out.

'Hello,' came a dull preoccupied reply.

I was about to go upstairs to my room and jump in the shower when I decided against it. Instead, I walked into my parents' en-suite and began filling the tub with steaming water and liquid soap. Amidst the noise of the running tap and the indistinct sounds of the TV, the pent-up tears started to fall. I climbed in and hugged my knees against my chest, immersed in the caressing water.

The shouting of my mother cut into my sobs.

'Sigi! You have a phone call. It's Danu.'

'Tell him I'm in the bath.'

My eyes rolled from the sound of his name.

I just couldn't accept what had happened.

Still emotionally boiling. I got out of the bath and headed to my room. turned on the air-conditioning and pressed 'play' on the tape recorder.

The sound of an acoustic guitar helped to swallow the last of my tears and I got dressed in a plain white t-shirt and light blue shorts. The drums followed, breaking into "Paradise City".

I sat at my dressing table and my eyes locked onto the poster above it. There he was, staring back at me, Axl Rose, the vocalist of Guns N' Roses. He dominated the wall, standing half-naked, wearing just his tight, faded blue jeans. I admired his slender tattooed body and his perfectly long, straight blonde hair flowing down to his waist. An American flag bandana covered his forehead, his signature look.

In the mirror, my face looked damp, and my eyes were red and swollen. I realised that I was still wearing my contacts and proceeded to take them out.

I put on my glasses – minus three on the left and four on the right – and they covered my puffy eyes efficiently. I brushed my black hair that fell upon my shoulders while I stared at my skinny cheeks with their protruding cheekbones and the oversized lips that I hated.

I'm not pretty.

I was skin and bones, and my honey-coloured skin was too dark for my liking.

So much for lightening cream.

I wasn't tall enough either, and now, I had lost the one precious thing that I had held so dear.

Brushing off those thoughts, I leaned over and grabbed the acoustic guitar that was resting against the side of my dressing table. I strummed and listened. A few strings were loose and out of tune, so I tightened them. I focused on the music and followed it on the guitar.

Soon I was lost in the energy of the song as it transported me away from the reality of my life. The voice of my mother screaming at me again from downstairs faintly registered. I ignored it.

When the song entered the part where the distortion effects kicked in, I strapped my guitar around my shoulder and stood up to face the mirror. I began playing ferociously, following the chords. I swayed and headbanged, admiring myself. When I held my guitar, I felt like I could conquer the world.

Someone was pounding on my door. It was Bulan, my eldest sister.

'Dinner's ready!' she yelled as she walked off.

I knew I wouldn't be able to digest any food, but I would need a good reason if I didn't appear at the dining table.

I put the guitar on my bed and killed the tape.

***

Downstairs, Bulan was already seated, scooping steamed white rice onto her plate. My father pointed the remote control at the TV to turn it off before taking his seat. My mother sat next to Bulan as she shouted to Umi, the maid, to fetch the chicken soup from the stove. My second eldest sister Matari was nowhere in sight.

'Sigi, bring some water,' my mother barked.

I silently took a few glasses from the table and filled them from the icy-cold dispenser. The water quality in Jakarta was undrinkable, so most families bought water in large plastic gallon containers.

We lived in a big two-story house in an upper-middle-class neighbourhood. Yet, we were either out and about by ourselves or locked in our bedrooms alone and private other than dinnertime when my father insisted that we eat together as a family. I wouldn't have had a problem with that, except that I detested my mother. The less time I spent in her judgmental and bitter presence, the better.

But we all loved our father. So I endured these family dinners, struggling to engage him in small talk while my mother dominated the conversation with her loud and idiotic remarks. If he wasn't home, I would take my meals separately at different times and in other parts of the house.

After handing out the water, I took my seat.

'What's wrong with your eyes?' Bulan asked.

I wanted to dowse her with the glass I'd just placed on the table.

Bulan, the 'good girl' of the family, the solid one, was seemingly unfazed by my mother's cutting and critical verbal blows. She was always acting like she was the peacemaker. She wore a short bob and thick glasses on her smiley, angelic face.

'I got smoke in them on the way home,' I replied shortly, trying to concentrate on my soup. Thank god Matari wasn't there; she wouldn't have let me off so easily.

'Where have you been all afternoon?' my mother started.

'I went to Kenari's, and then we went to the studio to rehearse.'

I did go to both, although I failed to mention that I also went to my boyfriend's place.

'Hanging out, wasting your time without accomplishing any-thing,' she said with her usual derision.

I decided not to reply and pretended to be preoccupied with my bowl of soup.

'How is Wanderlust going?' asked Bulan.

'We're going ok,' I replied curtly. I wasn't interested in furthering any discussion about my band over dinner.

'Hedi's wedding is coming up,' said my mother suddenly. 'It's the last Saturday of next month, and you will be attending.'

'I don't know if I can!' I protested, thinking this wasn't what I had in mind when I wanted them to talk about something else.

'Wanderlust might be performing that Saturday at the Jakarta Fair if we pass the audition.'

'Hedi's your cousin, for god's sake! You can't miss the wedding. Even Matari promised to come, and you know how busy she is now that she's the Head of Public Relations for Hard Rock Café[6].'

I pouted at my mother. Matari was the epitome of success, and I was the failed product, the black sheep. I knew how Matari operated, and she would cancel at the last minute and get away with it. That was ok with my mother because Matari was well-known and making loads of money. She was allowed to do what she liked in this household.

'Where is she anyway?' Bulan asked my mother. 'Working?'

'Of course.' My mother bestowed upon us one of her proud smiles. 'You know how dedicated she is, and that's why she's so successful.'

'She is a hard worker, isn't she,' Bulan added. 'Sigi, you should ask Matari if your band can play there.'
Inside, I was dying. Bulan was so naïve to think that a band like mine would have even the slightest chance at scoring a gig at the Hard Rock Café. They only invited big names.

Real musicians!

I was feeling the pain.

'No Bulan,' I said firmly. 'I don't think our band is ready for that yet.'

'Why not?'

'Because it's not a proper band,' sneered my mother. 'You can only dream about it, so you need to quit this childish hobby of yours and concentrate on your studies.'

'Come on, Mama,' said Bulan softly. 'I'm sure she'll do well someday.'

'*Bah[7],*' she mocked. 'You've heard the music she plays in her room, loud and annoying, not something civilised people listen to.

---

[6]The Hard Rock Café was a new and exciting brand café during the 1990s. Public Relations as department had just begun to emerge in Jakarta, making Matari and the café pioneers.
[7]*Bah* is an Indonesian expression to signify disagreement or scorn.

None of them has ever taken music lessons either, so how can you expect them to do well?'

And whose fault is that?

I sank back into my chair. I had asked my father a few years ago if I could enrol in guitar lessons after he had given me his old steel-string. It hurt my fingers and it didn't stay in tune for long, but I love playing. That's when he bought me a new one, with nylon strings.

But, before we'd even had a chance to discuss lessons, my mother had put a stop to it, claiming it was a ridiculous idea. To waste a lot of money on a hobby was madness, she said, and that it was better to sign up for an extra-curricular academic course.

'You wouldn't let me study music,' I decided to speak my thoughts.

'I never said that,' she replied coldly. 'I said it's not right to spend so much money on something that's not going to get you anywhere. But feel free to pay for the classes yourself if you like.'

Now I wanted to throw my hot soup over her.

'Remember Sigi,' she said, ignoring my bitter expression. 'Hedi's wedding, and you will be attending.'

I nodded in resignation. Not because I agreed, though. I merely wanted the conversation to end.

'When is your radio show with Elang? My friends want to listen in,' Bulan changed the subject.

'PV radio,' my mother went on and on. 'You should apply at Youth Act radio where your sister used to broadcast. Much more famous.'

Not only was I in an underground band, but I was also a broadcaster for an underground radio station. In the eyes of my mother, however, nothing I did was ever good enough.

'We're on every Friday night from eight to ten,' I mumbled heavily.

Throughout the conversation, my father, the introvert, had said nothing. He was the quiet type and most of the time, he didn't want to get involved with the ladies' dramas. This time, he spoke.

'There's still a couple of young people in hospital,' he said. His voice was deep and concerned. 'From the riot at that rock concert.'

'That was two months ago,' my mother gasped.

I tried not to look bothered while I slowly ate my food.

'I don't understand,' Bulan joined in, 'Weren't most of them were just teenage fans?'

'Yes, the papers said so,' he said. 'It's was on TV too.'

Why was my father bringing this up? Did he know I was there? Maybe somebody saw me and told him?

He pressed on. 'I'm glad I have three daughters instead of boys in times like this. I hope you weren't *lari-larian*[8] at that concert.'

As he spoke those last words, his eyes fell on me. I looked down at my glass and drank my water.

The silence was interrupted by the sound of the doorbell, a sign that my father had an ill child waiting for him.

'That'll be my patient.' He stood up to leave the table.

After the hospital rounds during the day, my pediatric specialist father worked his private practice at home, offering appointments between 7-8pm. I used the occasion to quickly excuse myself and dashed back upstairs to my bedroom.

***

---

[8]*Lari-larian* is a well-known Jakartan saying that loosely translates as 'running around, usually on the streets and most likely up to no good.'

Chapter Two

"Sweet Dreams (Are Made of This)"
Eurythmics

I locked the door and popped REM's latest album into the tape recorder. The plaintive voice of Michael Stipe in "Everybody Hurts" filled the room as I lay on my bed and stared at the ceiling.

I smiled a little, thinking whether I should make a phone call. I knew I wasn't supposed to, but the urge was so intense. My heart was accelerating at the thought of talking to him again. I turned over to look at the bedside clock. It was after eight. He would have finished dinner too.

The sound of knocking jolted me back from my thoughts.

'*Mbak*[9] Sigi, there's a phone call.' It was Umi.

'Who is it?'

'Mirah.'

Dragging myself off the bed, I went downstairs. The sound of a loud action movie in the living room indicated where my parents were.

Good, it will cover my conversation.

'*Hai*[10] Sigi,' said Mirah brightly.

I took a seat by the landline. '*Hai*, what's up?'

'Do you remember Soraya? ' she said excitedly. 'We all went to SMP1[11] together.'

'No, don't think so.'

'She came with me a few months ago to EMI studio.'

EMI was the place in central Jakarta to rehearse and record, and

---

[9]*Mbak* is an Indonesian form of address for a woman of similar age or younger.

[10]*Hai* meaning 'hello' or 'hi.'

[11]Indonesian junior and senior high schools are numbered rather than named. For example, SMP1 refers to Junior High School no. 1. SMA1 refers to Senior High School no. 1.

27

it was always full of young musicians, especially those from the underground.

'Oh yeah, vaguely.' A faint memory appeared, a girl who looked like a boy.

'She's finally agreed to come and rehearse with us, maybe in a few weeks' time. If she's any good, she can replace me as the vocalist.'

'Do you have to stop singing?' I sighed. 'Wanderlust was your idea and-'

'No, Sigi, the idea came from the three of us, you, me, and Kenari. And I'm not leaving until the end of the year, you know that. I'll still be playing bass.'

'And then what?'

'I know, but you've got to keep going. Soraya's been singing with Galih's band and she plays bass too. We'll find new girls if she doesn't work out.'

I smiled at the mention of Galih from junior high. He was the son of my mother's friend, and we had known each other since we were little kids.

'I haven't seen him for ages. I didn't know he had a band,' I said.

'He isn't as famous as ours, though,' she said cheekily. 'Anyway, Mum is giving me a horrid stare. Hopefully, Raya[12] will show up. Ok, bye.'

'See ya.'

***

Mirah, Kenari, and I were in a taxi on our way to Pid Pub, the notorious metal hangout in south Jakarta. Dirga, Mirah's boyfriend and frontman, was Hell's Fury, one of Jakarta's top bands, and they were headlining, along with a few others. My stomach was in a knot, as we drew closer to the venue. These older musicians were always a bit intimidating.

---

[12]Indonesians shorten names by using the last syllables, unlike English which shortens names by using the sounds at the beginning. Here Raya is short for Soraya.

'Let's get out here,' said Mirah, and, without waiting for our response, she told the driver to pull over.

We split the fare, and walked the remaining fifty metres to the parking lot.

'I can hear the music,' I said eagerly.

'More importantly, how do I look? Do I look ok?' Mirah replied.

She was wearing a black Anthrax t-shirt with shorts, black stockings, and black boots. Her shoulder-length straight hair fell open with a cute bang, complete with dark make-up and nude-coloured lip gloss.

'You look awesome,' said Kenari as she looked Mirah up and down. 'How about me?'

Her bleached strawberry blonde hair was striking when she wore it down. She combined her Overkill t-shirt with a dark blue flannel shirt worn loose, tight blue jeans, and dark brown chunky boots. Her eye make-up was simple, but her lipstick was bright red. I gave her a whistle.

'You don't look so bad yourself, Sigi,' Kenari said with a grin.

I smiled as I glanced down at the tight black shirt combined with tight black jeans and black ankle boots that I had agonised over earlier at home. A black and white bandana hung from my back pocket; an accessory inspired by Axl Rose.

Our sense of fashion was the sole reason we needed to travel by taxi. Even so, the driver had given us a number of suspicious looks in the rearview mirror. I could only imagine the fuss we would have caused if we had taken the bus.

The sound of thrash metal screaming from inside the pub was brutal! A light breeze carried the sharp and instantly recognisable smell of alcohol and weed, as bottles of Jack Daniels and joints were doing the rounds in the carpark. A group of guys were standing about; others were sitting on car bonnets. I couldn't see any girls although I noticed one of the guys making out with who knows, a girlfriend, or perhaps a groupie, in a vehicle under the harsh glare of the street lights.

'Business as usual,' Kenari chuckled. 'Should we join them?'

Mirah and I gave her a worried look.

'I'm joking,' she laughed. 'Let's go inside and find a good spot near the stage.'

'My thoughts too,' I nodded. 'Let's go in.'

The tiny pub was about half-full, the other half was bursting with eye-tearing smoke and the aggressive sound of a metal band. Mirah looked for Dirga, who took her away with him backstage. Kenari and I peered through the dim haze to see who we could spot.

'There're a few guys from the Jakarta International School. Gosh, they're so cool. Ooo, a few celebrities too, think I saw Cornelia Agatha and Sophia Latjuba near the backstage door,' Kenari screamed in my ear above the music.

'I saw them too,' I screamed back.

'And Trison and Jaya Roxx over there, with Robby Razzle, and Yachya Suckerhead.'

'Is Danu or Agam here?'

'No, I can't see them. Look, over by the sound system, there's Honda, Ilham, Ali, and Ungky. Want to go say hello?'

'Hey, Sigi,' Ali greeted me first. 'How have you been?'

'I'm great,' I said with a smile. 'How about you?'

Ali was one of the cutest boys in the underground. He was a vocalist, and his band covered songs from Skid Row. Some said that Ali couldn't really sing but he did look a bit like Sebastian Bach, with his white skin, tall, slender body, and long straight hair.

'Better now that I've seen you,' he winked. 'Where's Danu?'

'Not here by the looks of it,' I said shortly.

Thank god!

'Don't worry.' Ali looked me up and down. 'If anything gets too heavy, I'll be around.'

'Thanks, Ali, I'll keep that in mind,' I laughed.

The place was suddenly packed, full of the long-haired guys dressed in black who had come in from the carpark. Kenari and I were lucky enough to find a good position with a few other girls standing on some tables that had been pushed against the wall. There we waited, anticipating the madness that was about to take hold. We stared transfixed as Dirga came onstage, followed by the rest of the band.

'*Salam metal!*[13] ' he screamed, strapping on his guitar, and the crowd roared with anticipation. 'The first song is from D.R.I. This is "Enemy Within".'

The room fell into a commotion with the crushing speed of the song. Watching the guys slamdancing in front of us was overwhelmingly exciting. The energy never ceased to thrill, but I was glad that Kenari and I were out of their way.

Hell's Fury did a few more covers before playing their original songs. The powerful beat was savage, and Dirga was charismatic and intense. The pub became steaming hot, and the smell of sweat, alcohol, and cigarettes permeated the air.

Their last song, a cover of A.M.Q.A.'s "Bowling Balls", together with Kreator's "Extreme Aggression" and Metallica's "Seek and Destroy", was one of Pid Pub's anthems.

The crowd went crazy, their massive energy exploded as the guys slammed and shouted. Emerging from the smoky blur, Mirah pulled Kenari and I down from the table. We fell into the crowd, screaming lyrics and head banging. I noticed Ali was behind me. When we bumped against each other; it made me blush.

***

I had just arrived home from school and was having lunch[14] in the kitchen when the phone rang. I picked up, and then I wished I hadn't. It was Danu.

'Sigi?'

'What is it?' I hissed.

'Can I come over?'

'No, I have to study.'

'What about during the week?'

'No. I have a rehearsal and the radio show.'

'I can pick you up at the station.'

'No thanks.'

---

[13] *Salam Metal* loosely translates as 'Hail metal fans!'

[14] Indonesian schools often have two sessions. Students attend either the morning until 12:30pm or start at 1pm until late afternoon. Students also attend on Saturday mornings.

'How about Saturday night? Can I come over?'

'No, you can't. We're performing, I told you that.'

'Come on, Sigi,' Danu cried. 'At least let me take you home from the gig.'

'It's too far, Danu. It's in east Jakarta. Please, just stop it!' I paused, trying to find the courage. 'I want to break up.' I might have sounded a bit timid, but I said it.

'What?' He sounded incredulous. 'No, Sigi, you're just angry.'

'I've made up my mind. I want to break up.'

'No, you can't do this. Breaking up with me? This isn't right, at least not over the phone, not like this!'

'I've made it clear, bye Danu.'

I hung up quickly. I needed to call someone else, anyone, to avoid Danu ringing me back. The thought of that someone, the one I'm not supposed to call, came to mind again.

'Hello, yes, who is this?'

'Hello this is Mirah, *Tante*[15]. Can I please speak to Agam?' His mother had picked up, so I naturally lied about my name.

'Just a moment,' she said flatly.

Like all of us, Agam used to cover songs from the west in his first band Flatlining. He soon quit, and formed a new band that was going to write their own music. That band was Vortex, and they were a significant breakthrough in Jakarta's underground. They had a lot of diehard fans, and their gigs always sold out.

After the epic concert in April when they had opened for Metallica, without a doubt Vortex had become the top metal band in Jakarta, and the concert had also brought them national attention in the mainstream media. I felt proud of my underground connections, knowing full well that its leading man would soon be talking to me.

About two and a half years ago, we had met at Pid Pub. His mate Danu, a guitarist from another metal band, told him that he had fallen for me, and Agam encouraged him to pursue me.

Unfortunately, thanks to being with Danu, I ended up seeing Agam way too often since they were close friends. Whenever we

---

[15]*Tante* is a polite address for a woman older than oneself.

hung out, there he was, shadowing us with a few other mates. Somehow our attraction to each other had grown.

Lately, Agam began calling. This secret had been going on for months, even before the Metallica concert. We never did anything more, though, never even kissed.

'Hello?' His deep voice with its thick Batak accent made me giggle. 'I can't forget that sexy laugh,' he said. 'How have you been?'

'Oh, just busy. How are you?'

'I'm great. I thought it was Mirah, Sigi,' I imagined him shaking his head as he said my name. 'You and Mirah, you're the same. You're the naughty girls.'

'Not as naughty as you, *Abang*[16],' I teased.

'You know me well.'

'Too well,' I cut in quickly. 'You weren't even nice to me the last time we met.'

'When?' He sounded indignant.

'A couple of weeks ago at Pid Pub, you don't remember?'

'Yeah, I remember. You weren't wearing a bra.'

No man had ever dared to speak to me like that. Forget the high school boys. Not even the college boys I knew talked to me like that for fear of receiving a punch in the face. Then again, he was the king of the underground. Exception granted.

'When you came outside, you started screaming Si-gi, Si-gi and Danu heard you.'

'Danu was there? Oh shit,' he sniggered.

'Don't worry, he was ok about it.'

'Yeah, he also knows me too well.'

'I'd think you'd have more than enough girls.'

'*Bah*! I just fuck them.'

I was ashamed of my absurd jealousy. Although he was officially with a pretty girl named Berlian, god bless her patience, Agam had never stopped playing around.

'Anyway, what's new in your life?' I decided to change the subject.

---

[16]*Abang* translates as 'brother' and is used to address a male older than oneself.

'We're submitting our visa applications to the embassy soon, and if that's approved, we're going to America early next year.'

My heart dropped. For as long as I had known him, he had always talked about how he would conquer the world. The time was coming for him to follow his dreams. I was happy for him yet I felt sad too, thinking that one day he'd be far out of reach.

'How long for?'

'For as long as the visa, about six months.'

'Good for you,' I chirped. 'I'm sure you'll get it.'

'Thanks. By the way, am I going to see you at Retna this weekend?'

I smiled at the mention of another popular metal hangout in south Jakarta. It consisted mainly of uni students and teenagers congregating in front of a closed chemist shop. The place transformed late at night into the place to be, complete with a lineup of street food sellers that made the area vibrant.

'No, I won't be there. We have a gig.'

'Wanderlust,' he teased. 'Should I come and watch you play?'

'I've got to go,' I decided.

'Oh, come on, so soon?'

'Yes, I've got homework to do,' I smiled. 'Bye bye *Abang*.'

He let out the sound of a big smooch. I giggled and hung up.

Although he might be rude and loud, he was the most fun person that I knew. I went up to my room with him lingering in my mind, feeling a bit guilty, but my spirits had lifted.

***

Chapter Three

"Bad Reputation"
Joan Jett

The rehearsal was booked for four that afternoon, and it was going to be another long ride in the peak-hour traffic, this time from the centre of the city down to south Jakarta. I remembered to bring my Walkman and I stared blankly out of the taxi, listening to "Devil Gate Drive" from the 70s. Suzie Quatro was another secret of mine. The music transported me into the past.

Two years earlier, Mirah, Kenari, and I had tagged along with Dirga and Danu to an underground metal event at a basketball stadium. The usual big names were going to perform, but only two were really going to rock the stage, Hell's Fury and Vortex. The place was packed with hundreds of fans, and the music was aggressive and fast. The entire building, as usual, smelt of cigarettes and sweat.

It was difficult to distinguish between the boys and the odd occasional girl in the audience. Everyone was thin with long flowing rock 'n' roll hair, and had a similar taste in fashion with tight jeans and band t-shirts, mostly in black.

We swam through the heaving mass and escaped backstage. The top musicians were already there. Beautiful girls surrounded them with admiration and adoration, hoping that they might have a chance to be their girlfriends. We all loved these guys too, and we wanted to hang around them. Yet, even though Mirah and I both had a boyfriend, the three of us were still lumped together with the other girls as 'groupies', and we hated that. Unlike those girls, we loved the music, knew the music, and breathed the music; we didn't sell ourselves cheap.

We hadn't been there long when a deafening roar came from inside the arena. The huge crowd was agitated, the noise even louder than the kind of welcome usually reserved for major bands.

'Come on, we need to see what's going on out there,' Mirah had shouted and she pushed us out of the backstage.

We climbed the staircase and headed for the balcony to gain a better view. The three of us, Mirah, Kenari, and I, we all gasped with excitement.

'Look, look,' I cried with delight. 'Can you believe it?'

What the audience was totally going mad for was the four girls on stage. Yes, girls!

That was something we had never seen before in Jakarta's metal underground. It was definitely a man's world, and yet, there they were onstage, plugging in their instruments.

The drummer was large and angry-looking with long straight hair. By contrast, the bassist, with a short bob, was dark, pretty, and petite. The guitarist was tall and fair, beautiful like an angel. A minute later, also carrying a guitar, came the vocalist. She looked ordinary compared to the rest of the band, but there was something about her. She seemed intense. The four were wearing almost identical oversized band t-shirts with tight black jeans, and sneakers.

The crowd started yelling and throwing things. Cigarette butts, underwear, some even spat.

'Get naked bitches!'

'Leave, leave and go home to mummy!'

'Hey sweetheart, wanna see my pierced dick?'

I was shocked. The girls hadn't even started playing, and they were being attacked. After a few minutes, the vocalist grabbed the microphone, signifying that they were ready. Without a word, the drummer clicked her sticks three times, and together they opened with an intro to a thrash metal number from Kreator.

Then the magic happened. The screaming of degrading comments was silenced by the brutal music. The audience began to move as one in this giant, moshing, headbanging sea of black. They had fallen into a collective trance.

That day, Lavatory, this all-girl band, broke the boundaries in metal music. Four courageous chicks had kicked down the door of Jakarta's ruthless, male-dominated underground for women, and their captivating premiere performance made them famous.

Totally inspired by the courage of these girls, we decided to form an all-girl band ourselves.

Our boyfriends were opposed to this. They didn't want their nice sweet girls, who always listened to them and treated them like superstars, to upstage them. Good girls don't rock and roll; that was the popular sentiment. Yet, we moved forward with our plan regardless, even as we faced hostile put-downs and callous threats that we'd be dumped.

Because of our boyfriends, we knew what it took to get into the music scene. Underground bands started in awful run-down pubs, bars, and discos. Newcomers were never given a chance to play a complete set, let alone play for the entire night. They had to pay their dues by performing in small gigs where there could be anywhere from five to twenty bands playing, depending on the scale of the event.

Every new band was given an extremely limited timeslot to impress the crowd, and there might have even been an audition to prove to the organisers that they were worthy of that precious ten to fifteen minutes onstage. The newer the band, the earlier they played. The famous metal bands were always given the peak times towards the end of the event.

Once a band was known at these small stages, invitations would start to come from the Pensi. These were the high school events, a prestigious musical calendar that showcased up-and-coming bands across Indonesia, mainly underground bands, and the occasional major mainstream name as a guest star. We knew that we'd be on everyone's radar if we managed to perform on this circuit.

When we gathered later at my place to materialise our dream, I was introduced to Grace, a kind and charismatic classmate of Mirah and Kenari. She was pretty but unassuming in her casual t-shirt and jeans. With her long hair tied in a ponytail, she seemed stable and sensible.

I chose rhythm guitar because it seemed to be the easiest. Mirah wanted to play bass. Kenari was nominated as lead, and despite her protests, she finally complied. Nobody wanted to play the drums. After a lengthy discussion, Grace bravely became our drummer. That her younger brother had his own drum kit at home helped with her decision.

In our first line-up, we recruited Kamila, another senior student, as our vocalist. She was scrawny but pretty, with fair skin, long brown hair, and a fierce attitude. She was known as a rebel; she was always smoking and drinking, something taboo for a girl.

A fact we definitely exploited was that new bands were only given the time to play three songs. And so we gave ourselves three months to learn the three we'd settled on: "Anarchy in the U.K." and "God Save the Queen" by the Sex Pistols, and one from The Clash, "Should I Stay or Should I Go". We decided on punk, but not because it was our favourite genre. Punk was the easiest to play and we simply didn't have the skill to play complicated metal riffs and rhythms of Sepultura, Kreator, or Anthrax.

***

We owed a further debt of gratitude to Lavatory for one of our earliest gigs. We had been rehearsing for a while in the hopes of expanding our barely-there song list. By then, Kamila had left the band, so Mirah had become our vocalist as well as our bassist. She had also taken over as the unofficial leader of Wanderlust.

'Sigi, guess what? A friend is organising an event in east Jakarta. Lavatory were booked, but they've had a better offer to play in south Jakarta,' she told me. 'Wanderlust has been asked to take their place but it doesn't feel right. I don't think we should accept a gig they've rejected.'

'Beggars can't be choosers. We've had almost zero experience onstage. We need to take it.'

'I'm not so sure. It's going to be packed with guys who love 80s rock like Bon Jovi and Van Halen. And, it's in east Jakarta. That's not a great gig. We all know those guys don't have the look or sound,' she moaned. 'They aren't into punk; they aren't even into metal.'

'We still think we should take it,' I held firm.

When we arrived backstage that day, Mirah's fears intensified and her face was full of apprehension. 'I doubt they've even heard of punk.'

That triggered my anxiety.

'Don't be nervous, Sigi, although I am too,' said Kenari as she rubbed my shoulders. 'I keep telling myself this is going to be ok because no one we know is here. It won't matter if we make mistakes.'

'True, but I still hope we don't make any.' I exhaled and a cloud of smoke lingered around us.

'Oh, we won't,' said Grace, annoyed as she waved the smoke out of her face. 'We've rehearsed the songs, we've got this.'

The crowd started shouting insults as soon as we walked onstage. It had been a good decision just to wear casual t-shirts, jeans, and sneakers. No sound check was offered-they put us straight onto that battlefield. It was a pain trying to think amongst the horrid catcalling and derogatory comments and it took almost ten minutes to finish our checks.

Mirah's face was cool as she approached the microphone with her big white bass strapped over her shoulder.

'Hello, we're Wanderlust.'

The crowd pushed forward in front of the stage, demanding we leave. For a few seconds, Mirah appeared untouched, as if the aggressive reaction of these guys didn't bother her.

Then, perhaps she took her inspiration from the lyrics, she screamed back in response, 'Our first song is from Misfits. This is "Die, Die My Darling".

The ugly noise of the crowd was drowned out by the pounding raucous sounds of the music. Grace played the drums much more powerfully onstage than she did in rehearsals. Maybe she gave her all, knowing she only had three songs to get through instead of constantly banging away for two hours.

Kenari made a few mistakes. I could see that she was struggling, her face pale and her hands shaking. My fingers also slipped and so did Mirah's. The three of us didn't dare to take our eyes of our gui-tars for the entirety of that first song. Thank goodness for Grace. She was so solid we were saved by her confidence. Her energy was contagious and by the second song, we were somewhat at ease, and by the last, we were perfect.

The support of the crowd was shocking. When I finally dared to raise my eyes, I saw a few of them dancing. I was so proud of Wanderlust – we had risen to the challenge!

We began receiving offers to play in bigger shows in east Ja-karta and slowly we started to creep into events in the mecca of music-south Jakarta. We felt the joy of being onstage, performing, entertaining, and playing music that we knew most of our audience had never heard before.

The most intense excitement, a euphoria, came whenever we found flyers and posters of a gig with our name printed along with other bands. I diligently collected them all.

And, our boyfriends didn't break up with us either, although they refused to come and watch us play.

***

The taxi pulled up along the kerb in front of an impressive white colonial-style mansion, forcing me out of my reverie with a quick jolt into the present. The grand house was built in the Dutch era and it had been modernised by its current Indonesian owner. A leafy canopy provided by the mature mango trees shaded the back garden and the studio. Walking down the side of the house, I heard the faint strains of music.

I entered a large living area stocked with a couple of plastic chairs and a small table with a jug of water and a few cups. In front of the soundproof door at the other end lay two pairs of colourful All-Stars Converse sneakers. I recognised the shoes. Mirah and Ke-nari were inside.

I took off my sneakers and opened the door, to be slapped by the cool air-conditioning and heavy sounds.

Mirah gave me a big smile. 'You're here.' She turned to fix the strap on her white bass.

'Am I late?' I smiled back.

'Don't worry. Grace isn't here yet, and neither is Soraya.'

'Nice, so she is coming. That's great.'

'Sigi, grab the guitar and let's get into it,' added Kenari.

She had her black guitar strapped on and plugged into the effects board on the floor. She was trying out the mobile distortion effect. The sound wasn't what she wanted, so she squatted down and began adjusting it.

I grabbed a red guitar from the stand in the corner. I plugged it in and tested the volume. The strings were slack; it needed tuning.

'Did you book the session through Dirga?' I asked Mirah.

Her eyes lit up at the mention of her boyfriend.

Being an avid fan of metal, Mirah had been to a lot of gigs with him as they followed their favourite underground metal bands around Jakarta. The jealous girls at school used to put her down by calling her a groupie, but her popularity soon soared after becoming the frontwoman for Wanderlust.

I had great respect for Mirah; she was an outcast, like me. Only a more sophisticated one. I looked like a wild cat compared to her.

I knew her from junior high school, although we weren't close back then. We became friends once we were in senior high, despite being at different schools, when I would often bump into her and Kenari at underground events.

'Dirga is in Bandung, so I booked the studio through Mickey,' she said. He was Hell's Fury's lead guitarist.

The door opened. It was Grace with her big smile that always had a tranquil effect on us.

'Sorry I'm late,' she said as she quickly shut it behind her. 'I didn't have enough money for a taxi, so I had to take the bus.'

While she grabbed her wooden drumsticks from her backpack, I began comparing myself to the three of them. They all went to the same cool senior high school in south Jakarta called the SMA3. I almost wept to think of my lame second rate school.

We took off our school uniform shirts and put on t-shirts, still wearing our grey skirts, the standardised colour for senior schools. That there were no high school names printed on the skirts made us equal.

'Let's start with "What's My Name" from The Clash,' said Mirah.

The song opened with Kenari's lead and my rhythmic distorted chords, accompanied by the commanding drumming from Grace. Mirah joined in with the bass and began to sing. Kenari and I doubled up in the backup vocals.

I loved being here. All my pain disappeared, blown away by the energy of the song. The music made me feel special, just by playing it.

***

Chapter Four

"Pretty Vacant"
Sex Pistols

I never liked school, but the thought of what was happening afterwards gave me the energy to face the day. I planned to go to the radio station to get the playlist ready, and then I'd head down to south Jakarta for our rehearsal. After that, it was back again to central Jakarta for the live broadcast.

I dragged myself out of bed and headed for the bathroom. Just as I started to enjoy the warm shower, I was interrupted.

'Who's in there?' Matari yelled.

'It's Sigi.'

'Can you get out?' she snapped. 'I've got an important meeting!'

So typical of her.

'I just got in.'

'If you don't get out, I'll be late.'

As she banged again, I cursed. I decided to wash my face and skip the rest. I dried myself quickly and opened the door.

Matari's sour face was in front of me. She wore silk pyjamas, with a giant fluffy white towel thrown lazily over her shoulder. Her voice might be loud and demanding, but her body was less intimidating. She was shorter than me, the smallest, while I was the tallest of three sisters.

Her skin was the fairest, and she had small and deep eyes that hinted at a western lineage. They made her look like an outsider next to Bulan and me whom both inherited our father's honey-coloured skin and big eyes. Some said she got her looks from my father's mother who had a little Dutch blood in her. She had a funky-layered bob that was still in disarray, and she was wearing her Chanel glasses.

43

'You can finish your shower after me!' she ordered, hands on hips.

'I don't need to,' I said coolly.

She stared at me for a few seconds before pushing her way past and into the bathroom. She locked the door behind her.

As I entered the family room, I noticed Bulan sitting patiently with a towel on her lap.

'You'll have to wait until her Majesty finishes.'

'It doesn't matter *lab*[17] ,' Bulan smiled. 'She needs to get to work.'

I scoffed as I walked past. Ten minutes later, I flew downstairs in my high school uniform, carrying my backpack.

***

The big gate of SMA27 was crowded, with students milling around, joking and pushing each other as they headed towards their classrooms.

A mediocre public school full of second-grade rejects, students who have neither the brains nor the influence to be accepted in first-rate schools.

My heart dropped whenever I thought about what had brought me to this sorry school. For the first year, I laid low. I tried to avoid problems with the other kids and teachers, and I studied as often as possible. I decided not to make any close friends and just stick to those I knew outside of school, like the girls in my band. That was until Bara and her mates came along. She was a new student who had also transferred from another school. The minute I saw her, I liked her.

'*Hai* Sigi.' I heard her voice coming down the walkway.

Speak of the devil.

Bara was petite, but she was a powerhouse. Her face seemed a bit boyish, coupled with her short hair, and her voice was deep and loud.

'Where have you been,' she asked. 'I've been trying to call you.'

'Oh, rehearsals, gigs. It's always one thing or another.'

'So, when are you taking us to see you play?'

---

[17]*Lab* is commonly added to the end of a word or phrase for emphasis.

I stayed silent. I was secretive when it came to that other world of mine, and I didn't intend to share it with any of the students.

'I'm going to Reni's after school,' she said, changing the subject. 'Are you coming?'

'No, I've got a lot to do today. But I promise I'll try to find some time.'

The bell started to ring, and the commotion escalated. Girls were humming lame pop songs as they scurried along the walkways. Bara and I walked to class while some guys whistled, calling my name.

That annoyed me. Those boys knew nothing about the world or anything else for that matter. To me, they didn't exist.

'Still popular among the boys, I see,' Bara teased.

'Idiots,' I said as we climbed the stairs. 'The way they flirt. They either whistle or pass around porn cards.'

'What?'

'They do that in my class. Some of the boys pass these cards, like normal playing cards but with porn pictures on the back. Gross! And they passed one of them to me. I flatly passed it back. I've seen that kind of thing before. Accidently found my father's porn magazine, *Penthouse* it was called, in his drawer when I was a kid.'

Bara smirked. 'Well, that certainly doesn't happen in my class.'

'Maybe they just don't pass it to you.'

I could see that thought hadn't occurred to her.

'So, what do older guys do when they like you?'

'They say it to your face, you know, like a man.'

***

I found it especially hard to concentrate on my studies. I glanced at Esa's empty chair next to me. I missed her. I ended up scribbling nonsense on empty pages, doodling while my mind was busy plotting what to say when I next saw Danu because I couldn't avoid him forever. The only thought that came to mind was how bland he was.

Finally, at 12:30pm, the bell rang, and school was over. I took off out the gate and caught a *bajaj*[18]. These were three-wheeled vehicles, modified motorbikes with a closed compartment at the back to accommodate passengers. They were all over the city-a cheap way to travel. They didn't go that fast, and they were noisy and smelled of smoke, but they were convenient for short distances.

Fifteen minutes later, I arrived at Pasaraya Manggarai, a large mall in south Jakarta. It was lunchtime, and the mall was packed. People were heading for the famous food court. But that was not where I was going. Instead of entering the mall from the front lobby like everyone else, I went straight around the back, where the operational entrance was located.

The mall workers with different uniforms were busy going about their business, most of them on their way to lunch at the staff canteen. The parking lot was full of trucks loading and unloading goods. I quickly walked inside and headed for the elevator.

The industrial-sized lift was different from the ones used by the shoppers inside the mall. Those sophisticated lifts were equipped with air-conditioning and soothing music, compared to this plain grey and miserable one, complete with cigarette butts and crumpled tissues all over the floor. The grimy lift filled with workers took me where I wanted to go. Some got off at the different office floors, and I went straight to the top.

The doors opened to reveal a small empty room with a staircase leading upwards. At the end of the stairs, I opened the large door and heard the sound of people chatting amidst a thick cloud of *kretek*[19] smoke. I had arrived at PV Radio, short for Pure Voice FM.

The main room, or 'living room' as we called it, was full of comedians, announcers, operators, and fans. This station accepted all kinds of people. No door policies and no questions asked. We were all one big family.

PV Radio was initially an old-school comedy radio station. Almost all the great comedy groups[20] such as Bagito, Empat Seka-

---

[18]*Bajaj* is pronounced bha-jhay.

[19]*Kretek* is the name of the cloves used in traditional Indonesian cigarettes.

[20]Unlike in the west, group acts rather than solo comedians performed Indonesian comedy in the 80-90s.

wan, Diamor, and Patrio, used to broadcast there. More recently, the station started to emphasise music with programs dedicated to jazz, blues, and a rock show run by a young singer/songwriter called Elang Rahmanto. He had his own Friday night slot called PV May Rock. And, for the past three months, I, Sigi Putri, was lucky enough to be his sidekick. We played the latest music, talked about famous bands, and took phone calls from listeners. Occasionally, Elang would take out his guitar and sing a few songs for more entertainment.

Broadcaster Pandu was talking on the phone. He gave me a quick wave and continued his conversation, as I looked at him with admiration.

One of the oldest broadcasters at PV, he held a radio show every night of the week except Fridays. He had a golden, dreamy voice and his show Let's Go to Bed took romantic love song requests for the girls.

He complained a lot about the tacky music he had to play, but we knew he secretly loved every minute of it. The attention he got from his young female listeners was massive. Roses, candy, and love letters constantly arrived.

I walked past him and into the library at the back, supposing a small room with a few cabinets full of CDs and cassettes could be called that. I was pleased to see it was empty.

Closing the door behind me, I sat down at the wooden table that held a few music players. Alone, I suddenly burst into tears, a flood of emotional turmoil, as I rocked back and forth on the chair.

I thought back to the first night Danu and I met at Pid Pub. I was waiting outside with a few girls for the metal superstars to come out when the pub closed. And then, a thin, tall guy with fair skin and long curly hair began staring at me. I had seen him play but I'd never met him. He was cute and had a friendly smile. His friends were teasing him, calling out that he liked me.

Unlike most of the cocky metal musicians, he was humble and sweet. I immediately liked him. He was a singer and a guitarist, and he loved thrash metal. He called me the next day, and we started dating.

What brought me to tears now was the realisation that I had probably never loved him in the first place. It was clear that I'd only used him as a stepping stone to enter the underground, exploiting his metal connections and his protection to feel safe in the explosive male environment.

I wasn't that loyal either. I had been flirting with Agam for months behind his back and I'd also teased a few of his famous friends. Yet he faithfully stood by me as my serious boyfriend.

I had to pull myself together; there was work to be done. I wiped the tears on my sleeve and stood up to check out the music in the cabinet.

The library collection was a bit outdated although it had recently improved with Elang's demands to source new material. He also made the playlists for all our sessions, and would leave them for me to prepare, but he had been busy lately. As well as his college commitments, he was also recording his debut solo album.
So today I was charged with creating the evening's list. I had only chosen the playlist twice before, but according to Elang, I was pretty good at it-for a girl.

I pulled out a bit of glam-Whitesnake, Mötley Crüe, and Mr Big. Slow rock compilations for the ladies with Warrant and Bad English. The Seattle sound was not to be missed so I included some Stone Temple Pilots and Soundgarden. I had a few new cassettes from my own collection that I'd recorded a couple of weeks ago at Kenari's; Rage Against the Machine, L7, and The Clash. And, for a little bit of metal, Megadeth. The selection process continued until there were enough songs to fill our two hours on air. With the CDs sorted into neat piles, I began fast-forwarding the tapes to the specific songs so they were ready to roll when we needed them.

Reaching into my backpack, I pulled out some magazines Mirah had given me and set about collating the information. I summarised the music news, band histories, and new releases from the latest edition of *Rolling Stone* and the *NME* magazines.

When I had finished, I grabbed a CD from the pile. It was Mötley Crüe's 5th album *Dr Feelgood*, a 1989 hugely successful release. By 1992, the new grunge bands like Nirvana and Pearl Jam had overshadowed them. Yet privately, it was still one of my favourites. I decided to play "Don't Go Away Mad (Just Go Away)".

I rested my back against the chair and floated away with the intro, those guitar riffs, second only to the vocals of Vince Neil. His rendering of the lyrics, so in sync with how I was feeling, made me smile. I loved the way music spoke to me in the most unexpected moments.

Yes, what happened sucked, but I could do nothing to turn back time. I could only make amends to Danu, and myself, by firmly letting him go. I owed him a great deal. Besides, what happened wasn't entirely his fault. I was still languishing in my thoughts when the door opened.

***

Chapter Five

"Love Comes in Spurts"
Richard Hell and the Voidoids

Pandu burst in with what appeared to be a box of chocolates.

'Look what I got from a fan,' he said excitedly.

'Give me that.' I quickly stole the box from his unsuspecting hands.

Pandu was about to protest but stopped. He stared at me, looking amused as I ate the first chocolate I could grab. Greedily, I took a second while still chewing the first.

'You like them that much? Or are you hungry?' he said jokingly, snatching the box back from me. I managed to seize the third piece, though.

'These are mine,' he continued, stuffing the box in his backpack.

I threw him a sharp look, and after I finished the third, I lit a cigarette. 'What? You charmed all these girls with your soulful shit on the radio, and I can't enjoy the chocolates with you?'

'Stop being a smartarse. Hey, why are you looking so tired? Not enough sleep?'

'Sleep is for the weak,' I grinned. 'I'm feeling better now that I've got some sugar in me. And, I just had an epiphany.'

'Epiphany? I need an explanation. Next time though, right now, I've got to run.'

'Where are you going?'

'To grab a quick bite at the food court, and then I'm off to uni.'

'I'm coming with you,' I said quickly. 'Well, to the food court, not to campus.'

'No way,' he objected. 'I don't want to be seen eating with a high school girl. It might ruin my reputation!'

I laughed. At twenty-six, Pandu was probably the oldest broad-

51

caster, but he looked like he was about twelve, thanks to his soft short body. His facial hair helped only somewhat to look his age.

He was studying for his doctoral degree in psychology at the University of Indonesia, UI, as it's known, the most famous university in the country. Only real brains with good connections get into that top uni, like my sister Matari. She was a UI graduate.

'Come on, I hate to eat alone,' I said.

'Ok, but you and a cigarette? Who cares about my reputation? I'm sold.'

'Don't worry, I won't smoke in public. Let's go.'

I put my cigarette out in a nearby ashtray, grabbed my backpack and followed him out of the door.

***

The food court was packed, and we waited to score the first free table.

'You want to order?' he asked.

'No, you go ahead. Just whatever you're having.'

'I want *gado-gado*[21]. Is that ok?'

'Yep, whatever.'

'Spicy?'

'Medium, and an iced tea, sweet.'

As he walked over to the food stalls, I looked around and noticed a few people from the radio station. Comedians were eating together, plotting jokes, laughing at one table.

Jono, the station manager, was at another, having a serious business lunch with a group of people I had never seen before. Some of them gave me a curious look. I imagined him telling them that I was their youngest announcer. I was glad I wasn't smoking.

'Iced tea for you. Here we go.' Pandu placed the tall glass before me and sat down with his hot tea. 'So, what's going on?'

---

[21] *Gado-gado* is an Indonesian dish comprised of blanched vegetables, pieces of hard-boiled eggs, tofu with a peanut sauce, and served with lontong (steamed rice wrapped in a banana leaf). Most regions produce their own local variations.

'Just things in my head, but nothing I can't handle.'

'Like what?'

'Relationships.'

'Relationships?' Pandu repeated with an amused look. 'Of course, what else would teenagers be thinking of?'

'Don't worry, I think I've found the answer on my own.'

'Must be the epiphany,' he grinned.

'Yes,' I said softly as I fell silent.

Talking to Pandu was like talking to my father. They were both so bright and direct that I couldn't help but focus carefully on my words. He waited patiently.

'I realised I haven't been truthful,' I finally said. 'For the past two years, I pretended to have feelings, convincing myself and others to believe it. To accept that it was something real.'

Pandu's face was serious. He crossed his arms in front of his chest. 'So you're saying that you tried to manipulate the situation. Is that right?'

'To be short, I pretended to fall in love and failed dramatically.'

Pandu let out a little laugh. 'So, all this time, you didn't love that boyfriend of yours?'

'I thought I did, though, really. But the truth has finally come out.'

'That you don't love him?'

'Yes.'

'Why? I'm curious.'

'Ah, it's complicated....' I hesitated. I didn't know why I was confiding in him, but then again, if I didn't speak about it, I felt I might just go insane. 'I've been avoiding Danu for a while now. Managed to dodge him every time he called. But I can't do that forever. One of these days, I'm going to have to see him. And speak to him, honestly.'

Pandu was silent for a few moments. 'Remember how we met? I'd just finished on-air when you called the station.'

I did remember. I was in my bedroom listening to his show while I was doing some homework. The slow love songs were not to my taste, but I liked his voice, so his program had been another of my secret guilty pleasures.

'Well, PV listeners, I want to say thank you for all the requests that have been pouring in. I'm very sorry that we've run out of time, so the last request is for Tasya in east Jakarta. She said she was sad because she's been having problems with her boyfriend.'

I had rolled my eyes.

'So here's the song, especially for Tasya, and before I say goodbye, let me share a few of my thoughts. When it comes to relationships, commitment means being ready to support each other during the good and bad. Nite bro and sis, sweet dreams. This is PV Radio and Pandu Wijaya is out.'

His words had stirred something in me. I decided to phone the station.

'Yeah,' I said, back from memory lane. 'I asked my father if I could use the phone. I had to call to say that bad times should have a limit.'

'Yes, you did,' he chuckled. 'And you said, what if the other person isn't loyal, or abusive, or in a coma or something.'

'Or, all of the above.'

'But I only agreed with the abusive part. We argued for a while about that. I have to admit that I was curious to see what you looked like in person. I had to invite you to come in sometime, and I was shocked when you showed up in your high school uniform.'

'Really?'

'You were much younger than I thought you were. On the phone, you sounded like someone in her mid-twenties, but you still haven't answered my question. Why did you pretend to love your boyfriend when, in fact, you didn't?'

Before I could respond, two plates of *gado-gado*-vegetables, tofu, tempeh, rice cake, and a boiled egg with peanut dressing-arrived.

'Never mind, you don't have to explain,' he said.

I looked at him with affection. He was the one who pushed me into broadcasting after learning of my love and knowledge of music. That day he introduced me to Elang, and he also helped put my broadcasting demo together. He even gave it personally to Jono, the boss. I was instantly accepted.

'Let's eat,' he urged.

I nodded.

'So you're going to break up with him, huh?' he said after a while.

'I already did.'

'Oh, you did?'

'Yes, but it was over the phone. He didn't take it seriously.'

'I see. What finally made you do it?'

I was silent as I pretended to focus on my food. I didn't want to explain. It was too painful. He seemed to understand because he didn't push it any further. We continued to eat in silence.

'Pandu, what's true love?' I asked after we emptied our plates.

'Good question. All I know is that I'm very much in love with Linda, and I want to have little babies with her.'

'Lucky you! I don't think I'll ever feel like that about anyone.'

'Oh, you will, Sigi,' he said confidently. 'You will fall in love, trust me. None of us is immune to that curse.'

'A curse, huh,' I said. 'But how will I know if it's true love instead of whatever?'

'When you fall, you'll know. The question is-are you really looking for that right now?'

'What do you mean?'

'An open heart is vulnerable.' He paused for a few seconds. 'You'll risk getting your heart utterly and absolutely broken.'

'Don't you think I know that?' I said, feeling a bit offended.

'There-' he said.

'Oh, be quiet,' I scoffed. 'You're not even licensed as a psychologist yet, and you're already messing with my head.'

'Admit it,' he pressed. 'You aren't ready to fall in love. Past traumas, influences, who knows? Fact is, to fall deeply in love, you have to have an open heart, even with the risk of being hurt.'

'Tell me something. Have you had your heart broken?'

'Of course,' he said seriously. 'There are many factors when it comes to love, and it's not always perfect. It can be hellish too.'

'Then, what's the point?' I asked, suddenly craving a cigarette. 'What is the point of falling in love when, in the end, you end up hurt?' It all seemed too complicated, and I started to lose interest. 'You're right. Now I don't even know if I want to fall in love anymore,' I added.

'Of course you do. Everyone wants to feel alive, including you. You just have to be brave.'

'What if I get a broken heart? Can't just buy a new one in the mini-mart, can we?'

Pandu smiled and leaned back into the chair. 'Ok, let me explain love from my perspective. Love happens when you find a person who'll stand by you for the long haul, and no matter what the situation is, they will never leave you. You see, my opinion about love is still the same as that night on the radio. Couples must be together in good times and the bad, sickness and health, and all that.'

'Do you mean that this person will always stand by you, no matter what you do?'

'Except if you abuse them, of course.'

'What about if you cheat?'

'Yes.'

'You're insane,' I said cynically. 'Seriously? Would you forgive Linda if she cheated on you?'

'I'd be devastated,' replied Pandu, placing both palms on the very left side of his chest. 'Wait, hearts are located a bit more to the middle, not there.' He moved his hands comically, closer to the centre.

I gave him an annoyed look that made him grin. 'You'll take it sitting down if she cheated on you? You'd pretend that you didn't know and carry on as nothing happened?'

'I never said that. If she cheated on me and I didn't know about it, then, of course, everything is ok.'

'And if you knew?'

'I'd asked her to stop what she's doing and work on our broken relationship because there's no way she would cheat on me if our relationship were good.'

'You're mad,' I shrieked. 'I bet you a million rupiah right now that that's not the only reason people cheat.'

'Oh yeah? Name one.'

'Boredom.'

'True, but I'm sure if you're committed, you will try harder not to be bored. Actually, we're never bored with each other, well, at least not yet.'

'What if she's not ready to commit?'

'Then she shouldn't start a relationship in the first place, but really I'm curious. Why do you think she's not ready to commit?'

'Too young?'

'She's not that young anymore. Geez, Sigi, I think this is more about you than me, eh?'

I didn't know what to say.

'She recently told me that I was one of the hardest things in the world to find. You know what she means, finding that one person. And likewise, I told her that I'm pretty lucky to have met her too. We're blessed.'

I sighed. 'So how do I find this person?'

'All I know from my own experience is that it's like the old saying-when you meet that person, you just know. They'll touch you deep inside your heart without reason, and it just happens.'

'Right.'

'Look, Sigi,' he said as he leaned forward. 'I understand what you're going through. My advice is don't be too hard on yourself. You have a fantastic life, be grateful. And you're young, and you're bound to make mistakes. Your journey, especially when it comes to relationships, is just starting. So what if you don't love him? It's ok. It's fine to break up with him. You're allowed to change your mind.'

'Thanks, Pandu, you're right. I shouldn't over-think it.'

He winked. 'Exactly. Anyway, I've got to run.'

'But I have more questions.'

'What more is there to ask? Relax,' he said. 'Love will find you eventually, and when it comes, be brave. Ok, I've really do have to go!'

I sat alone, contemplating his words. Then I went back upstairs to the station and hurriedly lit a cigarette.

***

Chapter Six

"Rebel Girl"
Bikini Kill

The studio door opened during the final bars of "Lithium", and a girl quietly slipped inside. She sat down in the corner, watching. Now we had an audience, we closed the song with new-found energy. As the music faded, I gave the newcomer a curious look. I did remember her from EMI. Her face was still boyish, her expression straight. Her black hair was tied tightly at the back, and she was dressed in an oversized black t-shirt with the Ramones on it and ripped black jeans.

'Hey, you came,' Mirah greeted her. 'Everyone, this is Soraya.'

'Hello girls,' she waved slightly.

Her voice was deep and a little croaky, and her stare seemed a bit out of focus. She went around, shaking our hands. She was certainly something else up close. A silver spike protruded from her lower lip, and her eyes were red as if she hadn't slept for weeks. There was something wild about her. Unlike us standard brats, this one looked like trouble.

She reeked of alcohol and cigarettes, and her hand was cold and limp inside my grip.

'*Hai,*' I said weakly.

'So, you're in a band?' asked Kenari excitedly.

'Yes, I'm in The Upshot with Galih. You know him, eh, Mirah? You too, Sigi,' she answered. 'I'm the vocalist and the only girl, and I play bass as well. We cover the Sex Pistols, Exploited, the Dead Kennedys.' She pointed to her t-shirt, 'And the Ramones.'

'Yeah, we play some of those,' said Kenari. 'We're mainly punk, And a bit of grunge too, L7 and Nirvana. Do you like Nirvana?'

'No, I don't like grunge.' Her eyes were slightly closed with disgust.

59

We were a little taken aback at the unexpected shift in her demeanour and an uncomfortable silence hung in the air.

'People like grunge,' Mirah finally spoke for us. 'Every time we play "Smells like Teen Spirit", the guys slamdance. It's new, wild.'

Soraya was glowering. I couldn't help but feel a bit insecure.

Was she right? Was playing grunge really not cool?

'I know Nirvana are new, but as I said to you before Mirah, grunge just doesn't excite me. I'd like to stick to punk if you don't mind.'

Her tone offended me. I was about to take her down a notch or two, when Mirah spoke again.

'Alright, let's hear you sing,' she said as she turned on the bass that still hanging on her tiny frame. 'How about the Sex Pistols' "Anarchy in the UK"?'

'Sure.'

She grasped the mic stand from Mirah and positioned it in front of herself. She adjusted it a little higher, did the usual testing 'one two three,' and signalled with her chin that she was ready.

Grace banged the cymbal four times. Amongst the pounding beat and aggressive guitars, Soraya screamed.

'*Right…*!'

The force of her voice startled me; I couldn't believe what I was hearing. She was nothing like I had ever seen before in all my days of watching bands.

When it was over, Kenari looked at me, beaming. Grace was also smiling and, as for me, well, I was in awe. Her voice was powerful and robust, nothing like Mirah's lighter quality. She had copied the Pistols' English tone and accent almost to perfection.

Now we knew why she didn't want to do grunge; she was Johnny Rotten stuck in the body of an Indonesian teenage girl.

'That was great,' Mirah smiled with a look, half amused. 'Too bad you don't sing grunge though. It's kind of becoming our sound as much as punk.'

Soraya responded by moving the mic stand back in front of Mirah. 'That was fun, girls, but I got to run.'

'What's the hurry? We're not finished,' Kenari blurted out.

I was worried too. We probably weren't cool enough for her.

'I've got to get the bus and get up to central. I told the punks I'd be at their basecamp, and I'm already late. Let's keep in touch. You have my number,' Soraya said to Mirah.

She began putting the straps of her backpack on top of her shoulders.

'The punks?' said Mirah with a curious tone.

'You guys are welcome to join me. I'll introduce you.'

Kenari had an excited smile, but it soon faded as Mirah answered, clearly for all of us. 'We've got to rehearse, and we're playing tomorrow. Thanks for the invite, and thanks again for coming.'

'No worries.' Soraya opened the door and walked out.

'Ok, girls,' Mirah continued.

'Wait, I need to go to the toilet, sorry,' I mumbled as I quickly unstrapped my guitar. Without waiting for a response, I dashed out of the studio. She would soon be gone, and I needed that new girl.

***

Soraya was sitting in the living room, busy putting on her army boots, and I sat on the seat next to her. When she finished tying the laces, she grabbed a pack of cigarettes from her backpack.She offered me one, and I happily took it. She lit mine first.

'Sorry about that,' I said. 'Mirah meant well.'

'It doesn't matter. She's just a bit pissed off that I don't want to sing Nirvana shit. I've told her so many times, but she won't listen.'

'Nirvana isn't shit. They're great. Maybe not for you but for us they are.'

She took a deep drag on her cigarette, and exhaled. 'We met briefly with Mirah at that studio, but you don't remember me from school, do you? We were at the same junior high with Mirah, and Galih too.'

'I was there for the first two years,' I sighed. 'Then I was transferred after a bullying incident that involved some senior girls.'

Soraya looked at me differently, with more focus.

'That sounds horrible and don't worry, we never really talked, and we just smiled at each other once in a while when our paths crossed at school.'

I nodded awkwardly.

'This basecamp. Is it an underground hang-out?' I asked.

'Yeah, but it's not like the metal underground. This one is private,' she answered, eagerly. 'Galih introduced me to the guys from central. They're called the Young Offender, the first punk community I've ever known. They took their name from a song by Disrupted, an English punk band.'

'Young Offender? Never heard of them.'

'Of course, you haven't. You're always in the metal scene. These punks have different playgrounds that you've never seen. Smaller and newer, but much edgier.'

I kept my facial expression flat, but I couldn't deny my excitement.

'Come with me,' she continued. 'They aren't like the old, uni-educated metal guys in south Jakarta. These punks are the same age as us, and a few of them maybe a year or two younger.'

'Any girls?'

'No girls. I'm the first they've accepted,' she said proudly.

'Wow!' My enthusiasm was bubbling over. 'Young Offender, you said?'

'Yep, a punk tribe and band collective, a new underground for punk, hardcore, and alternatives. Hey, look, I've got to go. Are you coming?'

'No, I have to stay and rehearse. And I have a radio show to do after that.'

'You're a radio broadcaster?' She turned up her nose.

'Yes, at PV Radio. With this guy called Elang. Our session is PV May Rock. It's mostly rock and grunge, but we play a little punk too, well-known bands like the Ramones. Have a listen. It's on 101.6 FM.'

'Sure, whatever,' she said, unimpressed. 'I've got to run. Nice to meet you again, Sigi, bye.'

I watched her dashing out of the door while I sat mulling over what she had said. After a few more drags, I finished my cigarette and went back inside. The girls had put down their instruments and were standing around chatting.

'Personally, I think she's got great style.' I caught Kenari's last words.

'Yeah, you've never seen a girl so punk before, I get it,' said Mirah in an irritated voice. 'I know that she's my friend, but I'm ashamed of her. She was clearly high on something and was also a bit drunk if you girls noticed.'

What she meant was that Soraya had been smoking weed, something I had never tried. None of us girls used drugs or alcohol; we were all squeaky clean. I was a chain smoker, but that was about it.

'She's a badass singer, though. We have to admit that.'

'I'm with Kenari,' I added my thoughts to the group.

Grace, as usual, didn't say much. She just smiled and listened. Mirah finally turned to her.

'*Mbak*[22] Grace, what do you think?'

'I'd have to agree with Nari and Sigi,' Grace said, her voice soft and soothing. 'I'm sorry, Mirah, but we don't have much choice. We need a new vocalist if you're going to stop singing.'

Mirah's expression was gloomy, but she finally consented.

'I'll call her,' Kenari offered. 'Can you give me her number Mirah? I'll ask if she wants to join and let you guys know.'

'Alright,' she sighed. 'Let's just hope things work out for the best.'

We looked at each other with reassuring smiles.

'Now, back to "Lithium",' Mirah decided. 'We've got an hour left.'

***

Jakarta's late afternoon sky was spangled grey and light orange when we left the studio. I was waiting for the taxi I had called from the front office. I'd wanted to take the bus like the others, but I didn't have the time. I still had the show to broadcast.

'Smoking again?' said Grace with a disapproving look.

I just grinned.

'I'll tell Danu,' she added with a pretend hostility.

I threw my gaze away as I exhaled. I was tempted to say that I

---

[22]*Mbak* is an Indonesian form of address for a woman of similar age or younger.

didn't give a damn about what Danu would think but then I realised that it would provoke unwanted questions.

'I'm joking,' Grace snickered. 'You don't have to worry. But really, Sigi, you need to stop that disgusting habit.'

'Yes, Grace.'

'Where's Mirah?'

'She's still inside, on the phone.'

'Who's she calling?'

'No idea.'

'The Jakarta Fair organiser,' replied Kenari as she fixed her hair in the mirror of her powder compact. 'She wanted to see how we went in the audition.'

As Mirah walked from the house and along the pavement, she was glowing.

'We're in, aren't we!' Kenari squealed.

'Yes,' she confirmed, smiling as she put down her heavy backpack. 'And, they said they'll pay us. Not a lot, just enough to cover the transportation. Oh, finally, girls, we're finally getting paid. Isn't that awesome?'

'Wow, yes,' Grace mirrored back with her brightest smile.

'Eat your heart out, boys,' said Mirah. 'Wanderlust is here to stay.'

Kenari giggled. 'Oooh, this so exciting!'

The four of us began laughing, hugging, clapping, and jumping around, that was until we heard Grace's firm voice.

'Alright girls, hate to break up the party, but it's time to go,' she said as she glanced at her watch. 'You're good, Sigi, to get back to PV Radio?'

'Yes, you girls go ahead.'

Their houses were much closer than mine, with caring parents who wanted them to be home on time. We said our goodbyes, and they set off to the nearest bus stop.

I sat down on the shady verge and took another drag. I idly watched the smoke waft away on the late afternoon breeze and up through the leaves. I couldn't stop thinking about how we would have our first paid performance in just a few weeks.

It wouldn't be the best of gigs. The Jakarta Fair was a festival held every July to celebrate the anniversary of the city. We'd be entertaining what we and others in the underground called the 'common people'. It was a term we used to describe local Indonesians who were a bit old-fashioned and it wasn't only used by us. Rich Jakartans used it too, except for them, it meant 'poor people'.

These ordinary people were families and teenagers who had never heard of metal before, let alone punk. Their tastes were closer to the lame Indonesian pop music, classic rock ballads and *dangdut*[23], a retarded sort of music sung mostly by overly sexy trashy women that I couldn't stand. I imagined that they would probably just stare, not knowing what to make of us.

Sometimes, events like this take a band out of their comfort zone. The regulars who knew and loved the music we played wouldn't be there; neither would any of our underground mates. It was going to be nerve-wracking.

I put out the cigarette when a taxi turned and headed back towards me.

***

---

[23]*Dangdut* is a genre of modern music that draws upon Malaysian, Hindi and traditional Indonesian styles. It is extremely popular in Indonesia.

Chapter Seven

"Transmission"
Joy Division

Pasaraya Manggarai mall was buzzing with shoppers when I arrived. It had been a slow-going trip in the peak hour traffic. I jumped out of the taxi and made my way to the back of the building as fast as I could through the thronging crowds, where I waited for the staff lift to take me up to the radio station. When I entered the living room, Elang was already there.

'Hey, Sigi, you're in the nick of time.'

'Yeah, sorry, I'm late,' I said as I glanced at the clock on the wall. It was now 7:50pm.

I threw my backpack on the sofa and joined him standing in front of a long table where the CDs and cassettes I had organised earlier in the library were neatly arranged.

'I like your song list, but I've made a few changes if that's ok?'

'Yeah, sure.'

'We played Slaughter's "Days Gone By" last week, so I switched it to Live's "I Alone" and added Damn Yankees as well. The girls love them.'

I'm a girl, and I don't really like them.

'The songs from your personal collection are great, and I've added some of mine too, Alice in Chains and Silverchair, this new band from Australia.'

My mind was wandering. Elang was cute, but his taste in music was a bit boring. Then I realised that he was silent.

'Yes, ok,' I said.

He laughed.

My cheeks felt warm. Elang wasn't my type, but he was still cute nonetheless.

'I just asked you what prep you put together for tonight, and you said 'Yes, ok'.'

'Oh, sorry,' I said, feeling embarrassed. I moved to the sofa and pulled out the summary from my backpack. 'Here is it.'

As Elang gave it a quick read, I glanced at his face. He had small features, delicate cheekbones, and a small round chin. His dark skin was a little shiny under the stark light, and his layered, longish hair was swept neatly behind his ears. His face was handsome, earthy, and sweet.

Whilst I had a famous sister, he had this insanely famous brother, a jazz-fusion musician and singer named Bagas with a band called The Indo Project. This connected us, the fact that it wasn't easy to live in the shadow of a famous sibling, especially if you chose a similar path.

Elang was the frontman of a band called HALO he had recently formed with another PV broadcaster. From what I had heard, they infused ethnic and jazz sounds in their original rock songs. They weren't my style, but they were cool enough to warrant the recognition.

'Hey Elang, Sigi,' called Hestu, our skinny young operator, as he came into the room. 'How's it going? Are you guys ready?'

'You've prepared the cassettes, right Sigi?' asked Elang worriedly.

I nodded confidently.

'See you inside,' said Hestu as he grabbed the CDs and tapes from the table and disappeared into his booth.

We opened the soundproof door into the dimly lit broadcasting room. Two chairs were positioned on the left of the big glass screen that separated our broadcasting space from the operator's room. Pandu and I took our seats, as we watched Hestu behind the glass, checking his mixer.

On our table sat four microphones tied to a triangular stand on the mixer desk. The mixer itself was small, with just four slides to turn on the microphones. On top of each mic were the headphones we used to monitor our voices when we were live.

The apprehension started to creep in as usual, and my stomach tightened as we put on the headphones. My reading material and pen lay in front of me and I watched Elang place his on the table.

I glanced at him with envy. He looked so damn collected and relaxed. The thought of speaking to thousands of listeners always fuelled my anxiety, and I wished I had half his confidence.

To reduce the pounding in my chest, I looked out the window. The streets around Manggarai were a swirl of constantly moving traffic, their lights twinkling in the darkness. Under the stark glare of the harsh mall lights, the incessant lines of shoppers and vehicles never ceased coming in and out of the carpark.

My saving grace was that I usually performed well, intuitively, once we got going.

Hestu gave us his hand signal; he was ready. I took a deep breath. Here we go!

We heard the opening tune of PV May Rock, a short acoustic number that Elang himself wrote, played and sang. His voice was deep and strong, the vibe happy.

The night is young, the sky is bright,
You are on your own, and so why don't we
Listen to music, listen to us,
On PV May Rock right here and right now,
Only on PV Radio, yeah!

I honestly thought the song was terrible, although most people thought it was great. Then again, I wasn't most people.

After the opening, Hestu played the background music, an instrumental piece drawn from the sounds of classic rock. Elang and I slid the microphone button up to the 'on air' position.

'101.6 FM PV Radio, hello bros and sis, we are back with PV May Rock. This is Elang Rahmanto.' He gave me a look to speak.

'And this is Sigi Putri. Stay tuned! We're going to play you some great rocking tunes to spice up your Friday night and keep you company for the next two hours.' I returned the look.

'Let's open the show with something from Mr Big. This is "Addicted to that Rush".'

We slid the mic off, and Hestu launched the tape.

As the song came through my headphones, I thought about

their music. I had to admit that Mr Big was another of my guilty pleasures. I had never told anyone that I liked the band. They were too sweet and girly.

Yet I simply loved Eric Martin's edgy and soulful voice that could reach those crazy high notes, the 'sing along' melodies, the insanely skilful guitar solos of Paul Gilbert, and the crazy incredible bass of Billy Sheehan. The duet of Gilbert and Sheehan in "Addicted to that Rush" was epic, and Martin sang perfectly. They were a fantastic band.

Seattle grunge from the one and only Alice in Chains, "Man in a Box", followed.

I loved being at the station, playing great songs, talking about music, receiving phone calls, and playing requests. We continued like this, playing song after song, talking about life, and reading the latest music info.

We took random calls from our listeners. Hestu would screen them and send our runner to grab the requested song from the library. Hestu would then pass the selected call on to us when the tape or CD was ready.

'Hello, welcome to PV May Rock. Who's speaking, and where are you from?' Elang opened the line.

'I'm Yanti from West Jakarta. Hi to you all.'

Then she giggled. I couldn't help but smile. It must be exciting for her.

'Great, Yanti, what song would you like, and who is the song for?' I asked.

'I'd love you to play "You're All I Need" from White Lion. For my friends at SMA2 who are listening and for that special someone out there, you know who you are.'

I rolled my eyes. Requests like these bored me, girls with their slow rock ballads and desperate appeals to their not-so-interested boyfriends.

'Heeey, no name?' Elang teased her, and she giggled again.

'No.'

Elang gave me a glance and struggled not to laugh when he saw my disdainful expression.

'Ok, Yanti, I hope your friends and that someone special is listening right now. Here we go, just for you. This is White Lion with "You're All I Need".'

Elang and I went out for a quick smoke break while John White's high voice echoed through the speakers. I was glad when it was finally replaced with the eerie opening of Aerosmith's "Janie's Got A Gun".

We returned to the studio mid-song to find another caller on hold.

'You're listening to PV May Rock on 101.6 FM with Elang and Sigi. Welcome back, and looks like we have another caller. Sigi, do take over.'

'Thank you, Elang,' I said, as I slid the mic tab up on my mixer. 'Hello, this is Sigi. Who's calling, and where are you from?'

'Hi, this is Harlan from south Jakarta. First, I want to say hello to Elang and his band HALO.'

'Thank you, Harlan. The band's a team effort and the guys are listening in.'

'*Sama-sama*[24] Elang.'

'Ok, Harlan,' I said. 'What's your song-'

'Is this Sigi from Wanderlust?' He cut me off.

I paused in surprise as a tingling wave surged through me.

Elang seemed to sense it and gave me a warm smile. 'Ah, Sigi, we forget that you're in a band. An all-girl band, too.'

'I saw you on stage at SMA4 last year,' Harlan said excitedly. 'I was slamdancing the whole time. It was awesome. I'd never seen a punk girl band before.'

My spirits lifted; it was a great feeling. I wished Soraya was listening.

'Thanks for the support,' I said shyly.

'You guys were slamdancing?' asked Elang.

'Hell yeah, and the place was packed,' answered Harlan for me. 'I remember the crowd wasn't that nice to you girls, but when you played "I Want to Live" from the Ramones, wow, that was something else.'

---

[24] *Sama-sama* meaning 'You're welcome.'

'We love playing it too,' I said, smiling.

'That's fantastic,' Elang said with pride. 'Keep going, girls, never mind the rude boys. They secretly love you, I'm sure. And, as for you, Harlan, what's your request?'

'I'd like to hear Nirvana's "In Bloom" and say hi to all my friends at SMA68, my skater friends from Senopati Park, and to Wanderlust, with a big hello to Mirah.'

Of course, the pretty front girl always gets noticed!

'Thanks, Harlan, that's our last request for the night,' said Elang as he signalled to Hestu to play the required tape.

When the song was in its final bars, it was time to close the session.

'Thanks to all our listeners here at PV May Rock. We'll see you next week, same time, same broadcasters. This is Elang Rahmanto saying goodnight.'

'And this is Sigi Putri signing off, but don't go anywhere. Stay tuned for PV Blues Night with John from HALO. Bye!'

With that, the show was over.

'Wow.' Elang hi-fived me. 'That was awesome. Your band got a mention, and you are apparently famous,' he said teasingly.

'We're not famous,' I replied, trying to hide my own excitement. 'We're girls, so we attract attention.'

'It's not just that. The music you cover is new and hardcore. I should come and see you play someday.'

I bit my tongue about our gig the following day at a rundown bar in east Jakarta. If he ever came to watch us, it would be better to invite him to a more remarkable event.

'So, where are you off to?' I asked him while packing away my notes.

'I'm going home. You?'

'Yeah, it's been a long day.'

'See you next week Sigi.'

***

Chapter Eight

"Desire"
The Sound

July 1993

I was in the kitchen, grabbing a couple of *bakwan*[25] to take up-stairs. It wasn't long until the Jakarta Fair. Wanderlust was going to play! I couldn't stop thinking about it. When the phone rang and my mother answered, I took no notice. I switched off the light and headed back to my room.

'Hello, yes, who's this?' she asked abruptly. 'It's for you,' she called after me. 'Calling at this hour? No manners.'

I grunted. Probably Danu. I wanted to say that I didn't want to take the call, given I've been avoiding him for what seemed like forever, although it had only been about a month.

'Hello?' I said impatiently, putting the small plate on the phone table.

'Sigi, how are you?'

'Oh, hi.' I gave my mother a side look. It was Agam. 'What's up?' I lowered my voice.

'I'm at the mini-mart, across the road.'

The adrenaline kicked in. 'You're kidding.'

My mother stood firm, so I paused, take a bite of the delicious deep-fried vegies in batter. 'Hurry up and get to bed,' she demand-ed. I nodded. She seemed satisfied with that, and she went back to watch TV in the living room.

'Can you come now?' he asked.

'No. She's still up, so it might take a while.'

'I'll wait.'

---

[25]*Bakwan* are a favourite Indonesian snack, mixed vegetables deep-fried in batter similar to the Chinese dim-sum.

With that, he hung up. I put the phone down and sat there, grinning. The calls had begun a while ago, before the Metallica concert. Occasionally Agam would make the drive late at night from the south to central Jakarta and he'd call from a nearby phone box asking me to come out. I was so infatuated by his grand gestures and his cockiness that he knew I would agree because I never said no. If he announced his presence, I came running.

I flew upstairs, stuffing my face with the last *bakwan*. There was no sign of my sisters in the family room.

Thank goodness.

I quickly showered and changed into tight black jeans and a sheer, light yellow blouse that I knew he liked. I sprayed on perfume, checked myself in the mirror, and put on powder, mascara, and lip-gloss. As I brushed my hair, I couldn't help but notice how tired I looked. I decided to take my contact lenses out, put in some eye drops, and wear my glasses to cover my swollen eyes. I grabbed my wallet and cigarettes and threw them in a small, brown sling bag.

Clutching my sandals, I tiptoed down the stairs and peeked into the living room. My mother had fallen asleep in front of the TV. I slipped silently through the front door amidst her snoring.

***

I walked as fast as I could across the neat garden. The humidity hung heavy; the grass and the flowers in the pots glistened in the soft hue of the moonlight. I tried to open the metal security gate with the key I'd taken from inside. I was trembling so much that the damn thing fell from my nervous hands onto the path twice before I could finally put it into the lock. I cautiously crept out to the left and crossed the street.

The vulgar bright lights of the store came quickly in view. The carpark was crowded. My eyes searched for Agam and spotted him casually leaning against the front of his car.

He wasn't that tall, and he was thin yet with heavy bones. His shoulders were tight and toned. He wore his long and wavy hair down to his waist, making him quite a spectacle. Only college boys from south Jakarta had hair like that because teenage boys weren't allowed to have long hair in high school, and the majority of the uni guys from other parts of the city had no idea what metal was. His fair skin glowed along with his striking bleached blonde hair. It was hard for people not to stare.

I consciously paced myself and walked confidently up to him. He raised his chin when he saw me, his eyes narrowed, his lips half smiling.

'So naughty this Sigi, sneaking out of the house at bedtime to see a man like me.'

I smiled back.

No *'hello, how are you?'*

'You're the naughty one,' I replied coolly. 'Cruising in your father's car to see a little girl like me at this time of night.'

'Nice,' he smirked. 'We can both be bad then.'

'Maybe, but it might not happen if we stay here.'

He grinned as he opened the passenger door. I got in while he walked around to his side and sat behind the wheel. He put the key in the ignition and started the engine. The old Lancer sedan vibrated with a thundering sound as it came to life.

'Want to go to Menteng? We can order *nasi goreng*[26] and hang out.'

'Sure,' I said as we made our anonymous escape into the busy night-time streets of Jakarta.

***

We cruised along the main drag, Diponegoro Street, with its giant trees that lined the road in the city's centre. Its huge colonial-style buildings served mainly as government houses and international embassies.

The noise of his old car was humming in tune with the sounds of the street. I stole a glance at him. He was driving slowly with another half-smile.

---

[26] *Nasi goreng* is Indonesian-style fried rice.

Menteng Street was a short, wide road with a few office buildings, a supermarket, and a midsize shopping mall. Late at the night, it transformed into a young hip central Jakartan hangout with vendors along the roadway, working under their plastic tarps, serving cheap and tasty street food. The simple carts offered grilled satay, Jakarta-style fried rice, *pisang bakar*, and *aneka roti bakar*[27].

The street was full as we hunted for a place to park. The pavement was buzzing with life as people lounged around, chatting, and eating. They were relaxing on greasy plastic chairs and others were sitting on the paved and soiled steps leading up to the closed mall.

We liked to sit inside the car, so we had some privacy from the public. Jakarta might be a huge metropolitan city, but it could, at times, feel more like a small village because most people we knew gravitated to the same places. It seemed that one would always be recognised in this bustling city wherever they went. We called this phenomenon *Jakarta sempit*, meaning 'Jakarta is tight.' And tonight was just like the other nights – we wanted to remain unnoticed.

A few moments later, a middle-aged vendor came to Agam's side of the vehicle.

'Hello boss,' he said loudly, his big eyes looming at Agam.

'*Nasi goreng dua porsi Pak*[28],' he ordered.

'And for drinks?' Agam asked me.

'*Teh Botol dingin*,' I said. It was a popular brand of sweet tea in a bottle, served cold.

'*Dua Pak*[29],' he said while holding up two fingers. The vendor repeated our order and went off whistling.

Once we were alone, Agam pushed the end of the cassette back into the stereo. The chaotic sounds of Napalm Death seemed out of place, and he pressed 'stop' to eject it.

'Sorry,' he snickered. 'I don't have any other tapes with me.'

'It's ok,' I said. 'We can do without music, for now, I suppose.'

He manoeuvred his body to the left to face me, his left leg bent

---

[27] *Pisang bakar* is grilled bananas, while *aneka roti bakar* is grilled bread that can be sweet or savoury.

[28] *Nasi goreng dua porsi Pak*, meaning 'Two portions of fried rice Sir.'

[29] *Dua Pak* meaning 'Two bottles, Sir.'

on the seat, his right arm resting on the steering wheel. He stared at me with a big smile.

I had to look away. My eyes focused on my neatly-folded hands on my lap. Agam's hand touched my right hand, and it sent an intense wave of electricity right through me. I smiled shyly and decided to open the palm of my hand to receive his. I ventured to look at him.

He was larger-than-life, so good looking yet strange, so different from any guy I had ever seen before. His big penetrating eyes were usually fiery, but they were gentle that night. I liked his prominent long nose, and he had a masculine square jaw, a feature typical of people from Sumatra. His lips were perfectly full, a soft pink against his light skin.

'You're wearing glasses, the studious schoolgirl look,' he said in his deep voice. 'And I really like your honey skin. How hot is that!'

I rolled my eyes. Agam's brutal honesty was something we were all familiar with but I dreaded the fact that he was a notorious playboy.

His body was close. It smelt warm and natural with a mixture of soap and his own musky sweat. His gentle stare changed, his eyes twinkling.

'Bet you say that to all your conquests,' I finally said, my knees trembling with the tension.

'You're not a conquest. If I wanted to fuck you, it would have happened by now.'

I laughed. 'You are way too confident. What has stopped you?'

He responded by playing with my fingers, sending more electric shots through me.

'You see, I don't want to fuck you because I want to. I only want us to fuck if you want us to.'

'And that's different?'

'A thousand times different,' he answered. 'I don't want to manipulate you into doing what I want. It has to come naturally. And for that, I'm willing to wait.'

I didn't know how to respond. Thank god the vendor was knocking on Agam's window.

'Boss, the drinks, boss,' he said, handing over two bottles of ice-cold tea. Agam took them and passed one to me. He took a sip of his with his straw, and I did the same. The sweet tea instantly refreshed my dry throat.

'So, how did you guys form Vortex?' I decided to change the subject to the first thing I could think of.

'You know about that,' he laughed.

'I know, but I still love hearing you talk about it,' I swooned.

'Ok.' He straightened his back. 'When I was with Flatlining, I wanted to perform my own material. I tried writing with them, but it was too hard. I like unusual chords and playing around with time signatures, but they were so conventional. We tried for two years to write, but we only came up with two songs. One per year, how sad is that?'

'Did you ever learn music as a kid?' I asked curiously. We had never spoken about that before.

'No, I wish I had, though. Back then my parents couldn't afford it. And these days, my dad is just an ex-soldier who's a painter, and my mother has always been a 'stay at home' mum. They're still struggling just to send me to uni. Besides, my kind of music has never been exactly their taste so I ended up learning everything I know from Arief.'

'But they let you play in a band, though.'

'Of course,' he said with evident pride. 'Mum bought me my first guitar when I was only five, back when we were still in Aceh and dad was stationed in the local TNI AL[30]. Mum used to play us songs on the old gramophone, Skeeter Davis, Elvis Presley, and stuff like that.'

My parents were wealthy compared to his, yet his parents gave him the unconditional support he needed. That seemed so unfair.

'Anyway,' he continued. 'After leaving Flatlining I asked Arief if he wanted to make a new band. Then we recruited the others, then Arief left to make his own band, and we had to find a vocalist to replace him, and that's how we ended up with Ray.' His eyes began to wander again.

---

[30]The *TNI AL* refers to the Indonesian Navy.

I sighed. 'You're such an inspiration!'

'I'm just a nobody trying to make it in the world, Sigi.'

'You're not a nobody,' I said, patting him on the knee. 'You've made everything possible. Without you, we wouldn't have the underground.'

Agam was silent as he gazed at me. Those eyes were intense, as if he wanted to ravish me right there and then. I decided to grab my sling bag and look for my cigarettes and lighter.

'Hold that thought,' said Agam. 'I think the food is here.'

The vendor approached the driver's side window with a plate in each hand. I breathed a sigh of relief.

***

The fried rice was delicious, and Agam was gulping his down. By contrast, I was struggling to eat.

'What really happened at the Metallica concert?' I asked after straining to swallow a spoonful. 'My father said a few people were still in hospital. Is that true?'

'Maybe,' he said in between chewing. 'I don't know, but I'm glad you were safe though.'

'I wasn't a hundred per cent safe. There was one thing that happened.'

'What?'

'Yes. I got, well… I got touched up.' I paused as I drank a little tea. 'We were waiting in line to go into the stadium. Danu was in front of me, and then a mob crashed the line and pushed their way into us. These guys were out of control, and some of them started feeling me up. They rubbed up against my body, put their hands on me, down there, and grabbed my breasts. Thank god I wasn't wearing a skirt.'

'Oh, Sigi.'

'I tried to fight them off. I started smashing them, but there were too many. I was terrified.' Although the memory made me shudder, something made me want to confide in him.

'Bastards.'

'I heard the security whistles, so I held our tickets in the air and cried for help, and one of them took my arm and guided Danu and I through the gates.'

'What was the matter with Danu? Why didn't he help you?'

'It's ok, *Abang*[31]. I was still one of the lucky ones,' I said.

'True, you would have seen what was said about it on TV. Even the VIP guests were attacked; they were injured by the flying beer bottles and stuff too. By the end of the show, we all had to be escorted out in police cars,' he said.

'Wow, to be driven in a police car with sirens blasting! You must have felt like the President or something.'

He gave me another intense look that made me lose what little was left of my appetite. To distract him, I offered my half-eaten rice. He finished it quickly and opened the car door. Grabbing the plates and bottles, he whistled to the vendor. After paying, he jumped back in the car and shut the door.

I reached for my bag and took out two cigarettes. I offered Agam one. He nodded and opened his lips, a signal to put it there for him. I smiled and did just that, as he stared at me with that seductive smile of his. I lit the cigarette.

A cloud of smoke began wafting, circling up towards the roof, filling the car with a sweet smell of *kretek*[32].

***

---

[31]*Abang* translates as 'brother' and is used to address a male older than oneself.
[32]*Kretek* is the name of the cloves used in traditional Indonesian cigarettes.

Chapter Nine

"Typical Girls"
The Slits

Agam chuckled as if he was lost in some private joke.

'What's so funny?'

'Nothing.'

'Tell me.'

'Danu, two years with you, and you've given him nothing. You're saving yourself until you are married, aren't you? Like a good girl,' he said in a mischievous tone.

'I never promised him anything,' I replied coldly.

As a young Indonesian woman, I felt the social pressure to be a good wife, one who would bleed on her wedding night.

Agam shook his head with a smile and took another drag of his cigarette. 'Poor Danu, I feel sorry for him.'

His words were lingering in my mind when I realised that he was staring. I opened my mouth to protest, and he stopped me. 'If you were a good girl, you wouldn't be hanging around with guys like me. Or be in an underground band. You're a born misfit. Much more fun than a mainstream kind of girl.'

He winked.

'We're the underground music stars of Indonesia,' he teased. 'Can't be more anti-mainstream than that.'

'You're the underground star, not me,' I insisted. Given Vortex had been the only band to open for Metallica on the Asian leg of their tour, I knew he was right about that.

'Why not you? You should be. And, you will. You're a musician in an all-girl band. That'll sell tickets.' He leaned forward, smirking. 'Soon, it'll be time for you to have your own male groupies. Imagine that, having guys follow you around, willing to do what you want.'

'Seriously, who would marry that kind of girl?' I said, squirming. 'I want to have a husband one day and have kids and everything.'

Agam opened the ashtray in the dashboard and put out his cigarette. 'Yeah,' he said. 'We men are hypocrites. We want to marry a virgin while fucking around on the side. But don't take that to heart. There will be men who'll be cool enough, and you'll marry one of them someday.'

Now I was laughing.

He shrugged. 'I'm pretty sure of it. If he's not, he doesn't deserve you.'

I took one last drag on my cigarette and put it out. 'It's easier to carry on like that when you're a guy.'

'Look, you're a punk chick now. If you can survive in the metal underground, you're entitled to do whatever you want. You know, sex, drugs, and rock n roll!'

'Well, I'm going to be a punk chick that just does the rock n' roll part. You know I'm not interested in the sex and drugs bits. I'd like to think I joined the underground because of my passion for music.'

'So what are you doing in my car then, Sigi?' he laughed.

I just looked out the window.

'Oh well, I'd better get you back home. I'd love to cruise and talk some more, but I have to go to Ray's to do an interview. A reporter from *Hai Magazine* has been waiting since nine o'clock to speak to the band.' He smiled. 'And you, Sigi, you better watch out for the big bad wolves out there.'

I smiled too, and I believed him because the advice came from the most prominent wolf of all.

***

'*Terus! Terus*[33]!'

With the help of the screaming parking attendant, Agam slowly reversed out, handing him a 500-rupiah coin.

---

[33]*Terus, terus* meaning go, go. Indonesia has always used unofficial parking attendants in busy congested areas. These men help maintain traffic flow, and drivers pay a small fee for their service.

'Enough about me. Tell me more about your cute band. What's it called again?'

'We are not cute. We are fierce. And you know the name of my band.'

'Wanderlust.' He said our name with that grin of his.

I started pouting.

'Stop sulking like that with those lips.'

'My band is fine, thriving even. I'm hoping we can get through the audition for Hard Wire later this year. That's the event I really want for us.'

'Hey, Vortex is going to be a guest star at that. I'll be able to watch you on stage. How exciting.'

'Stop it. You've never wanted to see us before,' I said defiantly. 'You'll just tease us, telling us we're cute or something.'

'Why do you hate being called cute? It's ok. What's wrong with that?'

'No, it's not ok,' I said stubbornly. 'Who do you think I am, Melissa?'

'Who's Melissa?'

'You know, the child star that sings about *bakso*[34] sellers.'

Now I was sulking.

As we stopped at the red light, he reached for my hand. 'I was just teasing you, *Dek*[35]. I'm sure you and the band are as fierce as hell. I believe in you one hundred per cent.'

'Thanks, *Abang*, that means a lot to me.'

'Oh really? Why's that?'

'Because the rest of the time, you're full of shit.'

Agam burst out at that. I was swelling with pride that I could make him laugh so freely.

'But you like my shit conversation.'

'Well, maybe,' I teased. 'Or maybe not.'

---

[34]*Abang Tukang Bakso* is a famous Indonesian children's song about a man who sells bakso (Indonesian soup with meatballs).
[35]*Dek*, short for Adek, translates as 'sister', is a term that's used to address a female younger than oneself

'For sure you do. You wouldn't be cruising with me tonight or any other night if you didn't.'

'Shut up and drive.'

Agam chuckled. 'No, seriously. Any plans to write your own songs someday?'

'I don't know,' I said as I stared at the traffic ahead. 'None of us have learnt music.'

'Neither did I, but that didn't stop me.'

'Yes, but you've had years of experience, and you were taught by a friend. We haven't had anywhere near the amount of experience and we have no one to teach us how to write.'

'Why don't you ask someone?'

'I've tried. Nobody wants to teach a girl, and the majority of girls I know won't even look at a guitar, let alone play it.'

'I'll teach you. Come to my place.'

'Right!' I raised my eyebrows. 'You? Teach me guitar?'

'That's the intention. Let's see how it goes.'

'Nice try,' I laughed. 'No thanks. The point is we're still a long way from creating our own songs.'

'If I can do it, you can too. Just keep practising and get as many gigs as you can. The music will come out of you eventually, and you'll make a great song on your own, trust me.'

***

The carpark was empty when we pulled in to the mini-mart. Agam stopped over on the left, away from the bright neon signs. As he turned the engine off, he faced me.

'Thanks for coming tonight.'

'I had a good time.'

We were silent. I waited for him to speak.

'I remember the first time I saw you,' he finally said.

I gave him a knowing smile, 'Yeah, about two years ago at Pid Pub. Dirga introduced me to Danu, and then I met you.'

'No, I saw you before that.'

'Are you serious?' I began squealing. 'When? Where?'

'At One Feel studio, about a few months before we met at Pid Pub. You came with Mirah and Kenari if I remember rightly.'

As I thought back to that day, a memory resurfaced. It had been late afternoon, and we had dropped by to watch Dirga and Hell's Fury practise.

'Yes,' I said excitedly. 'I don't remember seeing you though.'

'I was in the lobby with Ray and a few of the guys when you all came out of the rehearsal room. Dirga and Mirah sat by themselves and you and Kenari walked straight past to the terrace outside.'

'So that's when you first saw me?' I said enthusiastically. 'Now, I want to know what you did after that.'

'Nothing. The guys rushed out to join you two but Ray insisted I stay inside with him. He told me that you were supposed to come to me. According to Ray, I had a reputation to keep. so I just stared madly at you through the window,' chuckled Agam.

'Are you serious?' I was shrieking. 'That's ridiculous. You're the one who wanted to meet me. You should have come to me.'

'I wanted to, but apparently...' His voice trailed off.

I rolled my eyes. 'And what sort of reputation was that?'

'You don't want to know.'

Oh yes, I do. That reputation ruined our chance. If only we had met back then.

I stopped myself. We were both single at the time. Things might have ended up differently between us, but I realised that it wasn't the right thing to say. It was too late. Agam seemed to understand what was going through my mind.

'*Adek*, how you made me feel that afternoon in such a short time, I can't explain it. All I knew was that I couldn't stop thinking about you. And we did meet, didn't we? Yes, a little too late, but I'm still glad we did.'

His eyes started to slowly trace my face, and I could see the emotion in them. I had to turn my face away and look out the window. My eyes were welling up.

'Don't be sad,' he said softly.

I was about to ask him why he gave up on me, why he let Danu chase me and why he chose to go steady with another girl so soon after but there was no point. I grabbed my bag and slung it over my shoulder. If I stayed too long, I might break down in tears.

I was about to say goodbye when Agam firmly held my hand. 'You are alright, aren't you, *Dek*?'

Somehow the innocent question cast a heavy feeling in me.

'What's wrong?' He pulled me closer. 'Tell me.'

I forced a smile. 'I… I broke up with Danu a few weeks ago.'

'Are you serious? He hasn't said a thing about it. Why?'

'I can't tell you why. You need to go and see that reporter.'

'But you can't just drop a bomb and leave. I want to know. Was it Danu's decision or yours?'

'It was mine.'

'What happened?'

'I'll tell you why when I'm ready.'

'This might not be serious, right? You two might get back together. Poor Danu, whatever he did, I am sure he didn't mean it.'

'Doesn't matter; it's decided.'

He stared at me to see if I meant what I said.

'It's serious,' I said with a fixed stare. 'Believe me.'

His gaze wandered to the window, and he sighed.

'Now go,' I ordered. 'Don't you have a reporter to see?'

His eyes found me again. 'He can wait.'

'It's ok, go.'

At that moment, I wanted him so badly that my heart raced, and my whole body tingled. Without warning, I took my glasses off and began to kiss him. I ran my hand down through his mane. I had always wanted to do that. I felt like I was floating. Agam gently tilted my head back as he softly pulled on my hair, and then he traced his lips down onto my extended neck. I felt a shock ripple through my entire body as he kissed me all the way down to my collarbone.

A thundering sound of motorbikes smashed into our private world. The noise of the engines and people talking and laughing in the carpark was enough to give me the strength to regain my composure.

'Oh god,' I said in shock.

Agam lent back against the door, catching his breath. 'Sigi, I'm sorry.'

'Don't worry about it.'

On the contrary, I was aching, wanting him to do even more to me, with me. Instead, we just sat there, looking at each other in silence. I reached out my hands and gently started to fix his hair. I wanted to kiss him again but thought better of it.

'I want to kiss you again too,' he whispered.

I smiled. 'That's probably why I told you that I broke up with Danu.'

'Still doesn't make it right. I have a girlfriend.'

'Don't try to tell me that you've been loyal to her all this time.'

'Yes, but this is different....' He paused and chuckled. 'Goodnight, Sigi.'

'Nite *Abang*.' I hopped out of the car. He waved at me before entering the road, the sound of Napalm Death followed in his wake.

I snuck back home and through the dark house up to my room. In the soft bedside light, I smiled as I got changed. Snuggling down under the covers, I couldn't stop thinking about how good he felt, and his words.

You see, I don't want to fuck you because I want to.
I only want us to fuck if you want us to.
And that's different?
Oh yes. A thousand times different,' he answered.
'I don't want to manipulate you into doing what I want.
It has to come naturally. And for that, I'm willing to wait.

What I couldn't tell Agam was that I wasn't the girl that I used to be.

I'm different now that I'm no longer a virgin.

***

Chapter Ten

"Dreams"
The Cranberries

In the days since the kissing incident with Agam, I had been constantly obsessing over it. I had sleepless nights. I had mixed feelings. A part of me loved it immensely, but the rest of me was utterly terrified of how complicated things might become.

Yet I couldn't stop thinking about how heavenly he tasted. My mind kept wandering, dreaming about how good it felt when those lips were on my neck and collarbone. I was flying with those thoughts when I heard shouting.

'Sigi, wake up, now.'

It was enough to pull me back to earth.

I glanced at the clock-6:30am. It was Saturday. Not just a regular Saturday, but the day of the Jakarta Fair and my cousin's wedding. I unlocked the door and opened it to face my mother.

A short lady in her mid-fifties, she used to be beautiful, my father had said. Now she was just a mess. Her face was so full of plastic surgery that we almost didn't recognise her.

'You have to get ready for school,' she said with a smug expression. 'I'm tired of having to wake you up. You have your own alarm clock. Papa and Mama are leaving now to help with Hedi's wedding. You're to come with Bulan after school. Uncle Yudi will pick you up.'

I nodded while mentally planning my escape.

'You look like you haven't slept.'

'I was up all night studying.' I lied.

'Hurry up and get in the shower.' Then she was gone.

I got ready as usual, but the plan was to skip school and head over to Kenari's. I stuffed a change of clothes in my backpack. Tonight, when I came home, I'd have to deal with the wrath of my mother. I knew Matari wouldn't attend the wedding either, and I thought I'd just tell my mother that it's not fair because she never goes off at Matari. Not that it matters to her. She goes off at me for whatever. She used to beat me with a broom when I was a kid.

I passed through the security gate in front of our house at exactly 7:30am. Instead of flagging down a *bajaj*, I went straight to the bus stop about twenty metres up the road. I hid behind the large tree by the kerb in case anyone from my family drove by. I thought about school. Cutting classes wouldn't matter that much. It was Saturday, just a half-day. But I knew I had to pass if I still wanted my father to call me his daughter.

Finally, the bus heading south came along. I took a seat at the back and turned on my Walkman. The music was from a new band from Ireland called The Cranberries. The first time I heard the album, I fell in love with the voice of the vocalist, Dolores O'Riordan. I wished I could sing like her.

I looked through the window at the busy streets of Jakarta. The album's second track, 'Dreams', started and I let out a deep sigh as I listened to the lyrics. They made me think even more intensely about Agam.

Why did I kiss him?

I shook my head anxiously. I had risked my clean, good girl reputation in the underground. Even worse, if Agam's girlfriend discovered this or if Danu found out, it would seriously hurt both of them. I reminded myself to stop before it went too far.

Yes, he might be a talented musician with an amazing intellect and be understanding and kind, but he wasn't everything to me. Damn it, he just simply couldn't become that.

***

Forty-five minutes later, I arrived at Kenari's. The large lush garden filled with tropical trees was quiet with just the faint rustling of the leaves. I opened the gate and went around to the back of her white, colonial-style home. I knocked, and after a few moments, she opened the door.

'Hey, Sigi.' She was still wearing her pyjamas, standing there with a half-eaten banana in her hand. 'I'm just finishing breakfast. Have you eaten?'

Indonesians always ask each other if they've eaten. It was a kind of courtesy, the beginning of the small talk, an opening line, although no one actually cared that much if one had eaten or not. Except for mothers-they cared. Not mine, though.

'No, I'm not hungry.'

I slipped off my shoes and followed her into her bedroom. Kenari was free to do want she wanted, with her parents out of town. She basically owned the house right now and we could hang out until it was time to go to the Jakarta Fair. She closed the door and sat on her bed.

'Are you sure your maid won't dob us in?' I asked.

'No, she's cool,' she smiled. 'I give her a lot of my old clothes and that keeps her happy.'

'Ok, great.' I opened my backpack.

I took out the black t-shirt and a pair of dark blue jeans and quickly changed into them. I pulled the bedroom chair closer to her, sat down, and wondered how on earth to begin.

'By the way,' I said casually as I opened a new pack of cigarettes. 'I have a secret.'

'Oooh, I love secrets,' Kenari's eyes widened. 'Go on.'

'Promise not to tell anyone? You cannot tell a soul.'

She nodded as she held her breath in anticipation.

'I broke up with Danu.'

I smiled when I saw her shocked expression.

'Gosh, Sigi, this is big news. When did this happen? Why didn't you tell me?'

'I'm telling you now. And, I've been secretly seeing Agam.'

'Oh, my god!' Her eyes were now wide open.

'It gets worse. I kissed him the other night.'

'What?' She sat gaping at me. 'You kissed Agam? Oh my god,' she gasped again. 'Did I just hear you right? How did all this happen?'

I lit a cigarette. 'Agam rings me but my mother always picks up,' I explained. I pulled an agonising face remembering the looks she would give me. 'Usually, we'd just talk but now and then he'd be waiting for me at the mini-mart and we'd cruise around in his car for a while.'

Kenari gushed. 'And you guys kissed? Come on, details, please. What was it like?'

I paused as the memory came rushing into my thoughts.

'Oh wow,' she said. 'It must have been good. Look at you blushing. He's a good kisser, eh? Who kissed who first?'

'I did.'

Kenari clapped her hands wildly, 'You kissed him? But…' she paused. 'Oh my god,' she said for the third time. 'What about Danu? What did he do? Is it because of Agam? Is he breaking up with Berlian too?'

'No, nothing like that. I didn't split up with Danu because of Agam.'

'Oh,' Kenari said. 'Then why did you?'

I was dying to tell her the whole story, but I couldn't find it in me to do it.

'I don't love him anymore,' I finally said.

Hell, I never did but I didn't want Kenari to know that.

'Really? Are you in love with Agam? Is that why you kissed him?'

'No, no,' I said, frantically shaking my head. 'I don't think so. I like him a lot. I'm a huge fan, but I don't think I'm in love or anything.'

'Are you sure? Danu is a good guy,' Kenari's eyes were still like full moons. 'And he's sweet and loyal to you. It's hard to find a guy with those qualities around here. You remember back when Jacob played around on me, right? Are you sure you want to let Danu go?'

Kenari had broken up with her ex ages ago. He was a gorgeous metal musician but he was also a cheat who shamelessly slept with every groupie he could get his hands on.

I exhaled, blowing the smoke up towards the ceiling. 'Yes,' I said firmly.

She smiled and gave me a hug, 'It's ok, you know I'll support you whatever you do. You don't look sad, though, for someone who recently broke up with her boyfriend. Let me guess, hmmm, it must be that kiss.'

I hid my face in my hands, and Kenari stared shrieking.

'I can't believe it, Sigi, you, kissing Agam from Vortex! He's not as handsome or as tall as Ray, but damn he's wild. That long, wavy blonde hair is insane. Where did you do it?'

'In his car at the mini-mart near my place.'

'That's crazy. You had a lot of guts to kiss him first.'

'I know. Don't even know where I got the courage from. But it was worth it.'

Kenari clapped and laughed, 'We need to tell the girls.'

'Nooo,' I squealed. 'You're the only one who knows about this. We're committed to other people, well, at least he is. Promise me.'

'Ok, I promise,' she said as she took the cigarette from my fingers.

She didn't usually smoke, but the news excited her. She took a drag and blew out the smoke without inhaling. She looked cute in her soft pink and green pyjamas, with a cigarette in one hand and that half-eaten banana she'd forgotten about in the other.

She was the daughter of a businessman from Manado, and her mum was a manager of a famous five-star hotel. She was of mixed blood, Javanese and English. That explained her fair skin, which made her popular among the boys. As for the oily skin on her face, she hated that because it gave her a little acne. She envied my smooth skin, and I envied her fair skin.

'So what now? Won't it be awkward when you guys meet in public?'

'I don't want to think about that,' I said as I leaned over and grabbed that banana. I took a bite.

'Be careful,' Kenari said with a wink. 'Don't let your feelings get out of hand with this guy. He's a total player, just like my ex.'

'Yeah, I just wanted to have fun, that's all,' I said quickly as I ate the last of the banana. I could feel my heart aching. Kenari was right. Once the feelings started with this guy, I was basically doomed.

Kenari shook her head with a knowing smile that irritated me.

'I want to hear the songs we've chosen for tonight. Can you play them on the tape?' I decided we needed to talk about something else.

She nodded and passed the cigarette back to me as she stood up and walked to the chest of drawers. She took out a mixed cassette, inserted it into the tape recorder, and pressed 'play'. The room came alive with punk.

'I better get into the shower,' she said as she grabbed a couple of towels.

I scanned the walls. Like mine, they were full of posters: Poison, Mötley Crüe, and a print of Sebastian Bach of Skid Row, the sexy rock star from America with an inviting smile. It was as big as my Axl Rose. We all loved their looks. But her passion for music was clear in the oversized Sepultura poster that took precedence on the opposite wall, along with an image of Kreator and a few other metal bands.

Her desk was in a mess. Paper, pens, pencils, coins, and cassettes lay cluttered about. Her bed was more or less in the same state, with crumpled blankets, an acoustic guitar, a few books, and dirty clothes. Tapes were scattered about too.

I looked out the open window and stood up to throw what was left of my cigarette onto the garden. I grabbed Kenari's guitar and put it on my lap as I sat back on the chair. I started to follow The Clash on the tape.

Fifteen minutes later, Kenari was out of the shower. Her strawberry blonde hair was wrapped in a white towel, her slender body covered by another.

'Hey, I have an idea. Let's call Raya,' she said as she got dressed.

She sat on the edge of the bed where the guitar had been. Her wet hair was down to her waist, falling over her plain t-shirt and jeans.

'Mirah said she cuts school a lot, so she might be at home,' she added. 'The phone is locked, but that won't stop us, though.'

The phone was in the living room, an old model with a curly cable attached to it. It sat on a small round table that came with a single chair. As predicted, it was locked. The usual manner of dialling was impossible, given the position of the padlock, strategically placed right in the middle. Not an easy phone to use.

Kenari was, however, an expert. She reached for her small book of contacts from the back of the table and checked Soraya's number. She sat down on the chair and picked up the phone.

She put it against her left ear and performed a series of rapid clicks with the 'on' and 'off' switches - six clicks for number six, eight clicks for eight, ten clicks for zero until she had 'dialled' the full number. In between each set of clicks, she paused a few seconds so as not to blend one number with the next.

I tried this method at home, but it was never successful. It was a good thing my mother had recently replaced our old phone with a new digital model. That had a plastic cover which hid the digits, and it was also fixed with a padlock. All I needed was a really slim screwdriver to press the numbers through the gap that lay between the plastic cover and the buttons below.

I watched in awe as Kenari succeeded and the call connected to Raya's number.

***

Chapter Eleven

"Sin in My Heart"
Siouxsie and the Banshees

We waited impatiently as someone picked up on the other end.

'*Selamat pagi*[36]. Can I speak to Soraya please?' asked Kenari, looking excitedly at me. 'It's you? *Hai, apa kabar*[37]. It's Kenari from Wanderlust.' She gave me the thumbs up. 'You didn't go to school? Same. Sigi is here with me. What are you doing? So happy you came to practice. Are you busy? Can we talk?'

I knelt down next to Kenari and pressed my right ear against the receiver. I could faintly hear Soraya's voice.

'Yeah, I'm not doing much. What's up?'

Kenari gave me a questioning look. 'What should I say?' she whispered.

I stared back at her with a blank expression.

After a few seconds, she spoke. 'We were wondering if you were interested in joining our band.'

There was a pause on the other end. Kenari and I waited nervously.

'I haven't decided yet,' she finally said.

'Ok,' said Kenari.

'Tell her that we might have a gig in Menteng,' I whispered.

'Oh yeah, and coming up, we might be playing at the Hard Wire festival, but we still have to audition-'

'No thanks.' I heard Soraya's croaky voice cutting her off. 'It's a metal event- no way! Mirah can handle that. Do you have any other gigs that aren't metal?'

Kenari gave me another look. I sighed as I took the phone from her hand, shooed her out of the chair and sat down.

---

[36] *Selamat pagi* meaning 'Good morning.'
[37] *Apa kabar* meaning 'How are you?'

'*Hai* Raya, this is Sigi. How are you?'

'Oh hey Sigi.' She sounded more cheerful.

Kenari kneeled next to me and placed her ear where mine had been.

'I heard you don't want to play at Hard Wire audition and that you still haven't made your mind up yet.'

'Sorry, but I don't like metal, you know that.'

'Yeah, I do,' I said. 'Tonight's gig at the Jakarta Fair will be Mirah's last as our vocalist. She's only going to be playing bass. Then after Hard Wire, if we get through the audition, that is, we're going to lose her completely.'

I looked at Kenari before continuing. 'So after tomorrow, we won't have a vocalist, and within a few months, we're not going to have a bass player either, and only you can do both, Raya. You're perfect. By the way, did you know that a few punk bands have been playing at some low-key metal events lately around Jakarta?'

The line went silent.

'A couple of bands have come up from Bandung[38] too, so we aren't the only punk band mixing with the metal guys. But we'll still be the first all-girl punk band,' I said smiling, hoping to change her mind.

Again, Kenari and I waited desperately.

'Perfect, am I?' Soraya questioned. 'If that's the case, I might consider joining.'

'Really? You would?' answered Kenari for me, screaming down the line.

'*Hai* again, Kenari.' This time there was a smile in Soraya's voice too. 'No, I said I'd consider and we need to get one thing straight. Don't expect me to be nice to those metal fans because they annoy me.'

'You can spit on them for all I care,' I said, unable to hide my own excitement.

She laughed. 'Let me think about it and I'll let you know.'

'Don't think for too long,' I said confidently. 'I know we're in

---

[38]An underground was also being established in Ujungberung, an area on the eastern outskirts of Bandung, a large city about 100km south of Jakarta.

the metal scene, but we're a punk band. We're flexible. Let me know if you find any other gigs we could play at.'

'Ok,' she replied.

I put down the phone.

'There you go,' smiled Kenari. 'She's considering it. Good news, right?'

'Why can't she just say yes though!' I rolled my eyes.

My heart started racing when I thought of the Hard Wire festival. It was one of the most prestigious annual metal events, and it was going to be held in central Jakarta rather than at one of the usual venues in the south of the city. If we passed the audition, Wanderlust, for the first time, would be playing alongside some of the biggest names in the underground like Vortex, Hell's Fury, Betrayer, Roxx, and Razzle.

That would mean I'd be sharing the stage with Agam, and he would see us on stage for the first time too. And Danu, he'd be there; I knew he wouldn't miss it either. That was a disturbing thought, given he'd always put our band down.

Like watching kindergarten, he had said!

I didn't know if I would even be able to perform without throwing up.

'What is it? Why is your face so pale? You're worried she won't join us?'

I gave her a reassuring smile. The last thing I needed was for Kenari to be nervous too. Besides, the audition was still a while away.

'No, everything's going to be fine. She'll do it, I'm sure.'

***

It was past noon when we set off from Kenari's. We stopped for a quick bite at a nearby *warung*[39] that specialised in *soto ayam*, a traditional chicken soup considered the comfort food of Indonesia. I couldn't eat much. I was nervous about performing at the Jakarta

---

[39] *Warung* are the street-side stalls that sell a range of goods from food and cigarettes to small household items

Fair later that evening. After lunch, we waited at a busy shaded bus stop.

'Off we go, back to central,' I said, lighting a cigarette.

Kenari took a folded piece of paper from her backpack. She opened it and began reading. 'Our soundcheck is at three, and we're on stage at seven.'

'We're meeting Mirah and Grace there, right?'

'Yeah, at the West gate at two-thirty,' she said as she put it back in her bag.

The Jakarta Fair incorporated everything from a food festival to amusement rides, various shows that included dance and music performances– and us, the up-and-coming young bands from all over Jakarta. I still wasn't that enthusiastic about playing for this audience though.

'Are you scared?'

'Not really,' I lied, as I gazed along the busy street.

'You realise that there's going to be a huge crowd?'

'Or none at all,' I said, waving my hands at the bus heading our way. 'Remember we're playing at the West Wing, and all the mainstream bands will be playing in the Square.'

'True,' she said as the bus came to a screeching halt in front of us.

The noisy *kernek*[40] screamed loudly, '*Kemayoran Kemayoraaan! Kosong mbak, kosong*[41].'

We quickly jumped on and made our way to the back of the bus.

'Hey,' Kenari continued as we took our seats. 'Didn't you have a wedding to go to tonight, your cousin's or something?'

'Yeah,' I said dully.

The bus rumbled along the busy main street, leaving a trail of thick smoke behind it.

Kenari smirked. 'You hate going to weddings.'

---

[40]*Kernek* are the bus conductors who used to ride the buses in this era, and they are still used in some regions of Indonesia today.

[41]'*Kemayoran Kemayoraaan! Kosong mbak, kosong*' loosely translated as 'Girls, there are still some empty seats on the bus heading to Kemayoran.'

'Yes, I do, especially if it happens to be at the same time as a gig.'

'Why do you hate weddings so much?'

'I don't know,' I sighed. 'My parents don't seem to be happy, especially my mother. I've rarely seen her satisfied with anything my father does. She was only nineteen years old when they got married, and then straight away she had three kids. Bulan told me that she might have been too young and I supposed that made her crazy and selfish.'

'But everyone got married at that age back then.'

'Yes, they did. I'll be nineteen next year. I seriously don't want to get married yet, do you?'

Kenari shook her head, smiling, 'No, I'm going to study in the UK. Don't have time for it.'

'Exactly, and how are you going to avoid, you know, doing it?' I said. 'We're Indonesian. We know it's not right to have sex before marriage, but I don't know if I can wait for that long.'

Kenari placed her hand on my shoulder as she blushed. She was still a virgin and that was probably the sole reason her ex decided to venture into other places.

'Yeah,' she moaned. 'It's always the same. Like when I was with Jacob. He was so hot but I couldn't go all the way with him. I still cry about it sometimes.'

We giggled. My lips tingled as I remembered the taste of Agam.

'I don't understand,' I said. 'And as for my mother, waiting until she married didn't make her a better parent. She's so selfish.'

'You always say that.'

'Well, she is,' I started. 'She only thinks about herself and what she wants. Like, she shops all the time for high-end stuff but never buys us anything. She gossips a lot and she hates anyone that has more than her, and she's always suspicious-'

'That's my mum too,' Kenari cut in. 'Always suspicious. What about your father?'

'He's a lot older than my mother and never talks much to us unless it's really important.'

'Geez,' sighed Kenari. 'Sounds like my dad too.'

The bus came to a stop. We were in Kemayoran.

***

The Jakarta Fair was buzzing with life, and more people would be coming after work.

'Where's the West Wing?' I asked, looking the map we received at the entrance.

'Here,' Kenari pointed her finger. 'See there it says west, next to the furniture exhibition.'

I put the map back in my bag, and we started towards the general area. It was located in an outdoor section of the Fair at the back of one of the buildings.

We strolled past the sea of stands and exhibitions that sold everything Indonesia had to offer. We saw local fashion, handmade arts and crafts, furniture, and traditional cuisine, all jam-packed into the colossal zone.

'We should have eaten here,' said Kenari, with a longing look at the steaming food.

My mouth watered as I smelled the aroma of *satay* on a nearby barbeque. Now I was hungry. 'Let's get something after the sound-check.'

I noticed Mirah waving at us from a distance.

She ran towards us with Grace trailing behind her. Both were holding paper bags full of hot snacks.

'What's that? Ooh, yes, please,' Kenari smiled as she opened Mirah's bag. She took out a *kue pastel*, a type of mince pie. I looked into the one Grace was holding and grabbed a *tahu isi*, fried tofu stuffed with vegetables.

'Grace and I have just been at the West Wing. Our soundcheck has been delayed for thirty minutes, so how about we hang out here?' said Mirah.

She led us towards a spare table. She was wearing a pair of cargo shorts. teamed with a light blue denim shirt. The rest of us wore jeans and t-shirts. As usual, we were wearing our All-Stars sneakers. We sat down on the empty bench.

102

'Ice tea for everyone?' asked Mirah.

We all nodded.

'By the way,' said Grace excitedly. 'Mirah is very nervous right now. Dirga might come and see us play tonight.'

Kenari squealed while Mirah's cute round cheeks burst into colour.

'No way,' Kenari's mouth opened in shock.

'Is he really?' I asked, trying to sound cool. The thought of playing under the watchful eye of someone like Dirga was nerve-racking.

'He didn't say point-blank. He said he was just joking,' said Mirah as she ran her fingers through her hair. 'But you know Dirga. When he jokes like that, it's usually-'

'True,' I said, finishing her sentence.

'So he's likely to show up?' asked Kenari. 'Oh, that's wild.'

Like Agam, Dirga had waist-length hair. Although it was black and curly, it was still a signature metal look. He would definitely draw attention.

'I don't know if he's actually coming,' Mirah said with a flat expression. 'I don't care. Whatever.'

Of course, she cared. We all knew it.

With that, she walked over to the stand to buy the iced teas.

'Look at her. She's panicking,' Kenari laughed. 'Imagine if he does show up.'

'She'll be pleased,' said Grace with a grin. 'By the way, Nari, did you skip school? I didn't see you this morning.'

'Yeah, we did,' replied Kenari, pointing at me. 'Sigi came over, and we spoke with Raya cos she skipped class too.'

'Really?' Grace arched her eyebrows. 'What did she say?'

'She said she'll consider it,' said Kenari.

'And we told her about Hard Wire too,' I added. 'At first, she completely refused but we told her about the metal gigs in Jakarta where a few punk bands have been playing. She didn't know because she never comes to our underground events. When I explained it would be Mirah's final performance, she said she would think about that too. But we have to pass that damn audition first.'

'Oh wow, she will?' Grace's eyes were wide. 'Do you think she'll say yes?'

'I don't know,' I replied.

'Why not?' asked Grace.

'We might not be edgy enough for her.'

'Have a little faith,' said Kenari. 'We're an all-girl band, and that's rare.'

'And,' continued Grace, 'Did you know we're rather famous for punk, even though we play grunge too. My friends at school told me.'

'When I was broadcasting the other night, a listener recognised me as Sigi from Wanderlust, you know, our punk band,' I said with a cheeky laugh.

Kenari clapped her hands.

'That's insane. Finally, we're famous.'

'We are?' said a surprised voice. Mirah was back. 'That's great. I hope you become really famous. I wish I could keep playing with you guys next year.'

We fell into silence as we all felt the same surge of emotion. Mirah had been a significant force in the band. Her popularity in the underground had helped us get recognised, and she had scored some of our best gigs.

'As for the vocals, I wish I could keep singing, but I've already promised my parents that I'll focus more on my studies for the rest of this year,' she said sadly. 'Remember how badly I failed some of my last exams? I almost didn't make it because of my bad grades.'

The only reason she had passed was because of her father's influence. He was a well-known singer and musician, but he had also said he was ashamed of her poor performance, and that it was the first and last time he would help.

Mirah was academically brilliant, but her involvement with Wanderlust and the amount of time she spent following Dirga everywhere in the underground were the reasons for her failure. She had to cut back to just playing bass, and cut back on seeing her boyfriend.

'We still have another few months before you leave, so we've still got time to stamp our name on the underground,' I stated firmly.

'Thanks. Hopefully, if we get into Hard Wire, you can keep the band going.'

'Provided Raya agrees to sing in the audition,' Kenari shook her head.

'Don't worry,' I said trying look confident. 'We have to make this gig count first. It's Mirah's last on vocals. Never mind the crowd, let's have fun.'

'Now we're talking,' Grace was smiling too.

'Geez, thanks, girls,' Mirah's eyes were on the brink of tears as the vendor placed our drinks on the table.

We leaned together around the table in a group hug.

'Long live Wanderlust,' sang Kenari. 'May our band become famous in Jakarta and right across Indonesia!'

We raised our bottles of icy-cold tea as a toast to our future success.

***

Chapter Twelve

The medium-sized stage had been set up with the sponsors' logos on a large backdrop that hung behind the drums. Backstage we were greeted by one of the organisers.

'Hey Mirah, what's up?' A thin young guy wearing a Jakarta Fair t-shirt came over. 'I'm Jaya. We spoke on the phone.' He shook our hands. 'Your soundcheck is after the guys from Kanisius High School.'

We looked up at the stage and saw five boys setting up and tuning their instruments.

'They're using their own gear,' continued Jaya. 'Fancy equipment that.'

Kanisius was a prestigious private Catholic school for boys, and the students were usually from wealthy families, mostly Chinese.

'What do they play?' I asked him.

'Jazz, what else,' he winked. 'I can't wait to see you girls, though.' With that, he disappeared.

We moved to find a seat as the boys started playing. I had no idea what the song was because jazz wasn't something I knew. They played well; those Chinese-Indonesian guys took their music seriously.

A few people clapped when it was over and we saw Jaya coming back towards us.

'Get ready, girls,' he chirped. 'Time for your soundcheck. Just one song. Can't finish late tonight, sorry, that's our license.'

As always, we attracted the attention of the crowd. A few guys even whistled. We grabbed the equipment we were borrowing from the side of the stage and plugged in the cables.

'Testing, one, two, three.'

The crowd was watching intently; most of them were musicians. I felt the adrenaline kicking in and my body began breaking out in a nervous sweat.

Grace clicked her sticks four times and we launched into the Sex Pistols' "Submission".

The audience stood still as we played while the sound engineer balanced the audio from the small mixer tent twenty metres in front of the stage. My hands were shaking, but I tried to keep my attention on what I was doing and I soon forgot about my surroundings.

When we finished, I was transported back to the present by a faint round of applause.

At least they're clapping.

We quickly packed away the equipment and headed off stage.

'Sex Pistols, eh? That was cool,' Jaya greeted us with a big smile. 'I heard you play grunge too. Are you playing Nirvana's "Smells like Teen Spirit"?'

'No, not tonight,' said Mirah.

'Shame,' he said. 'By the way, you girls are free to roam. The show starts at six and you're on at seven, so make sure you're back at least half-hour beforehand.'

***

We decided to look around the Fair, wandering about, talking and laughing, and looking at the goods for sale inside the various booths and stalls.

Yet I couldn't help feeling down. Mirah was leaving after Hard Wire, then Grace was going in the middle of next year, and Kenari six months after that. I had made a promise to keep the band alive, but I had the feeling right at that moment that I wasn't going to be able to.

Even though I was part of the band, I still felt like an outsider. Wanderlust was gaining notoriety as an all-girl band from SMA3, the high school where the girls went. And I, the outsider from a different high school, would be the only one left.

'Don't be sad,' said Mirah as she gave me a hug. She sensed what I was thinking about. 'You're the lucky one. Look at it that way, the adventures you going to have, the music, the rehearsals, the gigs, the guys… to be honest, I'm jealous.'

I smiled. Ah, the boys of the underground. The source of all our trouble!

'Not being able to see all those cute guys will probably be the saddest part of leaving,' I teased, and she smiled.

'Yeah, true, eh, but one thing about being in a band that I've realised, Sigi, is that the guys look at us differently now. They've always talked about their groupies whenever they got together. You know, this girl has big boobs, that other girl was good in bed, that kind of thing. They never talked about us that way once we formed Wanderlust.'

My eyes grew wide. There was no doubt that, as Dirga's girl-friend, Mirah was speaking the truth. She had overheard a lot of the guys talking.

She continued, 'Perhaps it's because we slowly won their re-spect. It took guts for us to be in a band, especially in this ruthless underground.'

'True,' I sighed. 'Thanks for letting me join.'

'Are you kidding?' she laughed as she gave me a push. 'The way you travel from central Jakarta to the south every week to practise? I think we should all thank you, silly.'

'Don't worry about it. I'm having fun.'

'Girls,' said Grace. 'It's nearly 6:30. It's time to head back.'

We turned around and began making our way past the packed stalls.

'So, no more boys?' I asked Mirah.

She laughed. 'No more boys except perhaps Dirga, sometimes. I have to pass the legacy over to you, Sigi. Please don't disappoint me.'

***

When we arrived at the West Wing, the stage was lit with colour-ful bright lights. The area in front was about half full with people were sitting on benches and a few others standing around watching the band. Roxette's "Joyride" was blasting through the speakers.

'You like this song?' asked Grace.

'It's always on the radio so I'm bored to death with it,' I grumbled.

She laughed as the song finished and people clapped cheerfully.

'Hello everyone, we're Buku Cerita. We're happy to be here at the Jakarta Fair. How are you all doing tonight? Have you been shopping yet?' smiled the female vocalist.

Mirah never made this sort of small talk with the audience, but I understood that it was necessary at a mainstream event like this.

'Here's a slow number from Extreme. This is "More than Words".'

We moved towards the right of the backstage. In the corner, musicians were hanging about, tinkering with the equipment. A few of them stared at us and I felt my nerves rush again.

They were all dressed in their stage outfits. The girls wore fancy dresses and makeup and high heels, and the boys had on shirts, trousers, and fancy shoes. And then there was Wanderlust. Four girls without makeup wearing casual clothes. I decided to reach for a cigarette just to add more fuel to the already fiery stares from these mainstream musicians.

Kenari mumbled in my ear, 'This place seems to be full of well-behaved misters and misses, eh.'

'Never mind them,' I said, trying to sound disinterested. 'We're different.'

'More like no skills,' she grinned. 'More like brats cutting school sort of different.'

'Hey, there you are,' Jaya appeared out of nowhere, his skinny hands holding a box full of bottled water. 'Want some?'

We each took a bottle.

'Two more bands, ok?' he said. 'I need to pass these out. I'll be right back. Stay here until I call you.' Then he disappeared again.

A moment later, we heard the sound of applause as Buku Cerita finished their last song. The MC took over and thanked all the sponsors.

'One more, and we're on,' Mirah sighed. 'Are you nervous?'

'Kind of. How many songs are we playing?'

'I've already told you like twenty times. We're going to play three.'

'Yeah, I know, L7's "Pretend We're Dead", Sex Pistols' "Submission", and The Clash, "Should I Stay or Should I Go".'

'Look,' Grace said, pointing with her chin forward. 'The Kanisius boys.'

We fell silent as we watched them walking eagerly with their gear towards the stage. My heart was thumping.

'I need to go to the loo,' said Kenari, looking a bit pale.

'I'll come with you,' said Mirah.

I stood mindlessly listening to the jazz; my understanding of it hadn't improved since they played at the soundcheck. With their third number drawing to an end, I moved closer to Grace. 'Are you ready?'

She was leaning over, pulling her drumsticks out of her backpack. 'Think so, you?'

I showed her my cigarette.

'You smoke too much.'

'I know. Why don't you go ahead on stage? I'll wait here for the girls.'

'Ok, don't be too long, and don't light another one.' She grabbed her backpack, and left me there.

When the cigarette was down to the butt, I threw it on the ground and stepped on it with my sneaker. I was trying to stay calm amidst the organised chaos backstage.

Then I saw him, thin, almost two metres tall. His dark brown hair was loose, covering half his face and curling down past his skinny shoulders. He quickly invited attention. His face was ordinary, but his fair skin, which looked even lighter against his black Kreator t-shirt, made him look different. He stood out like the Indo-Western mixed-blood boys do.

He walked into the backstage. His smile grew as he caught me staring at him.

'Hello, Sigi.' His light brown eyes were gentle and he stopped right in front of me. 'Surprise!'

'Danu,' I said weakly. 'You came.'

***

For a moment, time seemed to stand still. I felt a surge of emotions as Danu looked at me. Nervously, I glanced around to avoid him, but he didn't budge until finally I had to say something. 'What are you doing here?'

'To see you on stage, what else?'

'I thought you never wanted to see me play.'

He leaned in towards me. 'You left me no choice. It's been way too long, Sigi, and I needed to see you.'

'Who are you here with?'

It was unlikely that he came alone; Indonesians rarely did anything alone.

'You mustn't tell Mirah. I came with Dirga. He asked me to come, so all the more reason to finally watch you perform.'

'Now you're mocking me.'

'I'm not.' He grabbed my hands and held them intensely in his. 'Gosh, everything I say is wrong.'

I took back my hands. Just the thought of Dirga watching us made me anxious, and now Danu was here too.

'If you don't want Mirah to know that you're here, you need to go. She'll be back soon from the toilet.'

'Ok, we'll hang at the back behind the audience.'

'I didn't mean it like that. I'm just shocked. You've never wanted to see me on stage before.' I said accusingly.

'I'm allowed to change my mind.'

'Of course,' I replied flatly.

Why was I not surprised!

'Anyway, you need to take a hike, now.'

'Don't be so *galak dong*[42],' he winked. 'I'm still your boyfriend. I'll see you later, and good luck!'

---

[42]*Galak* means 'fierce' or 'fiery' *Dong* is a particle used for emphasis.

What?

I watched him turn and disappear out into the crowd.

Just in time, Mirah and Kenari were back.

'What's up, Sigi? You look pale,' said Kenari.

'I'm ok.' I paused as I realised that Mirah looked even pastier. 'Are you alright?'

'I'm always nervous.'

'Me too,' sighed Kenari. 'Let's hope for the best.'

***

The stage lights were hot and blinding as we checked our instruments and made last-minute adjustments. I tried to spot Danu and Dirga, but the audience was swathed in shadow.

My guess was there would have been around forty people standing in the front and another twenty or so sitting further back behind them.

I was struggling to breathe as I plugged in the guitar. When I tested the distortion effect, the sound roared across the open space. Looking up, I saw the girls were waiting. I nodded and Mirah, with her bass, approached the microphone.

'Hello everyone, we're Wanderlust from SMA3,' said Mirah with a flat voice. 'First song is from L7 called "Pretend We're Dead".'

Grace hit the cymbal four times. I kept my eyes on my guitar. My hands were shaking, but as usual, I felt more at ease as soon as we got into it. With its medium beat and heavy distortion, the song was from an all-girl grunge band we had seen on MTV.

This audience, however, wasn't filled with the kind of people that watched that channel. Nonetheless, we got a round of applause and a few whistles when we had finished. I felt my enthusiasm rise and it wasn't going to be as bad as I thought.

Sex Pistols' "Submission" came next. I decided not to care so much about the crowd and this song was more effortless. Finally, that was over too and we heard an even bigger round of applause.

The girls and I quickly glanced at each other to check our mood. I noticed Jaya giving us the thumbs up from the side of the stage,

113

a sign that we still had time to play the third song. I heard Mirah talking on the mike.

'Thanks, everyone, for the applause. Once again, we are Wanderlust from SMA3.'

She paused as if to take a deep breath. My heart stopped, as the crowd watched her intently. I saw her looking towards the back of the audience. I followed her gaze, and it fell on two faces, shadowy yet recognisable.

'Tonight is my last time singing with these girls.' Her voice was shaky. She never spoke much or interacted with our audiences; I felt for her.

'I'll still be playing bass with them. This is a great band, and it will keep going. Thanks for supporting Wanderlust. Now for our last song, here's "Should I Stay or Should I Go" from The Clash.'

With that, I opened with my chords. All eyes fell on me, and a rush of blood battered my nerves again. Thankfully, it settled once the others joined in and Mirah started singing. I felt a new energy and I began to relax.

It was an easygoing number, with playful lyrics that fit Mirah's situation. She powered through, knowing that this was her final song with Wanderlust.

I noticed a few people starting to dance. I couldn't help but smile. How we loved performing. This audience didn't know the music, but if some of them were dancing, we couldn't ask for more.

Then it was over. The crowd gave us a rousing cheer as I looked around and saw the girls smiling. We left the stage feeling exhilarated.

***

Chapter Thirteen

"I'm Set Free"
Velvet Underground

Jaya excitedly shook our hands one by one and slipped an envelope to Mirah before dashing off. We were still smiling from ear to ear. Finally, we were getting paid!

'Probably not much,' she said, tearing the envelope open. 'Sixty thousand. Not bad, fifteen each.'

'Yayy,' Kenari clapped her hands.

'Hello girls, all good?'

We glanced up as Dirga and Danu appeared. Kenari threw me a curious glance. I gave her a look of my own, indicating to be quiet.

'Hey baby,' said Dirga as he grabbed Mirah around her waist and gave her a warm hug.

Mirah was beaming. 'You came. How long have you been here?'

'Just before you started,' he said, smiling at the rest of us. 'It was a good performance, congratulations.'

'Really?' asked Kenari.

A compliment like that coming from a top musician like Dirga meant a lot to us.

Finally, we said our goodbyes. Grace and Kenari followed Mirah and Dirga. I had no choice except to walk the other way with Danu unless I was prepared to answer the unwanted questions that would come my way.

We headed out towards the carpark. People were staring at us. Maybe Danu's height and long hair attracted them. I secretly used to enjoy the attention we would get, especially outside of south Jakarta. Now we walked in silence until we reached the old Kijang.

'You brought your father's car,' I said as he unlocked the door.

'Yeah, he let me borrow it when he heard that I was coming to watch you. Great, eh, we don't have to take a taxi,' he said with a big smile. 'He likes the fact that you're in a band, strangely enough.'

'He's cooler than you,' I said flatly.

He opened the door to let me in.

'No thanks,' I shook my head.' I'm taking a taxi.'

'Don't be like that,' said Danu with a worried look. 'I'm here. Let me take you home.'

I glared at him with determination. At that moment, I would have rather been hit by a bus than take up his offer.

'I'm fine, and I'm leaving.'

I turned and walked away. I heard Danu bang the door and walk quickly to catch up.

'Sigi, come on, baby,' he nervously whispered in my ear. 'Why are you doing this?'

'You're asking me why?' My blood was starting to boil. I decided to stop walking and turned to face him.

'Let me ask you something. Why are you here?'

'To see you, to watch you perform.'

'Really?' I crossed my arms in front of my chest.

We stood looking at each other. The tension was so great that I could hear my own breathing.

'You were great,' he finally said with his usual cheery tone. It was so out of context that I wanted to strangle him. 'I like the distortion effect you used. You set it up pretty raw and edgy. I swear the whole Fair stopped to watch. Made me proud of you.'

'You're proud of me? Really? You said that I should quit and concentrate on school.'

'People can change their mind.'

That was the second time he'd said something of the sort.

I didn't reply. Danu's presence triggered a flashback, rapid and cruel. We were in his bedroom lying in his bed under the blanket, me nothing but panties on, him kissing and caressing my body, me trying to get lost in the feeling but too aware, too conscious that his hands were stripping me bare.

Blood!

In a split second came the blood, a splash of deep red against the white sheets.

'I have a question. After what had happened that day, how can you be so casual right now?' I demanded.

Danu's face dropped. 'It's not like I don't want to talk about it. I'm just waiting for the right time-'

'There is no right time,' I cut him off. 'What happened was horrible. How can you pretend like it's nothing, even for a second?'

I moved backwards to sit on the pavement, hidden behind a parked car. Danu followed and sat next to me. We sat in silence as I wept with my face buried in my hands.

He waited patiently as I cried. Images of the incident filled my mind-blood on his sheets, blood on his blankets. I had been hysterical; he had looked insipid, his jaw tense as he quickly took the bedding away.

I was left alone as he struggled to wash the blood out of the bathroom sink. I wished he had stayed with me. I wished he had hugged me, calmed me down, and told me everything was going to be ok. Instead, he left me alone to wash the stains, and I panicked, got dressed, and ran out the door.

The thought stopped my crying and I slowly raised my head. He looked worried as I regained a little composure.

'Let me get us a drink, and some tissues.' He walked off towards a small *warung*.

My chest felt empty and I realised that my face was wet, even my shirt was soaked.

When he returned, he handed me a small pack. I grabbed a few tissues and blew my nose. Then he gave me a bottle of cold water.

More silence.

I drank some water and lit a cigarette. I had never smoked in front of him before. He knew that I smoked and he didn't like it, so I usually abstained in front of him. At that moment, I didn't care anymore. He wisely said nothing.

'You took it,' I said after I had exhaled a few long drags. 'You took my virginity without my consent.'

'I'm sorry.'

'You promised to be careful, so I let you. I didn't know you were going to go that far. Then, then...' I paused. 'Now I've lost my virginity.'

'You were so excited. I thought you wanted to.'

'You didn't ask and I didn't give my permission.'

'I swear it was an accident, a misunderstanding,' he pleaded and reached for my hands. 'I know you're angry, but I'm still here. We love each other, don't we? Don't throw away what we had for so long away over this one mistake?'

I felt the pain in my lower lip as I bit down hard. I almost blurted out the truth, that I didn't love him and that I never did. I stopped myself in time.

'We'll get married someday.' He squeezed my hands. 'When I finish my studies and have a job, we can definitely do that. Look, Sigi, I'm trying to say that I'm deeply sorry for what happened and I'm fully committed to you one hundred per cent. You can trust me.'

I felt confused. Danu was looking at me with so much love that I was drowning in it. What was worse was that he mistook my silence as a sign of agreement.

He gave me a beaming smile. 'Let's take you home now. I don't want you in trouble with your parents.'

'I'm taking a taxi.'

'Come on, don't be silly.'

'No, Danu. Why can't you understand? I lost my virginity before marriage, and that's a big deal for me!'

'It was a big mistake, I admit that, but please, I'm begging you, let me be responsible for what I did.'

I stood up, and kicked a stone lying on the pavement. It travelled fast and made a loud clanging sound as it hit a nearby rubbish bin. Smoking nervously, I began to pace while I contemplated what to say. He continued to watch me from where he was sitting. I wanted so badly to tell him that I didn't love him, but again I managed to hold my tongue.

'I need to think things through,' I finally said as I threw what was left of my cigarette on the ground. 'But right now, for god's sake Danu, I can't be in the same car with you.'

'I can see that,' he said as he stood up. He cautiously held my two hands in his.

'I'll let you go,' he said gently. 'Be safe. And call me if… when… you're not angry anymore.'

I was too exhausted to argue.

'Bye Sigi, hope we'll speak soon.'

I snatched back my hands and walked off as fast as I could.

***

I woke up the next day feeling down and lethargic. It was Sunday. That meant the whole family was probably at home. I lay in bed, staring at the white ceiling, listening to the slow hum of the air conditioner. In the gap between the curtains, intense rays of sunshine were breaking through into the darkroom so it was probably about midday.

There was a soft knock on my door. *'Mbak* Sigi, you have a phone call.'

Umi's voice brought me back to reality. With considerable effort, I pulled myself out of bed and looked in the mirror. The girl staring back at me was every bit as worn out with red puffy eyes and messy hair.

'Who is it?' I asked with a raspy voice from too much smoking. I feared it might be Danu.

'Soraya *mbak.*'

I threw on a pair of shorts and t-shirt and opened the door. Bulan was hanging about, as usual, staring at me. She seemed amused and her lips formed a little knowing smile as she looked at me.

Matari came out from the bathroom with a towel wrapped around her head. 'Where were you last night? Mama was furious,' she demanded.

'Why?' I said defensively. 'Were you there?'

Matari shook her head on her way to her room. 'That's why she's furious.'

Without answering her, I went dashing down the stairs, only to be greeted by the devil herself.

'So you think you can just do what you like?'

Here we go again.

She was standing next to the phone. Clearly Soraya could hear what she was saying. I hated her for treating me like a child.

'What if you get married someday, and no one comes?'

My god, she could carry on.

'What if you get sick? Nobody will want to help because you don't care about anyone. All you care about is that bloody band. And what do you get out of it? I don't think they even pay you-'

'They did,' I cut her short, only to learn that I had just added fuel to the fire.

'How much, hmmm, one million, two million?' she sneered. 'My guess is less than a hundred thousand, divided by what, the four of you?'

I decided not to reply. She continued on about how stupid we girls were, and then she walked back into the kitchen, still muttering.

I sat down on the chair by the phone and picked up the receiver. 'Hello?'

'Hey, it's me, Raya.'

'Hi, thanks for waiting. Sorry, I'm guessing you probably heard her.'

She laughed, 'If it makes you feel any better, my mum's worse. Let's not talk about mothers. How was last night?'

'Nothing exciting, we got paid, though,' I sighed. 'Seriously, Raya, I want to keep the band going.'

'You shouldn't give up.'

'It's going to be tough.'

Soraya was silent for a second.

I was hoping she'd say she'd definitely join the band.

'Maybe you need a bit more support. Galih and I talked about it; we think you need to join our community,' she said instead. 'The Young Offender.'

'The punks you talked about at rehearsal?'

'Indeed,' she said, clearly with a smile in her voice. 'If you're free sometime over the next week or so, Galih and I will come and pick you up.'

'Oh hell yes, I'll make myself free.'

'Maybe next Wednesday, about three? Galih knows your place?'

'Yes, he knows where I live, but I'll meet you at the mini-mart near my place. I don't want my family to see who I'm with.'

'Why?'

'Too conservative.'

She snickered. 'Ok, we'll see you then.'

***

Upstairs, Matari was dressed and ready to go out. She was wearing tight blue Armani jeans, a loose white DKNY shirt teamed with a Gucci handbag, all originals. Who still used fake brands? That was something she looked down upon. Matari was stylish, sophisticated, and definitely expensive.

'I'm leaving,' she said after glancing quickly at her Tag Heuer watch. 'Oh, and don't go in my room. The last time you did, a few things went missing.'

Then she was gone, leaving behind a trail of expensive perfume.

And leaving me sorely irritated. Matari could make me feel insignificant, although I did, from time to time, go into her room to 'borrow' a few things. I decided to take a long hot bath downstairs. Feeling refreshed, I put on some Pearl Jam while I was experimenting with a different type of an all-black look. I drew black eyeliner around my eyes for the first time. I 'borrowed' that, too, from Bulan's dressing table, and I painted my nails black with the bottle I bought the previous week with Kenari.

As I stared at myself in the dressing table mirror, my eyes caught a glimpse of the photo of Danu and I that had long been wedged into the bottom right-hand corner of the frame. I was standing in front of him while he hugged me. We were both smiling, happy.

Now our relationship was over. I was alone. It felt strange listening to "Black", the voice of Eddie Vedder singing about lost love. It should have reduced me to tears, even a little perhaps. There was no sadness about it, though; I felt nothing.

If there was any feeling at all, it was the excitement of knowing that I would soon see Galih again. My mother used to visit his family. Then she had had an argument with his mum and soon after, the play dates stopped.

121

Nonetheless, Galih and I kept up our friendship right through primary school and into junior high at SMP1 until my mother transferred me to another school. After that, I never saw him and now he was in a band with Soraya.

In the mirror was a girl I barely recognised. This new girl was different, and she was a bit edgier, wilder, and darker somehow. I decided to crawl into her skin and apply this new 'me' straight away.

I took the photo from the mirror, set it on fire with my lighter, and threw it in the bin. I sat motionless, watching it burn.

***

Chapter Fourteen

"Something To Believe In"
Ramones

August 1993

I was consumed with meeting the Young Offender, the new punk tribe that Soraya had raved about. Alone in front of the mini-mart with a cigarette and a bottle of cold tea, I waited eagerly for them. That was until I remembered back to the night when Agam and I had been in this same spot. I caught myself smiling.

Those images quickly disappeared as maroon Civic entered the carpark. Behind the wheel was Galih, or Lih as we called him, with Soraya next to him.

I opened the back door and jumped in, welcomed by the cool of the air conditioner and the strong smell of tobacco. British punk was blasting through the stereo.

'Hi Sigi, we're getting some cigarettes and drinks,' Soraya yelled over the music. 'Do you want anything?'

'No, I'm good.'

Galih turned the sound down a little as he swung round to give me a big smile.

'Sigi, long time no see. I thought you'd disappeared from the face of the earth. What have you been up to?' he said. 'It's been what, four years?'

He hadn't changed. He was still softly-spoken with big, kind eyes. His skin was honey-coloured like mine, and his chubby cheeks gave him a kind of baby-face quality. Only his hair was different; it was short in the back but longer in the front.

'Yes, Lih, about that.'

'Where have you been?'

'I moved to SMP216, and now I'm in my last year in SMA27.'

'Me too at SMA4.'

'Yeah, SMA4 is famous, you know.'

'Like your band from what I've been hearing. How is that possible?' He winced as he continued. 'I've worked hard with The Upshot, and hardly anyone has even heard of us. That's how insignificant we are in this city, but that's about to change. East and central Jakarta are working together, and west Jakarta is planning to join us soon. We're going to be the biggest underground in Jakarta, even bigger than the south. Metal is on its last legs; it's time for punk and the alternatives.'

I was excited. 'For sure.'

'I heard you asked Raya to join you.'

'Hope that's ok.'

'It's fine. I've started a few side projects myself. Tonight is going to be historical. It's the first gig for one of our new bands, The Surrender; I play lead. I also play bass in The Myth. They're the first bands coming out of the Young Offender.'

The door opened and Soraya jumped in with a few plastic bags. She handed a bottle of a lemon cooler to Galih and took one for herself. The car filled with the sounds of gulping cheap sweet alcohol.

The old me would have disapproved of them for drinking, but the new me decided not to. Who was I to judge? I wasn't even a virgin anymore.

'Let's get going,' said Galih. 'We're off to Slammers.'

'Slammers?' I asked.

'Yeah, Slammers, short for Slamet Riyadi Street, where Satria lives, that's our basecamp.'

'Who's Satria?'

'You'll meet him. Are you ready?'

'Yes!' I said firmly.

***

Along the way, I learned more about Galih's adventures over the past few years. He had formed The Upshot with some high school friends. The band had been around for a while. They still hadn't played in the underground in south Jakarta, although they had performed at a few small gigs in east and central Jakarta.

At one of those, he had met Satria, a punk fanatic from SMA68. They started hanging out together and, through Satria, he met more punks from different schools. In time, the Young Offender was created. They had been going for almost a year with about a hundred members.

I had also heard about the growing interest in punks from a few people that I knew. The metal guys didn't think much of them; 'brats and losers', or even worse, some had called them 'unskilled players'.

I decided not to trust so blindly in what I had been told. There was a vast difference between those who lived in wealthy south Jakarta and the rest of the city, and I was starting to see those differences playing out.

Like the way Galih was often treated.

He had been studying at the Yamaha Music School since he was a kid. He certainly wasn't an 'unskilled player' at all.

'So what's it like hanging with the big guns?' asked Soraya.

'I know that you don't like them,' I said carefully. 'But the metal guys are ok.'

'They're the old,' she said. 'You should hang with us instead.'

I didn't reply. I couldn't just stop being part of the metal community. Those guys had opened the door to the underground and that had brought Wanderlust a level of notoriety in south Jakarta. It was something that the punks were yet to experience.

Then again, Soraya had a point. Metal was old. Soon those guys would be finishing university. They'd be forced to cut their hair and get a real job. Even Danu had spoken about it, that his days were numbered. The real world, in my case, could wait.

'Come on, Raya, don't be too hard on her,' said Galih.

'Yeah…' My voice trailed off. I wanted to say we needed Soraya to commit to us full-time.

'You can have her,' Galih teased. 'She's not a good singer anyway.'

Soraya hit him.

'Hey, stop that. You told me last night you might join them.'

'So you will?' I couldn't believe what I was hearing.

'No, I said I was thinking about it. Give me a bit more time.'

'Are you playing hard to get or something?' Galih teased her.

'Don't worry, Lih,' I said confidently. 'Got all the time in the world.'

***

Fifteen minutes later, the car entered a quiet complex. Yellow and green foliage littered the pavement and the empty road from the large trees extending from the gardens of the vast houses, all built in a similar colonial style. Galih pulled over and parked in front of one of them.

We entered the main gate and instead of heading to the front porch on the left, Galih led us down the right side of the house towards a second metal gate. He pressed the bell on the side of the wall. A few minutes later, it opened.

Satria, a skinny boy in his late teens, came into view. He had a loose smile and a chilled expression. I immediately liked him. It was only later that I found out that he was usually stoned. I just thought he looked calm and somewhat sweet.

'Hi Lih, Raya,' he said.

'Meet Sigi,' said Galih.

'Welcome,' said Satria. 'Come on in.'

The smile changed into a wide grin as he grabbed the bag full of coolers and led us around the back. The sound of hardcore punk was blaring out of a bedroom that opened out onto a small terrace and the garden.

The smell of weed, cigarettes, and a strange chemical smell hit as soon as we entered his room. It was about four-by-four metres, with a shadowy ambience. On the main wall was a massive banner of the Sex Pistols. Next to it was a giant Cocteau Twins' *Heaven or Las Vegas* poster. On the left wall was another poster, the black and white image of the Nine Inch Nails' *Head Like a Hole*.

Inside were five boys, and, the three of us with Satria, made nine. Some were sitting on the bed, while others relaxed on a mat on the floor. A few were on a three-seater brown leather sofa that was oddly positioned facing the back wall. Their faces were hidden as they sat with their backs towards the door.

Galih and Soraya squashed onto on the bed with the others and I was left standing alone.

The punks were dressed mostly in black. I saw silver spiked leather jackets, army pants and boots, and chains. The guys on the floor were doing each other's hair with spray paint, creating outlandish mohawks. That explained the strong smell. One was ripping his t-shirt and using safety pins to hold the slashes.

The whole scene looked so alien that I just stood there not knowing what to do.

'Hey, Sigi, have a seat?' said Satria as he poked one of the boys on the sofa to get up.

He stood and extended his hand with a bit of a smile. '*Hai*[43] I'm Abinaya. Everyone calls me Abi.'

'I'm Sigi.'

He had light skin and his hair was set in a deep blue mohawk. It stood strikingly above the shaved sides of his head. He wasn't thin like Satria. On the contrary, he was well built, toned and muscular, judging from how he looked in his tight white t-shirt, slashed black jeans and black army boots. I couldn't help but blush when he smiled.

Feeling a little anxious, I decided to take the offered seat. The boy sitting next to me turned his head.

'Panji,' he offered his hand.

I looked him over. My eyes fell onto his red, swollen bottom lip that was pierced in the middle with a single silver needle. His ears were red and swollen too, full of safety pins of various sizes.

That looked like it hurt!

'Welcome to Slammers,' Panji continued with a smile. 'We're getting ready for tonight. You coming with us?'

'Sounds fun. But isn't it a bit early? It's not even five o'clock.'

'We're all going to the studio to rehearse, then we'll be at the gig around eight. You should come along.'

---

[43] *Hai* meaning 'hello' or 'hi.

I was a little taken aback by the invite, this scary guy with his pierced lip and swollen ears. His chiselled face was masculine with high cheekbones. He wore a dark green tight shirt with a long dark red tie, the tip resting on his black jeans. Like the others, he was sporting a mohawk.

'I'll see what Raya and Galih are doing.'

'They're coming.'

'I'm not sure if I can. I've got school tomorrow.'

'So what,' Satria joined in.

He placed a plastic chair at the end of the sofa, facing Panji and I, looking cool with his dark grey t-shirt with Chaos UK written on it. His jeans were ripped, and the silver piercings on his left eyebrow glistened with sweat.

'Fuck school, come with us,' he insisted.

This guy was intriguing, a perfect mix between wild and stylish, handsome and rough; he was rugged, yet there was something regal about him.

I laughed weakly.

Satria winked and took a big gulp straight from the bottle he was holding before passing it to Abi. He took a big sip, too, swilling it back before handing on it on to me. I took the bottle and gave it to Panji.

'You don't want any?' he asked. 'It's red wine, Satria's favourite before he goes on stage.'

'No thanks.'

Panji took a long swig and offered it to someone on his right. 'You want some, Aquila?'

I couldn't see the face as he was leaning back into the sofa, holding a guitar. He refused the bottle with a gesture.

'Raya told us you play in the south underground,' Panji said, as Satria grabbed back the bottle.

Before I had time to answer, Satria cut in, waving the wine bottle at me. 'Who cares, cos metal sucks,' he said with a laugh.

It was the first time I was glad that I didn't have the skills to play the genre.

'So, are you coming tonight or what?' he asked after he drank some more of that wine.

'I need to go home first, but I'd like to. I'll see you guys there.'

'She only likes being with the metal guys,' came the scornful voice from the right.

'Not true,' I replied quickly. 'I'd like to hang with you guys too.'

'We won't believe you if you don't come tonight,' he said, his voice firm.

If Aqila had intrigued me, I was beyond curious now. It was a feeling, an instinct that I had, even though I still couldn't see him. I decided that I wouldn't be the one to lean forward first and show myself.

'Where's the gig Satria?' I asked.

'A discotheque called Voila. I know, a disco? Don't worry, there's definitely no disco. It's all bands. It's a show called The Blackhole. They put on gigs where punks can play and they invite other bands too that cover new groups like the Chilli Peppers.'

'I'll take you and Raya home,' said Galih, cut in.

I glanced up at his hair. It was now a light green array of tiny spikes that made his head look like a showy *durian*[44]. His t-shirt was ripped, with a heap of safety pins holding it together.

'I'll pick you up again later, that's if you want to come along,' he added.

'Ok.'

As I stood up, I was introduced to the guys on the bed. Hansel, the Chinese boy decorating his boots, was small and unassuming. Next to him sat Egan, who was equally small. His entire face was pierced with safety pins and spikes. Soraya was spraying his mohawk orange and the fumes were overwhelming.

'We're running out of spray,' she said as she shook the can. 'Sorry, Egan, looks like your mohawk won't be as bright as you want it.'

'And the safety pins, they're all gone too,' said Hansel. He was messing with his ear, poking at it or something.

'No worries. I'll bring some more from my place,' Galih replied.

I said goodbye to Panji who was standing over me. He was almost two metres tall.

Now I was able to catch a quick sideways glimpse of Aqila. He

---

[44]*Durian* is a large Indonesian fruit that has small spikes covering its tough skin.

was still sitting lazily at the end of the sofa with the guitar on his lap. His thin and long chest was bare. He was wearing just a pair of black leather pants and Doc Marten boots.

'Qila, see you later,' I heard Soraya say.

'Bye Raya.' He lifted his chin as he turned to face her.

Our eyes met in the dim light.

Before I had time to think, Soraya grabbed my hand and pulled me towards the door.

I glanced back at Hansel, who was burning a needle with the flame from a candle on the side table. He calmly poked his ear, piercing his flesh. Blood trickled down his earlobe and onto his neck, and he didn't even blink.

***

Chapter Fifteen

"Identity"
X-Ray Spex

'Who was that guy?' I asked Soraya once we were in the car.

'Which guy?'

'The one you said bye to last. Qila, I think?'

Soraya and Galih exchanged a meaningful glance, and I felt a pang … of something.

'She's already asking about Aqila,' said Soraya.

Galih smirked.

'Come on, guys, is there something I should know?'

'Well, yes, and no, Don't worry about it, eh,' said Galih

I decided not to take the bait. 'I like this tape you're playing. Lih, could I borrow it?'

Back then, a mixed tape was worth more than anything if it had songs that were hardly ever sold in the record stores of Jakarta.

'Sure, you can have it. It's called *Punk and Disorderly*, a compilation album, volume two.'

Soraya poked him. 'Hey, I've been asking for that tape.'

'Sorry, but I think Sigi needs it more than you. It'll broaden her horizons.'

She pulled a face.

'Ok, I'll make one for you too,' he said.

***

I was glad to find no-one at home. I sat on the chair next to the phone and quickly dialled Kenari's number-with the help of the small screwdriver inserted underneath the plastic cover.

'Hey, Nari, it's me, Sigi. You won't believe where I've just been and what I saw.'

131

'Did you go with Raya to Slammers? She asked me to come along too, but I had to stay home for my brother's birthday party.'

'Oh yeah, I did, with Lih too.'

I told her about how he and Satria had started the Young Offender punk community.

'That's wild,' Kenari squealed. 'So Satria is the leader, and Galih's the creator?'

'Kind of, they formed it together with a few other guys. I'll introduce you to them, but you need to get ready. We're invited to our first ever underground punk event tonight. Run by The Blackhole. You must come.'

Kenari began squealing, 'Are you sure? Those kids are shady.'

'No, they're not. They're cool, and some of them are actually cute. Don't think we need to worry.'

'Cute punks? Really?'

'Yes, they might look different but, you know how the metal guys are all in their twenties, well, these punks are our age. They respect us as a senior band, although we need to be careful when talking about the metal scene. Satria's like Raya. He hates metal too.'

'Are we going to tell them about the Hard Wire Festival that's coming up? That's metal.'

'They don't have to know about that, at least not yet. Anyway, Slammers was pretty cool. I saw one guy there, piercing his ears without anaesthesia or anything. He just jabbed at his ear with a burnt needle until it bled.'

'No way, and you call that cool?'

'I know how it sounds, but I'm bored with the metal guys. These cute punks with their mohawks and black leather jackets, it was exciting. Raya and I are meeting at the AH restaurant in Menteng Street at seven. Be there if you want to come with us.'

'I'll see you there.'

I ran upstairs with a gleeful smile.

Before I met the Young Offender, or the YO as they called themselves, I thought that my life was pretty exciting. I was different to everyone at school. I was a silent rebel, a misfit in a loud anti-social band.

Now I had decided that my life was lame. I desperately wanted to see them again. Hang out with them, talk to them, and see them perform on stage. The thought of being amongst the first girls allowed into this new and exciting underground world of punk propelled me into a state of euphoria.

***

An hour later, I was ready. I had been listening to the tape that Galih had given me, and I loved it. I stared at the mirror.

My hair was down to my shoulders, and I'd put black eyeliner all around my eyes, the look completed with a nude lipstick and lip-gloss. I decided to wear my contact lenses. I 'borrowed' one of Matari's black body-hugging long-sleeved tops, and I combined that with something I'd never worn before-my red tartan mini-skirt, the punk schoolgirl style.

I didn't have army boots; my classic black Doc Martens would have to do. My father had bought them for me a year or so ago. I never understood why he agreed. They were pricey and, in Jakarta, it was only a few guys who wore them, and, well, me too.

I checked myself in the mirror for the hundredth time. The mini-skirt looked a bit daring and, for a moment, I thought of changing it, but then I wanted to look good. Actually, I wanted to look hot.

***

The taxi arrived at the AH restaurant just before seven, and I took the stairs to the second floor to look for the girls. Soraya was already there, smoking. I took my seat in front of her and smiled. She looked back at me with a flat expression.

'What's up? Where's Galih?' I asked.

'He's still rehearsing with Satria and the crew at the studio. We're meeting them at The Blackhole.'

'Sure,' I said, grabbing the menu. 'We can share a taxi.'

She blew a long stream of smoke out of her pale, thin lips. 'What's that you're wearing?'

I didn't know how to respond, so I was glad that the waiter came by to take my order.

'A cheeseburger and a *teh botol*[45] please,' I said while trying to figure out why Soraya said what she said.

She looked more like a boy, as usual. Her long, straight hair was still tied back and she wore an oversized black Exploited t-shirt teamed with army pants and boots. Her skin seemed pale too, grey-ish even. Next to her, I looked like a cheerleader.

'What, Raya? You don't like what I'm wearing?'

'I'm not saying that, but it's girly.'

'What's wrong with looking a bit girly?'

'Nothing, whatever,' she laughed at me. 'It's not my style, and it's not really yours either.'

I glanced down-yeah, it was sort of short.

'My sister brought it for me from the States last year. I've never worn it before, but she said it was cool over there.'

Soraya flashed one of her scornful expressions. I quickly real-ised that was not the 'punk' thing to say.

'Look, Raya,' I said firmly, 'To tell you the truth, I'm tired of dressing like a boy all the time, wearing jeans, oversized t-shirts and sneakers simply because I'm in a boy's world. I'm trying a new look here.'

'Yeah, I get it,' she sighed. 'It's me. I hate it when guys look at me like I'm a doll because they're my toys, not the other way around.'

'I'm not a doll,' I said quickly. 'I might like to show some skin sometimes but I'm not a doll. So don't worry.'

We looked at each other with a better understanding.

My food arrived and I ate quickly while Soraya lit another ciga-rette.

'So, how did you become the vocalist with Galih?' I asked.

'I was surprised when he asked me to sing. I said yes in the blink of an eye because I had heard Galih was a wicked guitarist. We rehearsed at his place after school that day and The Upshot was

---

[45] *Teh botol* is a brand of a famous sweet tea in a bottle, served cold.

born.' Then she laughed, 'He said he asked me because he couldn't find anyone scarier.'

I laughed with her. She was a scary girl with an attitude, but she didn't intimidate me. My mother and sister had a level of scary that was more significant than any woman I knew.

'I'd never sung in a band before,' she continued. 'Though I think I'm ok. I can hit the high notes the boys can't reach and I can sing in the low keys the girls can't. We've started playing a few gigs.'

'What did I miss?' Kenari was standing next to us. 'Sorry I'm late,' she said as she sat down. 'I had to wait until everyone left my brother's party before I could get changed and escape.'

Kenari had also made an effort. Instead of her usual boyish look of jeans, t-shirt, and sneakers, she wore cargo shorts with a white tank top. Around her waist was a soft blue flannel shirt tied by the sleeves. Her bleached strawberry blonde hair hung down her back. She looked hot.

'I'll be damned,' said Soraya.

'What, no, don't be like that,' Kenari pleaded with her girly laugh. 'Sigi told me that there'd be cute boys and I want to look cute too.'

Soraya rolled her eyes. 'Are we scouting for boyfriends?'

'Come on, didn't you just tell me that the boys are your toys? You do play the game a little bit, don't you?' I teased.

Soraya smiled.

***

135

Chapter Sixteen

"Punk's Not Dead"
The Exploited

The Patra Jasa Building was a giant skyscraper looming over Jalan Gatot Subroto, one of the main roads in the financial district of Jakarta. It was home to private firms and a few good restaurants. It also held the Voila Discotheque, located at the top.

We stepped out of the taxi, and I felt a flush of adrenaline. When the elevator stopped at the 52nd floor, we were hit by a thick cloud of smoke and the purple glow of ultraviolet lights. The DJ was pumping out music I hadn't heard before; it was loud with the sound of brash guitars.

The place was packed with about a hundred teenagers, mostly guys, and a few girls. They were standing around talking and drinking but our presence didn't seem to bother them.

The interior was like nothing I'd ever seen before. The walls were covered in black cloth and painted with spiders, giant planets, ghosts, zombies, and skeletons. The colours glowed in the dark. It was as if we'd been transported into a weird hellish basement in another universe.

The air was eye-watering and I could barely recognise anyone in the murkiness. We decided to stand at the edge of the dance floor near the front of the stage, where a band was finishing their sound-check. The musicians were all westerners, the sons of expatriates or ex-pats as we called them, who were sent to work in Indonesia. Kenari and I exchanged an enthusiastic glance. We had never seen a *bule*[46] band perform before so we were pretty intrigued.

'Oh, Sigi, look, real *bule* and mixed kids,' Kenari shouted over the music.

---

[46]*Bule* is Indonesian slang for westerners.

I was beaming. The international school students were considered the coolest of all the teenagers in Jakarta. And, they were hard to get to know. To watch them play was beyond my wildest expectations.

'Hey, here's Lih,' Soraya said.

Galih approached us through the smoky haze with a guy I'd never seen before.

'Oi Oi Oi!' he greeted us. It was a sort of cheer punks used as a greeting, inspired by a song from the UK band Cockney Rejects. 'You came, that's great.'

'Hi Lih, meet Kenari,' I said as I ushered him towards her. 'She's our lead guitarist.'

'Not a very good one, I'm afraid,' said Kenari shyly.

'Galih is a badass guitarist,' Soraya proudly said as she turned to face him. 'What time are you on?'

'After this band, so I've got to grab my gear from the car. By the way, meet Ardi.'

With that, he disappeared towards the lift.

The new guy shook our hands. He was sporting long dreadlocks, something unique at the time in Jakarta. In fact, he was the first guy with dreads that I had ever met so I was pretty impressed. He was wearing a black t-shirt, green army pants and spiked black boots.

'I've never seen this crowd before, anywhere,' I said to him.

'This is The Blackhole,' he replied. 'The only gig that matters. They're connected with the bands from JIS, you know, the Jakarta International School, like the guys on stage. The Young Offender are always here when The Blackhole are on and this is the first time The Surrender is going to play.'

'What sort of music are the JIS boys into?'

'New stuff, mostly alternative rock. By the way, see those guys over by the side of the stage? They're the founders of The Blackhole.'

I glanced over at three guys in their early twenties.

'They look so cool,' I sighed.

'Do you want to meet them?' Ardi offered.

'Are you serious? Coming Nari?'

'You go ahead. Sigi. I'll stay here with Raya,' she said.

I followed Ardi. 'Sigi is in an all-girl punk group,' he opened.

'Wow, never heard of that in Jakarta before,' said a guy named Feizal. He was skinny and tall, and his eyes were fiery as he looked at me. There was something a little different about his accent and how he spoke.

'What's the name of your band?'

'Wanderlust,' I said. I didn't want to say that we also played grunge.

'You should play here,' Rudi joined in.

He was shorter than his two mates, but he was more stylish, wearing a simple white shirt and an expensive black leather jacket. He oozed charisma; I had a feeling he was in charge.

'We'd love to,' I nodded.

'This is Sigi's first time at The Blackhole,' Ardi said.

'That's great. We've been going for a while now. I used to study in San Diego, and there was a club that played dance music. They'd put on these wild events with bands and DJs every Saturday night. We've never had anything like that in Jakarta so I thought I would start something similar when I came back,' Rudi told us.

I was bursting with excitement.

Feizal continued, 'We started out with small crowds on a Friday night, and we've built a loyal following. Now we're on three times a week, Mondays, Wednesdays, and Fridays.'

'How do people know about it?'

'Mostly word of mouth. We put out flyers too at Pondok Indah, Pejaten, Blok M, Menteng and all the way up to Kemayoran,' said Feizal.

'Herry designs and produces all our advertising,' Rudi said as he tapped the shoulder of the guy standing next to him.

Herry smiled. He was skinny like Feizal, just a little geekier.

'He's so talented. Sigi. You see the paintings on the walls? He made them, all hand-painted,' said Feizal.

I looked in awe at Herry. 'That's so cool. They glow in the dark!'

'Rudi brought back a heap of paint from the States. You can't buy it here.'

'They look amazing.'

'Thanks, Sigi.' Herry grinned.

'And thanks to Feizal here, we have a lot of JIS guys into alternative who play at The Blackhole,' Rudi added.

'Oh, so you're an international student?' I asked Feizal in disbelief.

'Yeah, I'm Malaysian,' he replied. That explained his unusual accent.

'I better get back,' I said as I saw Kenari waving at me. 'Nice to meet you.'

'Nice to meet you too, Sigi. Let me know if you want to play sometime. Enjoy the show,' said Rudi with a compelling smile.

I hurried back with Ardi to Kenari and Soraya.

'Just in time,' Kenari said. 'The band is about to start.'

I gazed at the stage.

The vocalist was intense, his hair dyed with streaks of indigo blue. His fair *bule* skin was pale under the stage lights.

'Thanks for coming to The Blackhole!' he shouted to the crowd. 'We've got a great lineup tonight, including our guest band The Surrender from the Young Offender, our punk brothers in central Jakarta.'

He turned to a group of guys in the shadows just past the other side of the dancefloor. I saw Satria, Abi, Panji, Hansel, and Egan among them, fierce like colourful thugs. I was nervous just looking at them.

'We're The Rucksack,' the singer went on, 'And we're going to open with a song from the Red Hot Chili Peppers. This is "Knock Me Down".'

We moved further back to watch from the sidelines, as some of the younger guys started throwing themselves about in front of the stage. I noticed my foot had started tapping. The sound was infectious.

This band had a great stage act too, jumping around and somehow keeping the music straight. They were like pros. I felt a bit ashamed because we still weren't that good at performing.

When The Rucksack finished their set of three songs, the crowd gave them an enthusiastic round of applause as they left the stage.

The DJ filled the silence with more alternative music that I'd never heard before.

'The Rucksack's first song was from the *Mother's Milk* album, released in 1989,' Ardi said. 'Most people are more familiar with the Peppers' latest album, *Blood Sugar Sex Magik*, but *Mother's Milk* is better. Not so commercialised. Did you hear that thick baseline, wow!'

'Yeah, that was cool,' I was trying to sound as if I knew what I was talking about, except I didn't.

'Hey Ardi, can you give us a hand?' Galih had reappeared. He was carrying a guitar in a hard case, and a couple of big black bags. Ardi hurried over and grabbed the bags and they both jumped up on the low stage to begin setting up.

Soraya gave us a warning. 'Girls, I suggest you move right to the back because it's going to get fast and out of control.'

'How about you?' I asked.

'That's what I came for, so I'm staying here. I'm planning on pogoing!'

'What's that?' asked Kenari.

'You'll see,' she laughed.

'Well, tonight, I'm just going to watch,' said Kenari.

'Me too,' I agreed.

Kenari and I retreated into the dark haze.

'And, the moment we've all been waiting for. Let's call our guest stars up on stage. The Su-rren-derrrr!' yelled the DJ in a booming voice.

'This is so exciting!' Kenari let out a little squeal.

I felt it too. We were in this new underground scene with teenagers our own age who played punk and some of the funkiest music ever. I wished Kenari and I were on that stage.

Our anticipation grew as we saw the punks appear from the shadows and move across and onto the dance floor under the glare of the stage lights. They looked like they meant business.

Ardi was back with Soraya. The JIS boys were there too. Hansel still had dried bloodstains on him that had dripped from his left ear, down his neck, and onto his ripped t-shirt. He looked rather ghastly. Next to him stood Panji, tall and impressive. The piercings on his face glistened and twinkled. Abi with his bright mohawk was right behind him, wearing just his tight black jeans and a metal spiked black leather jacket that showed off his muscular chest.

'Who's that?' Kenari lifted her chin.

'You noticed?' I smiled, teasing her. 'Abinaya, he's sexy, eh.'

'Abinaya,' she said with dreamy eyes.

Satria and his mohawk followed and he jumped up on stage next to Galih. Clearly, he was the charismatic leader of the band, wearing a black leather jacket showered in silver spikes, light blue ripped jeans full of safety pins and silver spiked army boots.

At the back of the room in the dim light, another guy stood alone a little to my left. From the corner of my eye, I stole just the slightest of glances; his face seemed familiar. He had a black mohawk and was dressed in a tight long-sleeved shirt, a long slim black tie, black jeans, and Doc Martens boots, similar to mine.

'Who were you looking at?' Kenari's voice brought me back to reality.

'What?'

'He's cute,' she giggled. 'Who is he? He's looking at you,' she whispered.

I couldn't help myself. I had to look again.

He was indeed staring at me. It was Aqila! I turned my gaze away.

'I know him,' I said in Kenari's ear. 'That's Aqila. Met him this afternoon at Slammers.'

'Nice,' Kenari winked. 'He's cute.'

A few seconds later, Kenari snuck another peek, 'Oh, he's gone.'

I looked back and yes, he was gone. I peered around the club, but with a sinking feeling, I realised I couldn't see him.

I turned my focus back to the stage. The Surrender was ready. The drummer was another cute boy I hadn't seen before. He was bare-chested with a mohawk, a long chain with a padlock hanging around his thick neck. Galih looked impressive as he stood defiantly with his guitar. Satria positioned himself in front of the microphone. I couldn't stop myself gushing just a little. He was definitely fascinating.

'Look at Lih, wow,' I whispered to Kenari. 'And the vocalist, that's Satria, one of the leaders of the Young Offender.'

'So cool and handsome,' Kenari murmured. 'That jacket.'

'Oi Oi Oiiiii!' he shouted, and the room roared back with excitement.

'We're The Surrender from the Young Offender,' he yelled again. 'Don't forget the chaos!'

They opened with "Let's Start a War" from The Exploited. The crowd went mad on the dance floor. It happened so fast. They were slamming hard against each other, pushing and shoving, following the fast rhythm.

I was fascinated yet scared. This felt a lot rougher than the metal shows I was used to, although those could be wild too. Everyone seemed to be in a complete and utter trance, violently slamming to the aggressive beat.

Never mind the sharp edges of the spikes on their leather jackets or the chains wrapped around the back and sides of their jeans. Never mind the army boots. They were all under the spell of this music as if in a frenzy. My hair stood up and I hoped that Soraya would be safe in the middle of it all.

Hansel jumped up onto the stage and threw himself into a stage dive. Kenari grabbed my arm as we watched him land safely on the outstretched hands which pushed him this way and that above the madness.

Without warning, the crowd began surging hard and fast away from the dancefloor, with Hansel still crowd-surfing over their shoulders. I panicked and pushed Kenari to the side. She screamed as Hansel's boots travelled at a hellish pace towards me when someone else burst through, forcefully pushing Hansel and the swirling mass that carried him back towards the stage. I breathed in great relief.

My saviour looked at me and our eyes met for a second before he rejoined the crowd on the dance floor. It was Aqila.

The next song, a cover of Disorder's "Life", started with a deep bassline, followed by high-speed guitar chords.

I watched Raya and Aqila making these strange punk moves; oh, so that was pogoing. Aquila was pushing and shoving the crowd around him.

The Surrender's third and final song "Holiday in Cambodia" by the Dead Kennedys made the whole room vibrate. Everyone, except Kenari and I, was pogoing, slamming, kicking, moshing, and shouting very loudly.

Satria's voice often hit the wrong notes, but his energy and charisma more than compensated for the lack of vocal control. In fact, it added to his performance, to his ability as a punk frontman to own that crowd with every lyric.

Before we knew it, the song was over. There was a long cheer as The Surrender retreated off stage. The audience slowly dispersed back into the dark corners.

'What do we do now?' asked Kenari.

As we looked around, we realised that everyone we knew had left.

'They're probably outside. Galih and Ardi are still packing up. We can wait for them, or we can go look for Raya downstairs.'
'Downstairs?' Kenari's eyes were wide. 'How do you know she's outside?'

'It's the most likely spot, eh. Like at Pid Pub, everyone goes outside during the breaks. Let's go.'

Her eyes were sparkling with excitement as we stood waiting for the elevator. 'That was awesome,' she said. 'I was surprised no one started a fight.'

'Me too. I still can't believe that Raya was in the middle of all that. How brave.'

'Don't forget us,' Kenari said. 'We were there too, you know.'

'On the sidelines, yeah, and nearly trampled alive.' My heart skipped a beat as I remembered being saved by Aqila. We hadn't even been properly introduced but I was dying to be.

The lift door opened and we walked in.

'Ready to meet them, Nari?' I asked as the door closed behind us.

'Yes,' she smiled. 'I'm nervous, though.'

'Don't be,' I said with a straight face, sounding far more confident than I felt.

***

Chapter Seventeen

"Attitudes"
The Brat

Back on the ground floor, Kenari and I walked through the lobby towards the carpark where the punks were scattered about on the pavement, standing, sitting, drinking, and smoking.

I spotted Soraya with Satria and Panji. I lit two cigarettes and gave one to Kenari so she could pretend to smoke and lower her anxiety. We were, after all, going to hang out with the Young Offender.

'Hey girls!' Soraya was waving at us.

We waved back and headed over. Most of the guys had taken off their t-shirts and were walking around half-naked. There must have been about fifty of them. I felt a little embarrassed. I shook hands with some and introduced Kenari and myself as we moved through the group.

Looking down at me, Panji reached out to shake my hand, 'Sigi, glad you made it.' He seemed taller than I remembered. He was still wearing the same clothes, the dark green shirt now wet with sweat, his mohawk bent to the right. His nose and ears that displayed their piercings in full glory didn't appear to be so swollen.

'I was watching from the back,' I answered.

'I thought so. Was that you who almost got smashed?'

I laughed as Kenari gave me a bit of a look. 'By the way, Panji, this is Kenari, she plays lead for Wanderlust.'

'Hi,' Panji shook her hand as another appeared in front of her.

'I'm Abinaya, you can call me Abi.' He stood there with a grin, wearing just his black jeans. His mohawk was still standing.

'Stay away from him, girls,' said Soraya. 'That one's a *buaya*[47].'
'Me? I'm a good boy,' said Abi as he winked at Kenari.

---

[47]Indonesians use the word '*buaya*' meaning 'crocodile' to describe a player.

Her cheeks blush.

He laughed, gave us a quick nod, and moved on.

'Hey, where are you going?' Panji called after him.

'I'm trying to find iodine or alcohol or something. Aqila's wrist is bleeding,' Abi replied over his shoulder.

Aqila was injured? Was he ok? Where was he?

'Did you enjoy the show?' Panji turned back to face us.

'It was great, crazy but great,' I said while my gaze followed Abi. I saw him disappear in between some cars but the wounded one was nowhere in sight. 'Aqila's hurt?'

'Ah, that happens all the time. It's probably just a scratch from a metal spike. Don't worry. He'll be fine.'

'Where is he?'

'Not sure, maybe in Satria's car.'

Satria looked back at us with his big lazy smile. 'You should play here sometime.'

'We'd love to,' I said, glancing at Soraya. 'Provided Raya agrees to join Wanderlust. We need her.'

She looked back at me with a wry smile. 'Ok, let's talk about this. Why don't we go somewhere more private, just us girls?'

We followed her lead as we slipped between a couple of parked cars to the privacy of the pavement.

'To be honest,' Soraya opened after she lit a cigarette. 'It's not that I don't want to join the band. It is just that… you girls want to get into that Hard Wire shit and I'm dreading it. But, I also think it's important to break the metal stranglehold on the underground, so, yeah, I've decided to join Wanderlust.'

Kenari did a little clap and started jumping up and down. She had a huge smile. I was simply overjoyed.

'We can't thank you enough,' I said giving her a hug. She ignored it. 'So are you going to be ok with trying out at the audition?' I asked.

Soraya took another drag of her cigarette. 'I'm not thrilled, but someone has to do it.'

'You won't regret it,' I said. 'This is only the beginning. I promise we'll all go far together.'

Soraya finally let her guard down a little with a small smile and we headed back to the boys.

'Guess what, guys? We have a new vocalist,' I said, beaming.

'Oh, wow, you're going to sing with Wanderlust? That's great,' said Satria. 'We'll organise to get you into one of The Blackhole nights.'

'Yeah, we're planning on showing you guys how it's done' she laughed.

'Hey girls,' called Galih as he and Ardi took the gear to his car. 'Sorry to interrupt, but I have to go. Dad wants the car back. Who's coming?'

'I am,' said Kenari.

'Me too,' I said heavily. I really didn't want to go home.

'Stay here if you want,' offered Soraya. 'We're going to Slammers later.'

'School night,' I said with disappointment.

'Same,' sighed Kenari. 'I promised my parents I'd be home before eleven.'

'Who cares about parents?' Satria teased. 'Thanks for coming though. See you at Slammers again soon.'

We waved goodbye to the others as I skimmed the carpark one last time, looking for Aqila.

He was nowhere to be seen.

***

The next day after school, I went home to an empty house. After a quick shower and lunch, I dashed over to Grace's. Kenari was organising for the girls to meet that afternoon. When I arrived, they were waiting.

Grace placed a tray with four glasses of iced tea on her desk. 'Hi Sigi, girls, have one of these.'

'You haven't told them yet, have you Nari?' I asked.

'Relax, no, I haven't,' she said. 'We've been waiting for you.'

'Now that she's here, come on,' Mirah said impatiently. 'What's the news?'

'Soraya's joining the band!' Kenari said, rather triumphantly.

'Soraya's in,' I said at the same time.

'What? that's awesome.' Mirah's face said it all. 'She finally agreed?' How did this happening?'

Grace looked a little shocked. 'What did she say?'

'We were with her last night at this alternative gig called The Blackhole. She took us aside to let us know she'd made a decision, and she also agreed to do the Hard Wire audition. Can you believe it?'

'Soraya wants Wanderlust to break the dominance of the south and metal in the underground,' Kenari added.

Grace nodded. 'We all want to do that. There has to be room for us girls.'

***

Over the next couple of weeks, it was a struggle to focus in class. My thoughts were overflowing with Wanderlust. I dreamed of what our future might look like while I played around with designs for a logo. As for the Young Offender, I couldn't stop thinking about them either. I doodled their names alongside ours, and I drew their mohawks, chains, and safety pins in my journal.

My imaginative life was soon brought to an abrupt halt.

'Some rumours are floating around, started by that new girl Tania in second year,' Bara opened the conversation. 'Reni hates her.'

I rolled my eyes. There were seven of us girls in our group. We were rather notorious and a few feared us. It was something I never really understood. I didn't connect with the girls either, to be honest. Bara and Reni were the official leaders, but, in private, they often consulted with me. The rest followed along. Mostly we just did naughty things like cutting a class to smoke at the back of the school.

So Reni hates the new girl. That's nothing to do with me.

I couldn't say that. It would be considered against the spirit of being in 'a gang'.

'They had a big argument,' she continued. 'Tania has half the girls in her class backing her. There were only five of us against about a dozen of them. It was full-on.'

'Why are you telling me?'

'So you know. Reni's pretty angry.'

We were leaning against the metal railing that ran along the verandah while we talked. I saw Reni walking towards us with Anita, Linda, and Intan. Reni did look a bit tense; her short dark hair accentuated her dark eyes which signalled that, yeah, she was in some kind of rage.

'Uh oh, here we go,' whispered Bara.

'What is going on?'

'Just hear her out.'

Why should I?

I couldn't say that either.

Now Reni was right in front of me. She stared at me with the look of a broken, troubled girl, broken but pretty.

'You don't care, do you!' she said. 'You never want to know what's going on around here.'

'What is going on around here?'

'You really have no idea?'

'No, I'm sorry, but I never know what's going on. Talk to me *dong*[48].'

Reni decided instead to walk away.

I turned around to face the rest of the them. 'Someone just tell me what the hell is going on.'

There was an awkward silence. I gave each of the girls a questioning look.

'It was in the canteen, Tania and her mates,' said Anita. 'We could hear them talking about you, on purpose. Reni was fuming.'

'What do you mean?' I asked. 'Come on, Nita, what do you mean? What were they saying?'

'It was about you, Sigi,' said Intan. 'They were gossiping about you. All over the school, mean stuff.'

'What were they saying?' I had to repeat myself.

'I'm sorry, Sigi,' replied Anita. 'They've been saying you're not a

---

[48]*Dong* is an Indonesian particle used in a sentence for emphasis.

virgin and that you're having sex with senior guys from the universities in south Jakarta, and a lot of them too.'

There was another awkward silence.

'They're saying things like you're a slut,' said Linda. 'That made Reni angry,'

'Tell her not to be,' I said. 'I don't care. I know who I am, and I know you girls know me too.'

The bell rang. As we headed back to our classrooms. I was lost in thought.

The argument was about me.

I should have known. Trouble seemed to follow me wherever I went. Funny enough, I wasn't overly bothered by the name-calling. I had better things to think about.

During class, I wrote in my journal that I had finally found my place with the punks, a group of misfits. I had no idea who and what they stood for or believed in, but I felt drawn to them.

When the end bell rang, there was only one person I wanted to talk to.

***

I arrived at PV Radio around 1:30pm.

'Hestu, have you seen Pandu?'

'No, but if you're looking for smoking buddies, Emon and John are up at the rooftop.'

No Pandu.

I went upstairs, and Emon and John were there with their respective cigarettes. I gave them a friendly wave and lit one of my own.

'*Hai* Sigi,' said Emon with a big smile. 'You're early.'

I shook his hand but I dreaded his offer to kiss my cheek. I quickly stepped towards John.

He was kind of cute, with his long hair, fair skin, and chubby cheeks. Flirty by nature, he winked at me.

'Stop it, please,' I said firmly.

Like Pandu, they were psychology students at the University of Indonesia.

152

'What's the problem?' asked Emon. 'You look like the weight of the world is on your shoulders.'

They called me a slut at school.

'Where's Pandu?' I asked instead.

'He has to study, poor bastard, so I'm doing his program for him. You want a *curhat*[49] with him? I'm a good replacement for that too. You can talk to me.'

'Or me,' added John.

I mulled it over. Maybe I could ask for their advice.

'What if some younger students called you names and told lies about you all over school? What would you do?'

'Depends,' replied Emon. 'I'd probably ignore it.'

'Me too,' I said. 'I thought I'd just brush it off, but my friends are not happy because I don't want to do anything about it.'

'Peer pressure,' said John.

'I never asked to be in this group of girls. It just happened.'

'How many of them and how many in your group?' asked Emon.

'Seven girls including me, all in the third year against over a dozen of these second years led by a popular new girl.'

Emon and John both laughed.

'You don't seem to like your mates that much,' John noted.

'I do. The girls are loyal.'

'Then relax,' Emon said. 'Your friends like you, unlike that other girl who got her mates by, I don't know what, fame? Money? You don't have as many supporters, though it seems they're willing to stick by you.'

'I don't want to argue with them. I couldn't care less what they've said about me. But my friends are angry. I tried to calm them down and it doesn't seem to be working. What should I do?'

'You need Pandu for that. I'd just tell you to fight.'

'Yeah, me too,' said John.

'We're useless, aren't we?' said Emon. He was still laughing.

'Yes, utterly useless,' I grinned back. 'I appreciate you listening, though. Anyway, I need to go to the library.'

---

[49] *Curhat* is short for *curahan hati*, Indonesian slang meaning to confide in someone.

'We need to get back too,' said John, glancing at his watch. 'Come on, Emon, let's get into that script.'

We put out our cigarettes, and descended down the steep steps.

'What did they call you anyway?' asked John while opening the door.

'That's a secret,' I gave him a half-smile. 'And, I'm not sharing it.'

'Fair enough,' he said. 'You'll tell us eventually?'

I just looked at him.

If John or Emon, or any of the guys here knew what they were calling me at school, I was afraid they might be tempted to see if I lived up to the name.

***

My father had come home early from the hospital and he was watching TV. My mother was nowhere to be seen.

'Papa, can I use the phone please?'

Asking him when my mother wasn't around usually yielded positive results. He frowned, and his greyish hair glistened under the bright light of the living room. He went into their bedroom to retrieve the phone key.

'Not too long, or your mother will be mad,' he said, passing it to me.

'Thanks, Papa,' I beamed as I sat down, opened the padlock and began to dial Kenari's number.

'Sigi?' she squealed. 'I was just about to call. Guess who I went home with today from school?'

'I don't know, Sebastian Bach?'

'I wish. That'd be nice, come on, guess.'

'Just tell me. I'm not in the mood for games.'

'You know I always get a lift home with Dirga and Mirah. Today Danu and Agam were with them.'

'Really?'

'Yes! And Danu told everyone that you want to break up.'

A feeling of dread took hold.

'I know you said you had broken up, but I didn't think it were serious when Danu came to the Jakarta Fair and you went home with him,' she said.

'I didn't go home with him. I took a taxi. And I am serious. I told him again at the Jakarta Fair. He just won't accept it.'

'You should've seen him, Sigi. He was devastated, telling us over and over that he didn't know why.'

'He knows why.' I paused. 'What was Agam's reaction?'

'He didn't say much. Seriously, not like him. He was staring out the window the whole time. I bet he was thinking of you.'

'I hope he doesn't think he was the reason because he wasn't.'

'So, what was it?'

Danu took my virginity, and I was pissed off. I don't love him and never did.

'It's complicated. Just off that, I'm thinking of going to Slammers again soon. Want to come?'

'How can you manage that? Are you crazy?'

'I'll just sneak out as usual.'

'You are crazy,' she sighed. 'I'm so jealous. A big hello to Abi. Does he have a girlfriend?'

'Should I find out for you?'

'No, the cute ones are always taken. Do you like anyone there?'

I pictured Aqila's face. 'Not really,' I lied. 'Anyway, got to run. Can you and Mirah book the studio for us? Thanks, Nari.'

I put down the phone. Just in time because my father had reappeared.

'Finished?' he asked.

'Yes, Papa,' I smiled as I locked the phone and handed back the key.

Although I was dying to, I thought it probably wasn't wise to call Agam. I didn't know how to tell him why I ended the relationship, well, provided that Danu hadn't already told him.

***

155

Chapter Eighteen

"Hitch-Hike"
LILIPUT

I returned to PV Radio around six that afternoon, a bit earlier than usual. I asked around if anyone had seen Pandu. He had left a message to wait for him in the library. I thought I'd look through the new material that had been delivered. I was happy to see the new release singles were finally there and, to my surprise, some albums too. Music piracy was common in Indonesia, so record companies didn't like to give us full albums. It was different to America where they used charts like Billboard. We were stuck with the top ten or top twenty charts made by directors of major radio stations.

I was absorbed in Ugly Kid Joe's latest album *America's Least Wanted* when Pandu opened the door.

'Hey, Sigi!'

'Shhh.' Despite being happy to see him, I was listening to the chorus of their new single and I wanted to know if it was any good. After a few minutes, I turned the volume down and realised Pandu was standing like a statue.

'It's ok, you don't have to freeze like that.'

'You and your music,' he smiled. 'You're looking for me? What's up?'

'I'd like your opinion about a few things'

'I need to do my playlist first. Give me ten minutes. How about we have a chat over a cuppa?'

***

I waited in the staff canteen, a small narrow space at the back of the office. A table stood in front of a long window that was opened twenty-four hours a day because nearly everyone smoked.

There wasn't any food service, but we could make our own coffee or tea and eat there, usually takeaways bought from the food court downstairs. When Pandu came in, he fixed us some hot tea.

'How are you?' I asked.

'Not so good,' he said in a gloomy tone. 'I might have to cut back on my broadcasting schedule next month,' He carefully placing the two cups of tea on the table before sitting down. 'To just three a week. I need to finish my thesis if I want to graduate.' Pandu broadcast every night except Fridays and he once told me that being on-air was highly addictive.

'So,' he continued. 'What's bothering you?'

'I'm feeling a bit overwhelmed.'

In a few breaths, I told him what had happened at school.

'What did they call you that made your friends so mad?' he asked.

'Promise not to tell anyone here?'

He pointed his two fingers in the air, 'On my grandmother's grave.'

'This is not a joke.'

'Who's joking?' he said, struggling to look serious.

'Never mind. They called me a slut.'

'A slut? Weren't you called a prostitute at your last school?' he asked. I had shared that snippet a few months ago.

'Yeah, when those senior girls got at me by spreading rumours. They told everyone I was getting paid. My mother wasn't happy when a teacher called her about it. She had me transferred to let me know how frustrated and angry she was at my so-called troublemaking. Now at this school they say I'm doing it for fun.'

Pandu looked concerned as he reached for my cigarettes.

'I'd like to think that I've been doing ok at this high school,' I continued. 'I've managed to avoid trouble… until now. This time it's some juniors who are bullying me and talking behind my back. They're calling me a slut. I don't know if this is an improvement or not.'

'Girls are cruel to each other, huh?'

'At least at this school I have some friends. Back in junior high when a senior found out that a guy she liked had been flirting with me, I had to face those older girls alone.'

'What's happened now? What's going on?'

'There's a new girl who has a problem with me, but I have no idea why because I don't even know her. All I know is that her name is Tania. She came from a prominent Catholic high school in south Jakarta, and she hates me. The rest of them are just supporting her.'

'Oh, she's got her back up?'

'Nightmare, eh? My friends are hassling me to take her on. It was easier back at my last school. The seniors just locked me up in a changing room and screamed abuse.'

'Did they beat you up?'

'No, they just hassled me,' I said. 'SMP1 had a lot of spoilt rich kids. They weren't the type to get their hands dirty.'

'I've heard some horror stories about the girls in public schools on the outskirts of Jakarta. I can only imagine the catfighting, the scratching and biting.'

'And pulling hair perhaps,' I said with a smile. 'So lame, catfighting is not my thing.'

'Oh, it's totally my thing. Who wouldn't want to watch girls having a good old catfight?' He laughed at his own joke.

I looked at him.

'Ok, sorry. You'd rather avoid it?'

'Of course, but I don't think I have a choice.'

'You always have choices, no matter what. Doing nothing is also a choice.'

'I can't just ignore it. My friends are giving me a hard time. It's driving me nuts. I know them and they won't stop until I, I don't know, slap that bitch or something.'

'Then slap her,' Pandu grinned.

'Is that advice seriously coming from you, a psychology student who's about to become a doctor?'

'I'm not a doctor yet, so I'm allowed to give bad advice,' he smiled. 'And you are not my patient either, so yeah, slap her. I think it's a good idea.'

'Oh, god!'

'Look,' he continued. 'If this girl starts on you again, just slap her before she even begins. It will be a move so unexpected she'll be stunned and won't be able to do anything for a few moments. When that happens, you walk away. Nonetheless, I would prefer you invited her to a private chat to sort our your differences.'

'Right,' I chuckled. 'Anyway, you're a good friend. Thanks for helping.'

'I'm not sure if I helped much. All I did was promote violence. Anything else you want to talk about?'

I mumbled. 'I don't know.'

'You can tell me,' he said as he took a big sip of his tea. 'Entertain me, please. I need a break from all the research I've been doing.'

'Ok, sure. I kissed a friend a few months ago, the best friend of my ex-boyfriend. What's worst is my ex won't accept my decision to break up.'

'The one you pretended to love but don't.'

I gave him an annoyed look.

'Sorry,' he grinned. 'Go on.'

'We've liked each other for a while but we ended up in relationships with other people. Anyway, I thought I kissed him because I wanted to have some fun and now I'm afraid that I might have fallen for this guy. He's wild, and he's known to be a player.'

'So you settled for Danu. Why did you break up with him?'

'How can you tell me to choose a bad boy? He's going to break my heart.'

'I never told you to choose the bad boy,' Pandu laughed. 'Those are your words.'

'Sounded like it.'

'Look, Sigi, I'll tell you two things I know. First, young adults like yourself change their minds-a lot. Today you might like a guy you just kissed but then next week you meet another guy you like even more.'

My mind skipped to Aqila. 'Ok, what's the second thing?'

'Guys at the end of the day only want one thing, and that is-'

'Sex,' I cut him short.

'Yeah, it's all about sex. Guys, especially those older ones that you hang out with, will do and say anything to get you into bed. Don't trust them so easily.'

Don't I know that…

Pandu would be a good psychologist for sure and what he said clarified my own thoughts.

'Thanks, I'm feeling better, but I got to be on air shortly. You hanging around?'

'No,' he shook his head. 'Need to get home and back to the research.'

We finished our tea.

'Don't be too hard on yourself. I'm sure you'll handle the situation much better than you think.' His parting words gave me something to mull over.

***

Throughout the rest of the evening, I thought a lot about what Pandu had said. I survived the broadcast. We did an exciting show but I felt it lacked the usual punch, at least on my side.

Elang was his usual cheery self; I felt like pushing him off the building for that. There was something annoying about people who are always cheerful. Then again, he probably saved the show for us with his never-ending enthusiasm.

'How do you do that?' I asked after we closed our microphones for the night and walked out to the living room.

'Do what?'

'Broadcast with that level of energy all the time.'

'I don't know. Just doing my job.'

'It makes me feel a bit ashamed. Don't think I did a good job.'

'Not that I saw.' His gaze was wide as he started to clear the table full of the tapes and CDs Hestu had place there, ready to be put away. 'You sounded pretty normal to me.'

'Oh, that's a relief.'

'What's up?' he asked. 'Something I can help you with?'

'Not really, I just got stuff going on.'

Elang stopped his table-clearing mission, which was a lost cause anyway because he only made things worse. He gave me a good

161

look. 'I would love to stay and chat, but I got to run and pick up my girlfriend.'

'Go,' I shooed him away with a gesture. 'I'll put everything away.'

'Thanks, are you ok?'

'Yeah, don't worry.'

'Good. Try to have a little fun.'

I squirmed. 'Seriously, Lang, I'm quite capable of having fun.'

'Then show it,' he said. 'Have fun next time we're on the air. It's all about that here at PV Radio. I mean, if you're not having fun, then why are you doing this? The only one who's judging you is you.'

I nodded as I pushed him away.

'Goodbye, Elang, see you next week,' I said firmly.

He laughed and dashed out of the door.

While filing the music in the library, I thought about Pandu and what he said about teenagers. How they often change their minds about who they like. That made sense, but it also was also a little scary. It would be of no use to fight it, the way I felt about different guys, and the urge to get to know them.

Indonesian girls were encouraged to fall in love when they were young and stay together for years. I realised this path might be impossible for me. How was I supposed to hold onto love at eighteen for the rest of my life? I was young and ready to cruise. Besides, I wasn't marriage material anyway now that I wasn't a virgin. On the other hand, who wanted to get married when there was so much to accomplish in the future?

***

My father gave me a sign to sit with him at the dining table. He wanted to talk, so I assumed it had to be something urgent or I was in trouble.

'I never see you study. When are the exams?'

'December, I think,' I answered weakly. I knew where this was going, and I didn't like it.

'Why is it then I never see you doing your homework? You're always out after school.'

'I know, but I'm doing it,' I lied.

'You're rarely home. Where are you studying?'

'Friends places, the radio station before we go on-air,' I lied again.

My father's big eyes were staring at the wall. I liked him better when he smiled. Today, his face was stern.

He was fifty-four years old and fit, thanks to playing tennis twice a week. He was a hard worker who put in long hours in the hospital and he ran his home practice. He also smoked like a chimney.

'After you've finished school, remember that you'll still have to sit other exams too. The public university entrance exam is the most important.'

'Yes,' I mumbled, wishing I could light a cigarette. Apparently, my father did as well-he lit up his Kent and pulled an ashtray closer along with the table.

'How about the private universities?' He blew a stream of smoke in the air. 'What major? Which uni? Remember you need to choose three universities and see which ones accept you. They each have their own exams. There are long hours, long days ahead of you. I hope you realise that.'

I nodded without a word. I had to lie. I would have added more wrinkles to my father's face if he knew the truth. The moment made me understand why so many of my friends walked away from their bands. They must have been on the receiving end of a reality check like this from their parents too.

'Once you graduate high school and get into a good university, I'll buy you a car.'

I thought I didn't hear him right. 'Are you serious, Papa?' My eyes were wide open.

'Of course I am. But this offer only stands if you pass your final year. If you don't, the offer will be withdrawn.'

'I'll pass! For sure!' I said with a new sense of conviction. No more buses and taxis. Inside I was jumping for joy.

'Have you eaten yet? Eat something and start studying.'

I squirmed.

My father didn't say go study; he said start studying. He knew very well that I had barely touched the books for most of this year.

Yeah, that was my father, a man of a few words.

***

Chapter Nineteen

"Walls (Fun In The Oven)"
Crass

The inevitable finally reared its ugly head. I had to study and I knew that I was way behind. I swore, frustrated at the hell of my own making. I had to start cramming. Whenever I felt like giving up, I imagined the new car that my father had promised. That thought kept me going, well, whenever we weren't playing, that was. I was at my desk straight after school until late into the night.

I was in a deep sleep when I heard my father knocking on my door.

'Sigi, get up, you're late.' My father's insistent knocking increased into pounding. 'I'll drive you there. Get up, let's go.'

I wanted to throw something at the door but realised that would be pointless; the battle was lost before it had even begun.

We didn't say a word in the car. It wasn't often that my father drove me. He was usually gone by six.

'The hospital called. The operation was cancelled so I can take you,' my father said as if reading my mind. 'But I can't do this every day, waking you up and driving you to school. You need to start going to bed early and like I told you, you need to prioritise your education.'

'I can handle it. Don't worry.'

'If you get sick and you don't pass the finals, you'll have to repeat.'

I was starting to feel a bit agitated. 'I'll pass, Papa, don't worry.'

My father fell back into his usual silence. That was still better than if my mother had been with us. She would have gone on about it until my ears bled.

'*Ya sudah*[50],' he said as we approached the school gates. 'Just remember to put your schoolwork first. Are you listening?'

'Yes, Papa.'

'We don't want to upset your mama, right? Study hard, Sigi.'

Who cares about upsetting her?

I gave him a quick kiss on the cheek and dashed out of the car.

My father never treated us, his three daughters, like girls the way other Indonesian fathers do. He spoke to us without emotion or prejudice. He trusted us completely to be responsible without him hovering around. Bulan once told me that it had something to do with his Minangkabau heritage in West Sumatra.

My father had said that in the Minangkabau society girls are valued more than the girls in other ethnic groups around Indonesia. Having three girls was the highest blessing he could receive yet that fact was usually considered a huge curse for most Indonesian families.

In his culture, girls inherited land and went to the most prestigious schools. Another of their responsibilities was to come to the man's home in his village to ask his hand for marriage. They managed the family money, paying for almost everything including their own weddings, and they also made the most important community decisions.

That was because, my father had explained, the majority of Minangkabau men left their homes to find their fortune elsewhere. The women managed daily life to let their men seek greater opportunities across Indonesia.

And so, the men follow their *Rantau* tradition of wandering around the nation and sometimes beyond. Most of these men became known as tough businessmen, professionals, educators, scientists, even politicians. Our first Vice-President of Indonesia, Mohammad Hatta or *Bung* Hatta[51] as he was lovingly called by the people, was a Minangkabau-an anomaly back in the 1940s amongst the Javanese whose population dominated the nation and the po-

---

[50] *Ya sudah* meaning something has been completed which translated loosely in this context as 'Here we are!'

[51] *Bung* is the title given to a man of high esteem like a former Vice-President

litical playground. It was the reason that I had suggested we name the band Wanderlust; it was inspired by the *Rantau* tradition. The girls loved the idea.

Traditionally, these Minangkabau men were encouraged to conquer the world, and the women stayed at home, supposedly to guard and take care of their 'holy' land. How limiting! What if, as a woman, I want to do the *Rantau* too?

Yet I was proud of my father, whose achievements had surpassed everyone's expectations. A year ago he had become the Head of the Jakarta Pediatric Doctors Association. However, this meant he was even busier so we rarely saw him at home. The down side of this new position meant that my father increasingly left more of the parenting responsibilities to my mother.

***

I was five minutes late. My German teacher *Ibu* Tuti[52] gave me a sharp glance as I took my seat next to Esa.

'Hey,' I said to her. 'Great to see you back. How are you?'

I looked at her with compassion. Esa's face was still a little pale, and she looked like she had lost a few kilos.

'I'm fine now,' she said, smiling. 'It was bad, pneumonia, and now I'm a bit behind. How's your studying going?' she asked

'I've been trying but I'm a bit behind too,' I said as I took my German books out of my bag. Actually, my studies were in a disastrous state to say the least. As if reading my thoughts, Esa put her hand on my shoulder.

'Study bit by bit when you can,' she whispered as the teacher stood up from her desk and walked in front of the class.

'*Ruhe, bitte,*' Ibu Tuti said in a guttural voice. '*Wir wiederholen jetzt das Kapitel von letzter Woche. Bitte oeffnet eure Buecher.*'

'What the hell did she say?' I whispered in a panic.

'We are going to repeat last week's chapter.'

'I really don't see the point in this stuff. It's not like I'm going to live in Germany anytime soon.'

---

[52]*Ibu* is the polite term of address for a woman.

167

'Who knows,' Esa laughed. 'Maybe you'll marry a German someday.'

'*Ampun*[53] Esa, the things you say.'

'*Ruhe, bitte,*' Ibu Tuti barked. '*Bitte Seite zweiundreissig oeffnen.*'

Following her instructions, I opened my book to page 32 like everyone else, and tried my hardest to focus on what she was saying.

***

Finally, the bell rang to signal recess.

'So what's new?' asked Esa, putting her books back into her bag.

'I'm trying to juggle the band and catch up on my studies. But let's talk about that later. I need to get out, now,' I said, nodding towards the window at the back of the classroom.

I grabbed a pack of cigarettes and a lighter from my bag and put them in my pocket. Esa gave them a quick, uneasy glance. She hated me smoking, although she never complained whenever I dragged her to my secret spot right outside the classroom window.

We waited for the others to leave and then I climbed through the big window at the back by stepping on one of the desks. There was a small terrace where I could have a quick cigarette hidden from view, high up on the third floor, and I could see the alley below backing onto the garden. Nobody ever walked along there apart from the school gardener making his rounds.

Esa stayed inside, sitting behind the desk to stand guard. She was close enough that we could still chat.

'Linda told me about big argument Reni had with Tania and that everyone was getting into it,' said Esa. 'What's going on? She said they were calling you rude names.'

I exhaled.

Not this again.

'What are you going to do?' she asked.

I felt a surge of emotions rise up. There was something about Esa's honest questioning that rattled all my defences.

---

[53]*Ampun* means mercy. In this context, it loosely translates as 'Give me strength!

'Sigi, are you ok?'

She reached for my shoulder through the window. As soon as her hand touched me, my tears exploded.

I was standing with my back to her, but somehow she knew. She leaned out and whispered, telling me that everything would be ok. The tears came falling down my chest. My uniform was soaking.

Esa waited patiently as she gently rubbed my shoulders. Slowly the crying came to a stop. She passed some tissues as I took the last draw on my cigarette.

'Would you like to climb back in?'

'I think I'm going to stay here for a bit. I like the breeze out here.'

'Ok, but not for long, eh? Somebody might see you.'

'Don't worry. If you want to go find the others, that's fine.'

'No, I'm staying here with you.'

We fell into silence. I could hear the faint sounds of students chatting and going about their business.

'Why were you crying?' It seemed like Esa had to draw upon some strength, judging from the uncertainty in her voice.

'So many reasons,' I said, lighting another cigarette. 'For one, I broke up with my boyfriend.'

'Danu?' her eyes grew bigger. 'That's huge.'

'I know, please don't tell anyone. Then there's the band and gigs and rehearsals, PV Radio, and my studies. But that study is going nowhere because there is way too much I have to learn and I just don't think I can catch up. But fingers crossed, we'll pass the Hard Wire festival audition that's coming up. We just have to. But I don't know if I'm going to be able to pass the exams. Now I have to deal with a ridiculous argument at school.'

It had all came tumbling out in a rush.

We fell into another silence. She was just a simple girl; her whole life was based on home, school, and probably nothing else.

Her tiny body showed no sign of puberty as if she was still a twelve-year-old girl instead of an eighteen-year-old young woman. Boys and bands were the last thing on her mind, let alone a huge spat among the girls.

'Don't worry, Esa, I'll find a way. Thanks for listening.'

'Sigi, climb back in, now. I think someone is coming.'

Before I could respond, the sound of stomping along the verandah filled the room. My first instinct was to hide beneath the window.

'Hey, you,' said a sharp, girly voice. 'Where's that slut Sigi?'

I silently swore. I had a pretty good idea who it was. I wanted to jump back inside while my gut told me to stay put.

'So, where is she? We want her now!' the voice demanded.

'She wasn't in the canteen and we've looked all over for her,' chimed in a third.

'If anyone knows where she is, that would be you!' spat another in an even meaner tone.

Geez, how many girls were in there?

'I've just come back to school. I've been sick so I have to stay in here,' Esa said.

'Who cares? Just tell us where she is,' the first girl snapped again, her voice echoing through the empty class.

'Like I said, I'm in this room all day, so feel free to look around. Maybe she's hiding, go have a look. Maybe she's under the table or behind the door.'

I was proud my little friend wasn't so easily intimidated. I couldn't help but smile.

Another voice started on her. 'You know exactly where she is. We want her-.'

'Enough, Sherly,' said the first voice. 'Tell her and that other slag Reni that we're after them.'

Esa didn't reply.

They were laughing.

'You tell her that,' another yelled before the room was finally silent.

I peeked inside the class. 'Esa, are you ok? I asked in a panic.

'Just climb back in before anyone else comes.'

I did just that as I put my foot in between the scattered books on the table for balance and jumped onto the floor. As I took my seat next to her, I said quietly, 'Sorry you had to take that.'

'It was lucky that you were outside. You should speak to Reni and Bara about this. Let them deal with them. Try not to get involved. Don't you have enough problems?' she said.

'You don't understand, Esa,' I gave her a weak smile. 'I am involved. They've been calling me a slut.'

Esa looked shocked.

'If you really want to help, please stay out of this. I don't think you'd be much use in a fight, 'I sighed. This girl from such a different world to me had a big heart.

For the rest of the lessons, I felt like I was falling into a deep hole. If it wasn't for Esa who kept slapping my wrist to keep me awake, I would have nodded off at my desk. Finally, the bell sounded. I had survived another day of school.

'I'm going home right now. Thanks for everything,' I said with appreciation.

Without waiting for her response, I ran ahead of everyone, even the teacher. I ran, and I ran, down the steps, past the canteen, the classroom alley, and straight through the open school gate. I stopped a passing *bajaj* and without bothering to bargain, I jumped in.

***

I was sitting with the Wanderlust girls in the hallway of EMI, waiting to audition for the Hard Wire Festival. Groups of young guys dressed in black slouched on the white plastic chairs that lined the walls. Many of them leaned forward and stared.

'We've got one song, one chance, to prove ourselves!' Mirah whispered firmly. 'I hope this Pistols' "Steppin Stone" is going to do it.'

'It will,' Soraya hissed. 'The bands that have played since we've been here?' She rolled her eyes.

'I think you're right,' I said.

'We're the only girls and we're the only ones playing punk as well by the look of those guys.'

'I finally saw a couple of new punk bands playing last week in east Jakarta. That's given me some hope that punk is here to stay. And I want to show this panel what punk is!' Soraya was defiant.

'It's great to see a few more bands are getting into punk,' smiled Grace. 'We might strike it lucky and actually pass this audition.'

The girls smiled, including Soraya, her usual sour expression gone for a moment. Today she looked magnificent. Her hair was in disarray, sprayed in bright yellow, red and green. She wore a white shirt combined with a black leather vest covered with band pins, black ripped jeans and black military boots.

I chose a black t-shirt with a new leather jacket I had bought at Pasar Ular, a market in north Jakarta. Egan from the Young Offender had painted the words *Punk's Not Dead* in red on the back. He also helped me glue the spikes along the seams. The look was complete with that red tartan mini skirt, knee-length white socks and my Doc Marten boots.

Mirah wore black cargo shorts with torn black stockings and black boots. She used black smoky eye make-up, pale lipstick, and a chain necklace with a padlock pendant on top of a white ripped t-shirt. Kenari wore her slashed blood red t-shirt with safety pins, her lipstick matched her shirt worn over her black cargoes. No stockings-just her loyal dark brown leather boots.

Grace, as usual, opted for her casual style. She appeared in jeans, a dark t-shirt and blue All-star sneakers. Her hair was braided in two and her makeup was clean and simple.

'Wanderlust!' A man's voice echoed down the hallway.

'This is it, girls,' Mirah said confidently. 'Let's do this.'

All the equipment we needed was ready in the studio. Kenari and I hurriedly set up our guitar effects.

Under the watchful gaze of the five judges in the panel sitting behind the glass window, Grace banged her cymbals four times. Raya's eyes were fiery as she stared back at those judges. She stood tall, proud and insolent.

The intro of the song was heavy with noisy guitar distortions. Soraya gripped the mic stand firmly, one hand lower than the other. She bent down and tilted it forward. Her eyes were wide open, glaring. She grinned too, with a manic expression.

Grace's drum rolls were deep and powerful. With the guitar effects and Soraya's vocals, the music compensated for the lack of speed and complicated lines that the metal boys in the hallway were planning to offer.

The way Soraya sang was so obnoxious that I wondered what the judges thought about this boyish girl with colourful hair and psychotic glares, and a strange English accent. She jumped wildly about and waved about her mic stand, frantically shaking her head as if possessed by evil spirits. Grace's pounding drums grew more imposing, while Mirah was moving with the energy of any good English punk. I was starting to headbang, lost in the scandalous music when Kenari broke into her lead solo. Our sound was so cool I couldn't help but smile.

Soraya saved her best sneer to end the song, emphasising every word as she pointed her finger at the panel.

The guys behind the window stood up. They gave us a cheer and loud clap. I stole a quick glance at the girls; we had made an impression!

***

Chapter Twenty

"Smash It Up"
The Damned

It took my mother banging on the door and screaming to wake me. Once again, her irresponsible daughter needed sorting out to get to school on time and I could clearly feel her exasperation as she plodded back down the stairs to answer the phone.

'Sigi! Make it quick, you've got to get to school!' she yelled.

'Hello?' I picked up.

'Hey, it's me.' It was Bara.

'Esa told us what happened. They came looking for you?'

Great! Looks like I have no choice but to deal with this.

'Yeah,' I said rather impatiently. 'It isn't really your problem though because it's me they were after.'

'What should we do then? Leave you to your own defences?'

'I'm the one they've been calling a slut. Why can't you girls just let it go?'

'All I know is that the whole school is probably going to be waiting at the gate after school.'

'Sure, let them. We'll fight, and everyone can watch. Here's an idea. We should sell popcorn while we're at it.'

'How about we meet at the *musholla*[54] during the break?' she suggested, ignoring my sarcasm. 'We must talk about it, Sigi. See you there.'

I remembered what Emon had said at PV Radio, that I was lucky to have friends that backed me up.

'Alright. I'll be there.' I hung up the phone with a growing sense of dread. I decided to change my thoughts into something happier. I imagined the punks at Slammers, the music, the mohawks, and my mood lifted.

---

[54]*Musholla* is the Islamic prayer room at school.

Esa smiled at me as I came into class. The other kids were whispering, obviously talking about me. Good thing that Mr Tambunan, our history teacher, was late too.

'How are you? You look tired,' she said.

'I didn't sleep much. I was out late last night.' I'd only had a couple of hours of sleep.'

'Did you get any homework done?'

'No, I think I'm going to have to accept the fact that I'm going to fail.'

'You'll pass, Sigi. Don't worry!'

At that moment, Mr Tambunan arrived. His stern eyes quickly flew around the room and we were all silent. His face clearly showed that he meant business. I was screwed.

He began singling us out, asking random questions about Indonesian history. My heart was racing. I knew a little bit, but the last time I actually read the textbook, I couldn't remember.

He called my name and I wasn't able to answer all of his questions. For that, he gave me thirty minutes of detention after school. Even worse, I fell asleep at my desk I was abruptly woken by his booming voice and sent to the bathroom to wash my face. That display added an extra fifteen minutes to the detention.

By recess, I was exhausted.

'Let's get some fresh air so you can wake up,' offered Esa.

'We need to get to the *musholla*.'

'You want to pray? You?' Esa looked bewildered.

'The girls want to talk about what's supposed to happen after school.'

'Oh, ok, I'm coming with you.'

'No, I don't want you involved.'

She looked at me with her arms folded in front of her chest. 'I want to come. At least let me listen.'

'But I've got detention. I don't think those nasty girls will be willing to wait.'

'I'm coming anyway.'

We walked down to the first floor behind the sea of students, all heading in the same direction. Everyone watching us, and I was a bit nervous that we would run into Tania or one of her crew on the way, however, we arrived at the *musholla* without incident.

The five girls were there waiting. Bara signalled us to sit next to her. I looked around the room. Only a few other students were in there. We chatted casually while they completed *wudhu*-the Islamic washing ritual before prayer.

One by one, the students were immersed in their *shalat*[55]. That was our cue to sneak out the back to the small alley where we could hide.

'Come on, girls, seriously?' I said after I lit a cigarette. 'I have no time for this. I've got detention after school, thanks to Mr Tambunan. I don't think they'll wait for that long for me.'

'We'll wait for you,' said Bara as she lit hers. 'We're not letting you leave school alone.'

Fuck off and mind your own business.

With an umbrella in her hands and eyes determined, Reni continued the conversation. 'I bought this for you in case you need a weapon.'

I thought that she was being dramatic.

'You might not need it, I know,' Reni explained, reading my face. 'I want you to carry it, just in case.

'Thanks,' I replied kindly, as I took the umbrella.

She looked so pretty when her dark eyes twinkled.

'Why is Tania so pissed off at me anyway?'

Bara paused to gain our attention. 'There's a new guy who started school a couple of months ago. Apparently, she's obsessed with him. We heard that he likes you and he's been asking about you. Once *she* heard that, she was as jealous as hell.'

Boys. The same problem as in junior high. Fighting over boys was the lowest kind of action I could imagine.

'I don't even know who this guy is. It's all so pathetic.' My patience was being stretched, to say the least.

'What's his name?' Anita asked Bara.

'I don't know,' she replied. 'All I know is that he's from Tania's old school and he's in second year.'

---

[55] *Shalat* or *sholat* is the Arabic term for performing prayers.

'These desperate girls,' Reni sneered. 'What are they thinking? That if they hassle the girls these guys like, they'd win them over?'

I took a drag of my cigarette. 'Detention is forty-five minutes so maybe that's a good thing. Maybe they won't wait around for me,' I said.

'I don't think they'll go home,' said Linda worriedly. 'There're at least a dozen girls who can't wait to stick it into you, so I don't think they'll back off because of forty-five minutes.'

I threw my cigarette on the dirt, scowling as I ground the butt with my foot.

***

In class, time passed so slowly that it was killing me. When the bell to go home finally rang, the other students darted out while I had to stay back with Mr Tambunan. I felt like a trapped animal. It was a long forty-five minutes. To fill the time, I began plotting what I could say, what I could do, to insult and belittle Tania.

As the detention drew to a close, my mood was dropping and the desire to escape was increasing. Reni and the girls were waiting when I came out of the classroom.

'What are you doing here, Esa?' I asked. 'You know you're not supposed to be here.'

'Well, I am,' she said firmly.

'You're not coming with us. Go home.'

'I'm going to watch from the sidelines.'

'Let her come,' said Bara. 'She can take care of herself.'

As we walked through the school gate, Pandu's words came rushing back to me, echoing in my head like a twisted mantra – *just slap her*.

And there they were. The girls were waiting on the street, sur-rounded by what must have been more than half the school.

Tania stood in front of her mates, obviously wound up, ready to smash me. She was tall and her long brown curly hair cascaded around her glaring face and down her shoulders. She was a pretty girl, but her smug expression killed her good looks.

In a show of aggression, she put her hands on her hips as our eyes met.

I kept on walking, my girls behind me. I played with the umbrella, swinging it around, tapping it on my left palm, while I looked her right in the eyes. She had a disdainful smile. I decided not to smile at all.

All eyes were on us and I quickly sensed the ridiculous nature of what was going on. It was surreal like we were in a movie. It was so absurd that I wanted to laugh.

Finally, I stood in front of her, the serpent and drama queen she was.

'What's with the umbrella?' she scoffed. 'Afraid of the rain?'

'I thought I might have to protect my face from your flying spit.'

The students around us started to giggle, making those kinds of '*uuuuh*' sounds that teenagers make.

'You wanted to see me? I don't have much time, so cut the crap and get to the point.'

'I heard you got detention. How fitting! I wonder why. Let me see. Maybe they caught you smoking somewhere in the back alley? Or maybe because you fell asleep during class, again, or maybe because you're just a stupid bitch with bad grades?'

'You're talking crap.'

'Everything about you is CRAP.' Tania's voice escalated. 'You're nothing but a slut and you're failing too. The thought of you hanging around like a piece of shit for another year? Do us a favour, fuck off and move to another school.'

The crowd began cheering, laughing at both of us. I could see that this ridiculous carrying-on was going to go back and forth for a long time.

So I made up my mind. I was going to cut it short, out of my own exhaustion, boredom, and wanting to be free of Tania and her foot-soldier mates.

'Answer me slut. Don't just stand there like a fucking idiot!' she demanded.

'I'm not in the mood for talking.'

'*Oooooh*,' the students jeered.

'Sluts don't talk, they just, well, *do*, don't they,' she laughed.

The crowd jeered again.

'Stop saying that I'm a slut and a piece of shit or I'm going to slap you.'

She laughed again. 'You? Slap me? Not even my father slaps me.'

'Go ahead,' I said as I passed the umbrella to Bara standing nearby. 'Try me.'

'You… are… a… slut!' she said slowly, with precision and a vicious provocative smile. 'And, a piece of shit!'

At lightning speed, I did it.

I slapped her!

I did it without thinking. I just did it the way my mother used to do it to me. A sudden, sharp, heated slap on the face.

The sound reverberated around the students as she screamed. She stood there, looking at me, pathetically holding her red cheek in her hands. Time slowed down. It seemed frozen in the silence and I could hear my heart pounding.

'You slapped me,' she whimpered. Her lips started to tremble and her eyes became teary. Pandu was right; she had fallen into shock. 'You slapped me,' she suddenly screamed again, more loudly.

Uh oh.

That was my cue to get going, but before I left, I gave her a sorry look. I nodded to my girls to take over. I kept walking without looking back and calmly got into one of the waiting *bajaj* lined up along the kerb.

I turned and looked out through the transparent plastic window at the back. Reni was provoking her; she was good at that-until Tania's friends finally dragged her away. My girls gave them a loud laugh.

As we drove off, I saw Esa on the side of the street waving with a grin. She gave me a victorious thumbs-up.

It was time to focus on the band!

***

Chapter Twenty One

"Come As You Are"
Nirvana

September 1993

School was much quieter after the slapping incident. Fortunately, I rarely saw Tania again. It wasn't a nice thing to slap another student yet the teachers went about as if nothing had happened. I heard that the reason was due to Tania. She didn't want to report it to the school.

She had been expelled from her previous school for bullying and causing a huge drama and so she stayed silent to avoid the possibility of being kicked out again. I could only think about Wanderlust and the Young Offender, and so I gave her no further thought.

Mirah had organised an acoustic session at my place that afternoon and I pushed through the back door and scurried up to my room. I had enough time for a bite to eat and a quick shower.

Umi must have let them in as I soon heard the sound of feet running up the stairs. I threw my door open to see Raya with Grace, and with Mirah and Kenari behind them carrying their guitars.

Kenari was screaming. 'Sigi, Sigi, we passed the audition for Hard Wire!'

'No way,' I was screaming too.

'Yes, one of the organisers phoned.'

'Crazy hey, we passed the audition. Can you believe it?' said Grace breathlessly. 'And, Mirah, it's your last time onstage. This going to be massive.'

Mirah clapped her hands, equally excited. 'Imagine the crowd, it's going to be huge, a few thousand or so, maybe more. I am so glad I'm only playing bass.'

Soraya's face was flat. We knew how much she still despised

metal and now she was about to play in a metal festival, and an important one at that.

'Thanks for being here,' I said to her. 'A few punks should turn up so it might not be all bad.'

'Yeah, let's get it done.'

I glanced over at the calendar on my desk. Our biggest and best gig would be in just a few weeks. My stomach started twisting and turning.

'We've got three songs, as usual,' Kenari added. 'Mirah and I thought we'd do Two Sex Pistols and a Nirvana. Isn't it cool we have Raya?'

We were beaming. The fact that Soraya finally had agreed to sing Nirvana was beyond our expectations.

I hit 'play' on the tape recorder. The drums and bass resounded around the room. We followed with our guitars while Soraya's rough voice took control of the songs.

Grace sat, beaming and I was ecstatic. With Raya as our front-woman, we were going to rock that festival.

***

An hour and a half later, we were satisfied. These days Soraya led the practice, although Mirah still managed our schedules.

'Well, girls, I've booked the studio for the next two Thursdays and then the following Sunday. After that it's D-day,' she confirmed.

'Fantastic, by the way, well done today, Raya,' I said.

'Thanks.' She didn't offer me much more than that.

'I need to run, in about five minutes,' said Kenari as she took a quick glance at the Swatch on her wrist.

'Me too. I'm coming with you,' said Mirah. 'I've got a heap of homework to do.'

'I'm going home too,' Grace chipped in.

'Are you coming with us, Raya?' asked Kenari.

'No, Slammers, isn't too far away. I'm heading over there.'

Kenari squealed again. 'Are you ever going to take me?'

'Come now then. I don't know who will be there, but Satria and Galih should be,' replied Soraya.

Kenari was thinking about it. 'Sigi, what are you doing?' she asked.

I wanted to go more than anything, but my father's voice filtered through those thoughts.

'The amount of work I need to revise scares the shit out of me. I'm going to have to give it a miss.'

'I've an idea,' she said. 'How about we all go just to say hi, just stay for five minutes? What do you think?'

'Good idea,' Soraya agreed. 'Sigi, are you in? What about you Grace?'

'I know myself,' I said with a sigh. 'I won't want to leave after five minutes, so I'd better skip it.'

Grace shook her head. 'I'm taking the bus home. See you, girls.'

'And, I need to study. I'll grab a taxi,' said Mirah firmly.

'No, you won't. We'll share the cab and we'll just stay for five minutes, I promise,' begged Kenari.

Mirah caved. 'Alright then, five minutes.'

'Yay, come on, we'd better get going. See you later Sigi,' Kenari said.

As we said goodbye to Grace, I beat back my common sense. 'Hell no, I'm coming with you.'

***

By the time we arrived at Slammers, it was already late afternoon. The place looked deceptively quiet, but once we stepped out of the taxi, fast and raucous punk music could be heard emanating from the back of the house.

'Full house, the front gate's open. There must be a gig tonight,' said Soraya with a smile. 'There's Satria's car.' She pointed at a dark blue VW convertible in the driveway. 'And that's Lih's, the maroon Civic.'

'Look,' Kenari said as she stared at the pile of jackets and shoes scattered about on the front terrace.

'They're probably getting ready now,' I added

'Will they be dressed in their punk gear?' asked Kenari, clapping as she jumped up and down. 'Will we get to see that?'

'Oh, Lord, why do I get the feeling that this is going to take more than five minutes?' said Mirah.

'Here we go, girls,' said Soraya.

She led us along the path down the right side of the house, and through the second gate. As we approached the back garden, we heard guys talking and I got a familiar whiff of the spray paint.

A number of punks were sitting around outside. Some of the faces I already knew. They were engrossed with precisely what I saw them doing the first time I came to Slammers-building mohawks with glue, spraying them with the colourful paint, attaching spikes, and piercing their bodies.

Ardi was there, as well as Hansel, Abi, and Panji. The latter had a big smile as soon as he saw us.

'Hi Panji, where's Satria?' Soraya asked.

'He's in his room with some of the others sorting out the flag.'

'I'd love to see it.'

'Go and have a look. Galih, Egan and Aqila are in there too.'

Aqila, I remembered that he had been hurt. I was about to follow Soraya when Panji caught my hand.

'Hey,' he said. 'How are you, Sigi? Abi and I are trying to decide which colour to spray our mohawks.'

'Hi, let me introduce you to our bassist first. This is Mirah,' I said.

'Hello Mirah, I'm Panji,' he said as he shook her hand. I could tell from her blushing cheeks that she was in awe of him.

With his mohawk, Panji was almost twice the height of Mirah. The piercings on his nose and ears had healed and his lean abdominal wall was as ripped as his t-shirt.

Kenari and Mirah were quickly engrossed in conversation so I snuck off. At the doorway to Satria's bedroom, I peeked inside before I closed the door behind me. The music was loud. and I squinted to adjust to ultraviolet light. The sofa had been pushed up against the back wall, and a makeshift table now stood in the middle of the room, with a few silhouettes standing around it.

A vast black flag with a circular logo drawn with white glossy paint, lay on the table. Dominating the central point was a swastika, and on top of that, a hand, pointing in a Nazi-like salute. A chain formed the outer ring.

The look of the flag stirred something dark inside of my soul.

'Great, isn't it!' I heard a voice on my left. It belonged to Aqila.

'Hey,' I said shyly, grateful for the low lighting as I tried to focus on the flag.

'What's with the swastika and the Nazi salute? You guys believe in the Nazis or something?'

'No, not the Nazis, not their idealism, if that's what you mean,' he said categorically. 'We just borrowed a few elements to convey a sense of anarchy.'

I glanced up at him but he was staring at the flag.

'We wanted to use the symbolism of the PKI, you know, the hammer and a *celurit*[56],' he continued, mentioning the name of the now-banned Communist Party, the PKI, from the 1960s. 'Then we thought it might be too controversial. We settled on this instead.'

'Oi Oi Sigi,' said Satria. He was standing just a little further along. 'How do you like our new flag? We're making this version in red and white[57] too.'

He looked at me with a grin. Next to him stood the fierce Egan. He gave me a quick glance and then went back to concentrating on the flag. He was holding a big brush in one hand and on the table sat a few cans of paint.

'Satria gave us the idea for the design and Egan has done some great work painting it,' Galih said enthusiastically. 'Now all he needs to do to finish it is to write the words Young Offender underneath the logo.'

'I will if you guys just give me a bit of room,' muttered Egan.

The circle of admirers dispersed. Out of the corner of my eye, I watched Aqila and Galih go back to the garden with Soraya behind them. I stepped out with Satria, leaving Egan to work his magic.

'Are you coming with us tonight?' he asked. 'Big night, The Surrender's going to compete in the Grand Final of the Jak Rock Festival.'

---

[56]*Celurit* is a type of Indonesian sickle.
[57]Red and white are the colours of the Indonesian flag.

'Oh, wow, where is it?' That sounded exciting.

'At Manari Café, a new place for the underground in Gatot Soebroto Street. There's even a few new punk and alternative bands from south Jakarta going to play like New Disease, Soul Kitchen, No Names, and Bottoms Up. And famous judges too. They're top mainstream musicians, you know, Arthur Kanaung, Bens Leo, and Doddy Katamsi.'

'Wish I could come along,' I said in dismay. 'But we just called in for a few minutes to drop Raya off. The rest of us need to get back home.'

'It's still early. If you can't come now, come along later. We'll be here after the gig until morning.'

'Tempting,' I said. 'We'll see, thanks, though.'

Mirah was still in conversation with Ardi and Hansel, and she waved to signal that she was ready to go. I looked around for Aqila, but he was nowhere to be seen. I was going to say goodbye to Soraya except she had gone to the *warung* to buy cigarettes.

Kenari was with Abi and Panji, helping them spray a mohawk, to her great amusement. She put the Pilox can down and said her goodbyes to the boys.

'Looks like we're going now, unfortunately,' I said to Satria.

'Why don't you stay?' said Galih suddenly. 'I can drive you home.'

'Thanks, Lih, but I really do need to study.'

'Want me to pick you up after the gig?'

I nodded without thinking.

Looks like somebody is going to sneak out again tonight.

'I'll call you about eleven.'

As we walked through to the front yard, I noticed Aqila talking to a few guys I didn't know on the porch. For a brief moment, our eyes locked.

'Hey Qila,' Satria called out from behind us. 'These are the Wanderlust girls. Have you been introduced? Girls, this is Aqila and his mates from The Revolver.'

Kenari, Mirah and I shook hands with them.

The Revolver was Aqila's band. He was the vocalist, with Bastian the drummer, Azis on guitar, and Dafa played bass.

Aqila and I were finally introduced.

I stole a quick glance at him. In the afternoon light, he had a face shaped like that of Agam's with sharp lines and a strong jawline. Most probably the same roots from the Batak people in Sumatra, only his skin was darker. He had a prominent nose and lively dark eyes that darted around while he touched his chin with his long fingers. He wore a black and white Subhuman t-shirt, black jeans, and his Doc Martens. His hair lay dishevelled and messy on his cheeks.

'Wanderlust, coming with us tonight?' he asked.

'Next time,' I said.

'Aqila and his band do covers of the Sex Pistols,' said Galih, hoping to convince me.

'Cool,' I said, as I turned back to face Aquila. 'Hey, I heard you got hurt at Voila. Are you ok?'

'Hurt?' he asked with a puzzled look.

'Your wrist,' I said.

'It was nothing, just a scratch.'

'A scratch, uh-huh. He was crying like a girl on the night,' snickered Dafa.

'I was not,' said Aqila.

'You were,' Bastian said.

I grinned at the thought of Aqila crying like a girl.

'I was not!' Aqila was now quite annoyed, given the tone of his voice.

'Yes, you were!' insisted Azis. 'I saw you.'

While they were teasing him, I observed his mates. Bastian looked like a simple boy next door with his neat and short haircut. I liked how he laughed and how his eyes laughed with him. Azis had short hair but not cut as neatly as Bastian's. He seemed the oldest with his short beard, and I liked the hint of sweetness in him. Dafa wore oversized glasses and was tall and thin with attractive features.

As for Aqila, he was, in my eyes, damn hot. He had the same honey-coloured skin as me. I usually didn't go for guys like that. Yet, there was something about him. I dreaded going home, leaving them, leaving him.

***

Chapter Twenty Two

"Just Go Away"
Blondie

Galih dropped me off and I scurried up to my room to hit the books. It wasn't easy to concentrate. I kept seeing Aqila's lively eyes. There was definitely something about him, but I couldn't quite put my finger on it. I studied well, though, memorising a few pages of history and geography. Before I knew it, it was eight o'clock.

'*Mbak* Sigi,' I heard Umi's voice call through my door. 'Are you going to have dinner?'

'I'm still busy. Tell them to start without me.'

'There's nobody home. Just you.'

'Where is everyone?'

'*Bapak, Ibu*[58] and Bulan went to your uncle's. Matari isn't home yet.'

I wasn't hungry, however, I knew Umi wanted to tidy the dining table and go to bed.

'Leave a bit of food on the table. I'll come down soon.'

'Yes, *mbak*.'

Given I was intending to hang out with the punks until the early morning, I decided to lay down for a few minutes. That was a mistake. I dozed off in an uneasy sleep and into a nightmare. My mother was screaming with hatred and disappointment when she had found out that I wasn't a virgin anymore. I woke up sweating and agitated.

I washed my face and made some hot tea. With all my might, I forced myself to sit back at my desk and start work again.

After a while, I decided that I was hungry and went downstairs

---

[58] *Bapak* and *Ibu* are polite terms of address for a man and woman. Here Umi is referring to Sigi's parents.

into the kitchen. I looked at the clock-9:48pm. I ate alone at the table, reading my history book. None of it stuck in my head.

Just as I was finishing, the phone rang. A smile spread across my face. Galih was early.

'Hello?'

'Sigi, it's me, Danu.'

'Oh.' A sense of dread kicked in.

What now!

'Hello,' I said dully.

'Come on, don't be like that. We're in Menteng and just finished dinner. Can we come over?'

'What do you mean 'we'?'

'Just me and the boys. Can we?'

'It's late,' I said calmly, trying to breathe in spite of a racing heart.

Was Agam with him?

'I know it's late, but I just want to say hi, to talk to you for a few minutes. Can we?'

I glanced around. My parents wouldn't be home for a while, and my sisters were nowhere to be seen.

'Alright, but you can't stay too long, I need to study.'

'Great, I promise. I'll see you soon.'

The only reason I agreed was the thought that Agam might come with him.

Suddenly I realised the state that I was in and headed upstairs. I looked in the mirror and the reflection of a girl with an oily face and messy hair stared back. After a quick shower, I browsed through my wardrobe and chose a simple white t-shirt and khaki cargo shorts.

I turned on the radio.

'Alright, *brur and ses*[59], this is Let's Go to Bed with Pandu Wijaya on PV Radio. That was one of my favourite bands Living Color with "Love Rears Its Ugly Head",' about the way a woman can change from hot to cold.'

---

[59]*Bru* and *ses* are Indonesian for 'bro' and 'sis'

His dreamy voice filled my room. I snickered. Of course, Pandu had to be the one on-air.

'Girls, if you're listening, go easy on us guys. If you don't love us anymore, just say so. Don't keep us hanging on.'

Pandu could still mess with my head, even when he was on the radio.

He was right, though. I should tell Danu the truth, that I don't love him. Just as the song was finished, the doorbell rang. I raced downstairs. As Umi was about to walk to the front door, I stopped her in her tracks.

'It's my friends. I'll get it. Thanks, *mbak* Umi.'

She nodded and went back to her quarters at the far end of the house. I took a deep breath and headed to the door.

***

Four guys were standing there, leaning against the pillars of the front porch, Danu, Agam, Dirga, and Ray.

'There she is. The wander girl,' Ray laughed.

'Hey guys,' I said.

'You look pretty tonight,' Dirga winked.

'Thanks. What's the honour of you guys dropping by?' I asked, trying to sound cool. None of the girls I knew, with the exception of Mirah, had ever been visited by the most famous metal musicians in the underground.

'We got dragged here by your boyfriend,' smirked Ray. 'I always go to a girl's house alone. What did you do to him, Sigi?'

'I need a cigarette,' said Agam.

He smiled coolly. I smiled back as coolly as I could muster.

'I'm going to the *warung*[60] out the front,' he added as he headed back towards the street.

'I'm coming with you,' said Ray. Dirga followed in their footsteps. They were leaving me alone with Danu. Then again, it was inevitable. I invited him to take a seat on the porch chairs.

---

[60]*Warung* are the street-side stalls that sell a range of goods from food and cigarettes to small household items.

'I don't have much time. I've got homework to do and my parents will be home soon.'

Danu's hair was loosely tied at the back. He looked clean and fresh, with a white Slayer t-shirt, blue jeans, and thongs.

'I know. I just wanted to see you. I really miss you.'

I took a deep breath as Pandu's words echoed through my head. *If you don't love us anymore, just say so.*

'Danu, you know what I want.' I took another deep breath. 'I do hope you understand. I'm sorry.'

'Why? Because of what happened at my place? I want to be responsible, Sigi. I want to marry you someday.'

'There's no need to feel so responsible that you have to marry me.'

I was silent, dying for a cigarette, but I didn't have any.

'I love you so much,' he desperately added. 'And you love me too.'

I decided to answer him with all the honesty and courage I could muster.

'No. I, I'm so sorry to tell you that I…,' I paused. 'I don't love you anymore.'

The look on Danu's face when it registered showed a mix of shock, heartache, and confusion. His eyebrows hung low, his lips even lower.

He took out a cigarette from behind his ear and I was surprised because I had never seen him smoke before. He didn't light it. He just played with it, staring at it and crushing it a little with his long fingers.

For a while, he sat there, looking at his cigarette.

'Say something,' I finally broke the silence.

He reached in his pocket for a lighter and lit the crumpled cigarette, took a deep drag and blew the smoke up in the air. He looked at me with a sad smile.

'I thought so,' he sighed. 'You never really loved me even from the beginning, or at least not as much as I loved you.'

That was a shock for me; I never thought Danu knew.

'I couldn't believe my luck when you used to tell me you loved me too. I'd never had a girlfriend like you, so pretty and cool, brave and smart, and a virgin. I was the luckiest bastard in the world. And I took it just like that. I keep beating myself up over it.'

'It was a misunderstanding,' I said.

'Yeah, a misunderstanding. That stupid move caused me to lose you. It's ok if you hate me. Guess I deserve it.'

'I don't hate you,' I said. 'I just feel like I can't keep seeing you. That's all.'

After a long drag, he exhaled.

'Danu, I-'

'Let me say this. You're too good for me, Sigi. Of course you don't want to be with me anymore. You'll have a lot of adventures before someone catches your free spirit. Thanks for the good times. I will definitely miss you.'

This time I couldn't hold my tears.

'Hey, baby, don't!' He quickly put his cigarette on the ashtray and held my hands in his. 'Don't cry over me. I'm not worth the tears.'

'You're a good man,' I whispered, struggling to get the words out. 'You were never angry or sad, even when I was carrying on and acting like an idiot.'

'One thing you're not is a fool,' he said, wiping my wet face with his fingers. 'I'm so sorry for going too far.'

We hugged each other as I lay my head on his shoulder, inhaling his scent for the last time before we broke our embrace.

'I'm going to say goodbye before I start crying too. I love you, baby, always have, always will. Doesn't matter if you don't love me back. I had the best time of my life with you.'

He stood up and walked away without looking back.

I watched the three guys across the street move on from the *warung* back to the vehicle. Danu unlocked the doors as they waved goodbye. Agam give me that half-smile before getting in, but I didn't smile back. The car was soon gone, buried in the blur of passing traffic.

***

I went inside and up to the family room, filled with competing emotions, sad and yet relieved. And it had been the wrong time to see Agam again. Now I wasn't sure how I felt.

I glanced at the clock. It was almost eleven. The sound of the front gate opening meant my parents and Bulan had returned. How depressing tonight had turned out to be.

Another hour passed. and the phone still didn't ring. My parents had already gone to bed. I stayed upstairs watching TV with Bulan and she soon headed off to sleep too. I was left alone, flooded with disappointment. I glanced again at the clock, 12.40am.

Finally, I gave up, went into my room, and sat at my desk. I needed to sleep yet I dreaded the morning would come too soon. I noticed my diary with a pile of cassettes heaped on it. It had been a while since I wrote anything. Sliding it out from under the tapes, I wrote, and wrote, and wrote.

I wrote about my frustration over my studies and my fear of not passing the exams. Failing everything would be a significant humili-ation-and torture. I imagined having to repeat the same classes with the same hateful girls for another whole year while my friends had moved on with their lives. I wrote about Danu and our dismal end.

It dawned on me that I was single.

Hearing the phone ring, I flew downstairs. My father was just opening their bedroom door when he saw me. He picked up any-way.

'Hello? Who is this?'

The person spoke.

'Why are you calling after midnight?'

The person spoke again.

'Alright, but not too long. It's past one, you know.'

He handed me the phone. 'It's Soraya,' he said and headed off to bed.

I took the receiver while trying to hide my smile; Soraya was cruising with Galih. Of course, it was much better for a girl to call me at this hour.

There was just enough time to quickly get changed into an all-black outfit. I put some black eyeliner around my eyes to look bolder. Then I did the usual. I crept through the family room and downstairs, stealing the house key on the way as I disappeared into the darkness.

Galih and Soraya were sitting in the shadows at the side of the mini-mart, drinking coolers. They were also dressed in black, their hair sprayed in different colours. Galih's shirt was torn, tied together here and there with safety pins. They both wore magnificent army boots with silver spikes. Thank goodness the place was deserted. For sure, they would have attracted a lot of attention.

'Hey,' I said to Soraya. 'What did you tell my dad?'

'That I've been admitted to hospital, so I won't be at school and I needed you to tell the teachers.'

'Good one.'

'You ready to go?' asked Galih.

***

Chapter Twenty Three

"I Wanna Be Where The Boys Are"
The Runaways

At almost two in the morning, the outline of mohawks could be seen in the dim streetlights. Slammers was still packed. I got out of the car, exploding with excitement. The normally quiet road was full of punks milling around, like that night outside Voila. Soraya and I, again, seemed to be the only girls. As usual, nobody paid us any attention, just a quick glance, and they went back to talking among themselves.

'Oi Oi Oiii Sigi,' Satria gave me a loud cheer. 'I was wondering when you were going to show up.'

'Hey, Satria,' I smiled. 'How was the Jak Rock Festival?'

'It was awesome. The Surrender won first prize for the best new band. Can you believe it?'

'Wow, that's amazing, congratulations!'

'Too bad you missed it.'

With that, he began introducing me to a few more of the punks before he wandered off. Ren seemed the craziest. He was renowned for his channelling of Sid Vicious from the Sex Pistols and he had more piercings on his face than the others, five on his bottom lip alone and even one through his tongue. He was clearly high on something. His best friend Radit was the drummer for The Surrender. I remembered him from Voila. His looks reminded me of Abi, that fair skin and full lips. Alongside Radit, Bayu had a mainstream appearance with his short haircut, dark skin, and big glasses.

Ardi, Soraya and Galih, along with Panji and Abi came over and joined our conversation. We talked and joked, but my eyes were scanning the street for Aqila.

'Hello, I'm Eki,' said one as he joined us. I instantly liked him. He was short with a slight frame, and I couldn't guess where he was from. His fair skin and face were not Chinese or Indonesian; he was more like a mixed ex-pat kid. He had long, wavy, light brown hair, light brown eyes and a friendly smile.

'What music do you like?'

Oh god, here we go.

'I don't know a lot yet when it comes to punk music,' I answered shyly. 'Only the Ramones, Sex Pistols and The Clash, you know, very basic. Lih gave me a compilation tape, and I liked all the music, but I don't know some of the bands on it.'

'Oh, the tape I gave you? That was *Punk and Disorderly*,' said Galih. 'I'll have to make you a photocopy of the album cover so you know the tracks. If I remember rightly, it was The Blitz, Abrasive Wheel, The Insane, The Mob, Chaos UK-'

'I'll make you a mixed tape,' Eki cut in. 'I won't give you a compilation like Galih did. That's just lazy. I'll make you one with an excellent selection.'

'Like a nice boyfriend,' Ardi winked.

'I want her to know the latest, you know, the songs that are hard to find,' Eki said defensively. 'I don't do this for girlfriends. Besides, she's an underground radio DJ. She should know these bands.'

'Arhh, so sensitive,' Ardi teased. 'What are you going to give her?'

'Fugazi, Jane's Addiction, Sonic Youth, and she should listen to industrial as well like Ministry, Skinny Puppy, Front Line Assembly, and Revolting Cocks.'

'Cool stuff,' Ardi agreed, his long dreadlocks covering most of his face.

'By the way, Sigi, were you at our gig the other night?' asked Eki.

'No,' I said with regret.

'You should have seen it. We played in a new venue called Hot Spot, a small pub in south Jakarta next to Lebak Bulus Stadium. The South Sex guys organised it.'

'Really? The South Sex? You played in the south? With South Sex? Who are they?' This was big news to me.

'They've just formed their own community in south Jakarta. It was crazy, different punks hanging out together, about one hundred and fifty of us. The Surrender, Revolver and The Myth played and the rest were their bands. The headline was The Idiots.'

It was starting to look like the domination of metal in the underground was about to be presented with a serious challenge.

'How did the Young Offender meet these other punks?' I was breathless with anticipation.

Galih answered, 'From our t-shirts.'

'What do you mean?'

'After school, we wear band t-shirts,' explained Eki. 'Not the usual rock or metal t-shirts from the shops around here. Everyone wears those!' He pulled a face.

'You mean like the ones you guys are wearing now?'

'Yes,' said Galih. 'Satria made them.'

'Really?'

'Yeah, he and Egan and a few other guys. They have a t-shirt printing machine.'

'Wow!' I gave the boys a big dreamy look.

'We started getting recognised by punks who were into the same music as us because of our t-shirts,' Eki continued. 'We met some of the South Sex at a record store in Blok M. I had on a Fugazi t-shirt, and they were freaking out. They told me they had just formed their own punk community. We kept in touch so we'd all know what was happening in the punk underground that's been building right across the city. And now we've been able to collaborate in gigs like at the Hot Spot.'

'We've grown from strength to strength since we started forming our own bands,' said Ardi. 'It began with hanging out at Satria's and the Young Offender was born on the thirtieth of September last year.'

'That's the anniversary of the PKI,' I mumbled.

I remembered Aqila had told me that they had wanted to use the PKI logo from the banned Indonesian Communist Party. They changed their minds, however, because they thought it might be too controversial and invite trouble from the police or even the military.

Panji interrupted my thoughts.

'You know we're always at The Blackhole. You should come again,' he said

'Maybe, if I can, I will.'

'Sigi has to study,' said Soraya, pouting.

'And you don't?' Ardi laughed.

'I'm a genius. I don't need to study,' said Soraya laughed, obviously drunk.

'Well, I am no genius,' I said as I looked away.

'Come with us, fuck studying,' she insisted.

Aqila emerged with his band mates. I kept my cool and pretended to listen to the conversation instead.

'Oi Oi Oiii!' he yelled, as he began handing out packets of cigarettes and coolers. I walked away. I didn't know why. It seemed the exhilaration at seeing him was too much to handle. I sat down next to Satria in front of the gate, but he didn't say anything. He was lost in thought. The others were busy amongst themselves. That gave me a few moments alone to watch.

Aqila was telling jokes, complete with comical body gestures, and the punks were laughing. I felt my cheeks blushing. He was so good-looking, even from afar. Under the faint street light, he looked rather dashing.

His eyes caught mine.

He entertained the guys with a few more jokes and then he slowly detached himself from the group. I watched him casually walk towards me.

'Sigi,' he said. 'How are you?'

When he sat down next me on the footpath, I could smell him, just slightly. There was a mix of leather, musky sweat, and, surprisingly, the clean smell of soap.

'I'm good, thanks. How was the gig?'

'Great.' He took a drag of his cigarette.

I took a drag of mine too. His dark eyes were wandering, taking in the street.

'I saw your band perform once,' he started.

'You did?'

'Yes, a gig at SMA8.'

'What did you think?' I asked nervously.

'Cool, but with Raya, you'll be a lot cooler.'

Didn't I know that!

'Wanderlust has played mostly at metals gigs, eh?' he asked.

'Not always. We've played on the Pensi circuit and some uni events.'

'Ever been a guest star?'

'No, we still just play three songs, occasionally four. Most of the time, they put us on early. Sucks to play just a few songs, but you know we all have to share the stage with a heap of other bands. We've got about twenty-five covers in our playlist, and I wish we could play them all at the one gig.'

'You're dreaming,' Aqila teased. 'Not even guest stars get that much time.'

'Yeah, but at least they get to play about eight to ten songs.'

'Still not enough, though, is it? We know over twenty songs since we formed last year and we never get to time to play them either.'

'Yeah, you have to be a major mainstream star for that,' I added.

'Or a mainstream cover band that plays in big cafes,' he said with a grin.

He was definitely cute.

'What's been your biggest audience so far?' asked Aqila.

'That was probably the Pensi at SMA6. About five hundred, I think.'

'By the way, I saw a poster the other day for the Hard Wire Festival at Menteng next month. Your band was on it.'

'No way,' Satria was suddenly awake. 'Metal is shit, Sigi.'

At least Soraya hadn't told them. But I still felt like a thief caught red-handed. Damn posters!

'Well maybe, but we're going to be playing punk.' I didn't say that we were also considering Nirvana. They didn't need to know that.

'We should come and support you,' said Satria.

I was shocked, and it must have shown on my face because they were laughing at me.

'That's a nice idea, thanks, but I don't think it'll be your scene.'

'Why not?' Satria teased. 'I want to see those metal guys with their long hair and check out their celebrity girlfriends.'

'Then come. Don't let me stop you,' I said. Maybe reverse psychology would work. Perhaps I had learned something from my student workmates at PV Radio. 'Bring everyone.'

'Speaking of everyone, you remember that fight, eh Lih?' laughed Abi and he, Galih and Eki sat beside us. 'Back when Satria and the guys first met Aqila and they were all dressed as full-on punks.'

'At Kali Pasir with a local street gang.' Galih sniggered.

'A fight?' My eyes were wide.

Eki scoffed. 'Nothing we couldn't handle.'

'Hmm, maybe not,' said Aqila. 'I remember that metal event ages ago organised by Mustang Radio. I was there to see Antiseptic and there was this huge fight, a heap of punks against even more metalheads.'

'Really?' I couldn't believe what I was hearing.

'The organiser asked Antiseptic to stop playing right in the middle of the first song. They thought it was too hardcore and that really pissed us off,' he added.

'Don't worry. We won't come,' said Satria, laughing as he lay back down on the pavement.

A few others laughed too before they walked away, everyone except Aqila and I.

'Don't take any notice of him,' said Aqila. 'You know how he looks down on the metal community. Don't take it personally.'

'It will be our biggest gig ever,' I whispered, not wanting anyone to hear, but I actually had nothing to worry about. Satria had passed out due to too much wine and who knows what, and the rest were busy talking amongst themselves.

'There's probably going to be around five thousand people. I'm as nervous as hell.'

'I can come and support you if you want. I'll bring some friends too if you like, definitely not Satria, though.'

'Thanks, but we'll be fine,' I said with a smile, touched by the sweet gesture.

We sat in silence, smoking and watching the others banter about.

'Thanks for saving me,' I said after a while.

'Huh?'

'You know, the Blackhole event at Voila. Remember when Hansel was crowd-surfing? I would have gotten a boot in the face if it weren't for-'

'Oh, that? I'd forgotten about it,' he said as he looked away.

I felt disappointed.

'What I do remember was you wearing that red tartan mini-skirt.'

I punched his arm. 'Are you criticising my choice of fashion?'

'No, not at all,' he grinned. 'By all means, wear what you like.'

'How is your arm?' I changed the subject, trying to hide the warmth spreading over my cheeks.

'It's ok,' he said, pulling up the sleeve of his leather jacket to show me an ugly scar. It was about five centimetres long. 'It bled a lot, and then it was swollen for a few days. Ren stitched it with a needle and thread.'

'You're kidding?' I said with a horrified look. My hair was standing on end. No wonder he had been crying like a girl. 'Why didn't you go to the doctor?'

'What for?' he laughed.

These boys were nuts.

'Let's go catch up with the others.' He put out his cigarette with his Doc Marten, stood up and gave me his hand as he pulled me up, his grasp solid but tender.

I stole a quick glance at my watch. It was almost five-in the morning!

'Oh, I've got to go.' I said in shock. 'It's so late.'

'Come on, I have to go too,' answered Galih.

We said goodbye to the few remaining punks still hanging about on the street. Aqila lifted his chin to me; I gave him a smile in return.

***

Chapter Twenty Four

"Cool Schmool"
Bratmobile

October 1993

I woke up early on Saturday morning, anxious and tense. Hard Wire Festival was finally here, the most prominent underground event in Jakarta this year, and Wanderlust was in the lineup. We had come this far!

When the girls arrived, they were excited and ready to slay. These were the moments that I really enjoyed, together with them in my room with the music on full blast, talking, giggling, putting on makeup, and trying on clothes.

'How many people will be there, do you think?' asked Kenari, trying on yet another of my t-shirts.

'I don't think it's going to be full, but at least half, for sure,' I replied. 'Maybe a good few thousand!'

Mirah joined in. 'Once I thought about the fact that it's in central Jakarta, I think a lot more people are going to come than if it was in south.'

'True. Menteng Stadium is central, easy for everyone to get there. So there should be a lot of people,' added Soraya.
Her tone suggested that she had warmed, at least a little, to playing at Hard Wire.

'Provided the promotion was done right,' chipped in Grace.

'I think it was. PV Radio has been advertising it, so has Mustang FM,' I said confidently. 'Guess we need to get ready for the biggest crowd we've ever played in front of.'

'What a way to say goodbye to Mirah,' said Grace.

Mirah smiled, although she looked a bit sad.

'Alright then,' said Kenari. 'I want to wear this t-shirt Sigi. Is it ok?'

I nodded in approval. She stood out with my dark yellow top, ripped black jeans with safety pins, and her favourite dark brown boots. Her long strawberry blonde hair was now a fiery red and she wore winged eyeliner and bright red lipstick to match.

Mirah chose to wear her cargo shorts and I decided on my red tartan skirt. And as for Soraya, she looked more punk than ever; I was proud of her. Her mohawk was red, green and blue and she teamed that with a full spiked leather jacket, ripped black jeans and green army boots. Her eyeliner was black and heavy and she wore dark blue lipstick-she was fierce! Even Grace tried to look a little more extreme. Her blue jeans were slashed and the ends of her fingers emerged from the black biker gloves that covered her hands.

Mirah was putting on a pink lip-gloss. 'I'm finally going to play on the same stage as my boyfriend. I'm scared to death.'
'Wanderlust and Hell's Fury performing at the same event. Who would have thought?' laughed Grace as she brushed her long hair.

Mirah blushed.

'And the rest of the south bands,' sniggered Soraya.

'Yeah, all of them,' I replied with a sick feeling. 'Vortex, Razzle, Roxx, Flatlining, Morbid, and a few JIS bands, and Lavatory.'

'Lavatory,' said Soraya in a rather derogatory tone.

'They've been our inspiration and they've got skills, I mean, real skills. Of course, we're nervous,' said Mirah.

'We're totally different!' Soraya was indignant. 'We're punk, and, do I have to say it - g-r-u-n-g-e, *yuk* - and they are, *ugh*, metal.'

'What?' Mirah sneered back at Soraya. 'You think it's easy to play metal?'

'Raya's right,' I said quickly. 'We are different. We've got nothing to worry about.'

After a quick lunch, it was time to go.

***

Menteng Stadium stood proudly in the middle of Jakarta, where it had hosted some of the most important football matches in Indonesia. It was used for concerts and festivals during the off-season.

We arrived mid-afternoon to do our soundcheck. The major bands had done theirs the night before, which left us, the smaller bands, to finalise ours before the show started. We entered the stadium and looked at the stage in awe from the lobby. It was huge. It had been erected on the opposite side of the vast football field facing the main entrance. The sound system was of international standard. The lighting was in place, ready to make the stage come to life as soon as the sun went down.

'I never thought I'd see this day,' Mirah said, her eyes were huge. 'That stage is enormous.'

Grace grabbed her by the waist and hugged her.

'Perfect for the last gig,' she said.

Mirah nodded more excitedly this time.

I walked forward in silence, absorbing the spectacle. Mirah was right. The stage was one of the biggest I'd ever seen for an underground event. Crews and officials were running about, looking diligent and important.

There were a few familiar faces I recognised from a distance, mostly musicians with their roadies and a few diehard privileged fans. The masses would follow soon. They had been gathering on the street outside waiting for the gates to open when we arrived,

'Wanderlust,' A male voice echoed throughout the large foyer.

'Hey, Tio,' Mirah said with a smile, 'What are you doing here?'

'Working,' he said while pointing his finger proudly at a laminated identity card hanging around his neck. 'I'm the Liaison Officer. Basically, that means I'm a slave to the bands. I'm assigned to take care of you. The other guys are jealous.'

'How about Lavatory?' asked Mirah. 'Don't they have their soundcheck too?'

'They did theirs last night.'

Damn, clearly they were one of the headlining acts.

'They were boring if you ask me,' he winked. 'Always playing the same metal shit. I'd rather hear you girls.'

Soraya's frown turned into something that looked a little pleased.

We instantly liked Tio with his dark skin and lively black eyes that twitched each time he got excited.

'By the way Tio, this is Sigi, she plays rhythm and I'm on bass. Grace is our drummer, and Kenari, our lead guitarist. And this is our vocalist, Soraya.'

Tio's outstretched hand was eager. 'I'm so glad you passed the audition. The first time I saw Wanderlust play, I knew then that you'd go far, eh, Mirah?'

His eyes twinkled again. 'I can't wait. Ok, follow me. You're the last band to do your soundcheck.'

He led us across the field and into the backstage area behind the two-metre-tall stage. We climbed the wooden stairs and quickly understood the scale of the place as we gazed around in awe. We plugged the borrowed instruments into the sound system. Every sound we made was so amplified that we knew there would be no room for error. If we were to play a wrong note, we'd never get away with it. The pressure was on.

As usual, we attracted attention. Guys stopped and looked, and the only thing I could do to allay my nerves was to not look back at them and stay focused on the tasks at hand. We played "God Save the Queen" from the Sex Pistols. Soraya wasn't as loud and energetic as she usually was. It must have been nerve-wracking for her too.

We headed back down the stairs and Tio was ready with two large plastic bags. 'Here you go, girls. A few snacks and some bottles of water. You'll be on stage around five-thirty if everything goes on time. Hang in there, and come and get me if you need anything.'

'Wow,' whispered Kenari in my ear. 'They gave us food.'

We headed up another set of stairs behind the backstage area to relax on one of the stone benches that formed the seating for the stadium. It was a prime position from where we could watch all the goings-on. As we ate and chatted, I noticed that the main gate on the opposite side of the field had opened.

Metal fans were pouring in and the grassy area was quickly filling up. There were even a few punks too. At a metal event! I smiled as I wondered if they had come to see Wanderlust play.

The crowd was mainly guys, but I managed to spot a few girls here and there too, trying to disguise themselves under loose t-shirts and caps like I used to. A shiver ran through me as I remembered the assault I had endured at the Metallica concert. Then I realised while I might have been part of that sorry audience, here I was one of the performers. That sent a shot of adrenaline through me.

From the stage, the voice of the MC blared out of the sound system.

'Welcome to Menteng Stadium!'

The words were from an enthusiastic male, but we couldn't see him from where we were sitting.

The crowd began cheering, and fans started flooding closer to secure a spot in directly front of the stage.

'Welcome to the Hard Wire Festival. We've got the best of the best from Jakarta's underground. They're ready to rock the stage, so are you ready?'

The crowd cheered again.

'Are you rea-dyyyy?' he screamed again, and they roared in return. 'Let's welcome The Dark Soul!'

The band opened the event with a cover of Metallica's 'Master of Puppets.'

'Do I have to endure this shit all day?' moaned Soraya. 'It's killing me already.'

Grace laughed.

'Look,' Kenari squealed. 'The guys from the south, they've arrived.'

From our vantage point, we could see them filing into the backstage. Older guys in black with long flowing hair, these metal stars didn't carry their equipment. They had roadies for that, the younger not-so-cool guys with short hair. These musicians paraded their girlfriends on their arms-the finest, fairest celebrity girls in leather boots and oversized sunglasses.

I saw the Razzle boys, the Guns N' Roses of Indonesia. Robbie, their vocalist, was gorgeous. His long wavy brown hair caressed his shoulders and fell all the way down to his waist. His mixed-race face was model handsome, and he had made the right decision not to copy Axl Rose in terms of fashion. He wore a simple t-shirt and jeans, but his voice and how he sang was a dead ringer of the real thing. He was with the three other guys from Razzle, all of them surrounded by pretty girls.

Behind them came Roxx, totally glam with big hair, leather pants, and eyeliner. They were also surrounded by their girlfriends and their crew.

'I think I can taste back what I ate for lunch,' said Soraya sarcastically. 'Look at those girls with them. Just pathetic.'

'Oh, come on, Raya. Don't you think the boys are magnificent?' said Kenari dreamily. 'Robbie's so hot I'm melting.'

'They are cute,' smiled Grace.

'Ugh!' Soraya shook in disgust.

'Look,' squealed Kenari again.

The guys from Vortex and Hell's Fury had arrived, wearing simple black outfits. Mirah stood up to get a better view.

'Hey, they're carrying their own gear and there's a girl with them,' said Soraya, half-smiling and somewhat impressed. 'I like them, a little perhaps.'

'Did you notice who she is? That's Diah Pangabean,' Kenari chirped. 'She's dating Ray, the Vortex vocalist.'

Soraya nodded flatly in the direction of the sexy actress. She was probably the most famous of all the celebrity girlfriends of these rock stars.

I wasn't paying any attention. I only had eyes for Agam. He looked extremely fierce that day, wearing a black tank top, tight black jeans, and black sneakers. His toned upper arms looked sexy as he carried his guitar case, his expression serious.

'How come Agam never brings Berlian, that girlfriend of his?' asked Kenari, rather innocently.

'Who's Agam and Berlian?' asked Soraya.

'That's Agam,' said Grace as she pointed him out. 'Guitarist and leader of Vortex.

'Berlian's his girlfriend. She's just a senior high school student like us,' added Mirah.

'My guess is that he never brings her so that he can pick up other girls,' said Soraya cynically.

Inside, I was aching. Soraya wasn't attacking me because she didn't know that I had been seeing him in secret, although it had been a while since I last saw him alone. Grace and Mirah meant no harm either because they also didn't know. As for Kenari, well, she could have been a bit more sensitive. I quickly reached for my cigarettes. Grace looked at me disapprovingly, but I ignored her. I needed one right now.

'Sigi, look, your ex is here with Dirga,' said Mirah in a low tone. Indeed, he was. Danu, with Dirga and the boys from Hell's Fury. I rolled my eyes, him again.

'The girls from Lavatory are here too,' said Kenari.

We watched them proudly carrying their own equipment, walking with their famous rock star boyfriends. They were wearing clothes like we used to wear when we performed-metal band t-shirts, tight jeans, and sneakers. Their big drummer came in first and she looked like a tank guarding the other three.

One by one, the cool bands and their crews from south Jakarta began mingling in the backstage area below while we watched unseen from above. They were moving in and out of the marquees and liaison officers were frantically running around trying to accommodate them all.

'Hey girls,' Tio called out as he made his way along the row of seating towards us. 'How're you doing? Can I get you anything?' Mirah turned towards us. 'Girls, do we need anything?'

'No.'

'Good, I can sit here and be completely star-struck. Look at them all down there. So cool.'

'Don't you have work to do?' teased Mirah.

'I only have to take care of the opening bands.'

'Gee, thanks for reminding us of who we are,' she laughed.

He laughed too.

'Oh, look at Dayan from The Stupid with his girlfriend, Sophia Latjuba. She is divine. And the celebrity girls. Wow, there's Cornelia Agatha. That's my future wife, you know.'

'You wish,' we laughed at him.

'Diah Pangabean, Ria Wibowo, Ayu Azhari, and Karina Suwandhi,' Tio swooned as his eyes twinkled. 'Even Krisdayanti is here. Lucky bastards, those musicians, what have they got that I don't?'

We all laughed again. Tio was skinny and geeky; he knew the joke was on him.

He couldn't stop gawping at the backstage crowd. 'Flatlining and the boys from Painful Death, Alien Scream, Mortus, and Commotion of Resources. I better get going. The next band will be on soon. Get ready, girls, because you're on after them.'

***

Chapter Twenty Five

"Boys Keep Swinging"
David Bowie

'Are you going to say hi to Dirga?' Kenari asked Mirah.

'No, my man's busy,' she answered quickly.

We all knew that she was feeling insecure. We saw Dirga making small talk and laughing with some of the pretty girls down there. I couldn't help but sympathise.

Danu stood out among the crowd because he was so tall, although he lacked the charisma of the others. By comparison, Ray and Agam clearly demanded all the attention; musicians, girls, officials and the media were constantly fawning around them. Hard Wire's management greeted Agam first while the other rock stars and celebrity girls went for Ray and his girl Diah.

I gushed as I spied on Agam who seemed to be speaking seriously to the Hard Wire team. Then, his head lifted, and our eyes locked.

Flashbacks of that night in his car filled my mind for just a split second. It was enough to make my heart pound. His eyes laughed, and he gave me that half-smile of his. I smiled back shyly.

'Agam,' Kenari whispered. 'He was staring at you. Let's go and say hi.'

Nothing seemed to escape her.

'No, I don't want to. Danu's there and I want to avoid him.'

'Oh my god, you must be a wreck.'

'Tell me about it.'

'I need the toilet, now,' she whispered.

'Yeah, let's go,' I said, standing up. 'Anyone else need to go?'

'Not me,' Soraya shook her head.

'Me neither,' said Grace. 'I'll stay with Mirah and Raya and wait for Tio. Don't be long.'

Kenari and I began creeping undetected through the backstage crowd towards the toilets. I frantically tried to light a cigarette when Tio blocked our path. Next to him was Dirga. 'Let me introduce you.'

'We know each other,' said Dirga with a warm smile. '*Hai* girls, looking confident and ready.'

'Thanks,' said Kenari returning the smile.

Dirga tapped Tio on his shoulder, 'You make sure Wanderlust have what they need and that everything is ready for them onstage.'

'Yes, sir,' said Tio eagerly.

'Are you nervous?' Dirga asked us.

Kenari and I nodded in sync.

'I'll help you out with the soundcheck later. Right now, where's my girl?'

'She's up there on the stone benches behind the stage,' said Kenari as she pointed.

'I need to get up there too,' said Tio. 'Come with me.'

***

Unfortunately, there was no way to go to the toilet quickly in a music festival as big as this one.

'Damn it,' said Kenari. 'The lines are massive.'

I was dreading it. At least a dozen teenagers were waiting in each line in front of the six portable toilets at the back of the stadium. Sighing, I followed Kenari to the end of one of the queues.

'How come there's no 'girl only' toilet?' whispered Kenari. 'Do we really have to use the boys' toilets? They're always so filthy, so gross.'

'Don't make me think about it,' I muttered in disgust. 'The organisers don't even think to put toilets backstage, so why would they think about us girls?'

'I guess that's because there's not many of us here.'

I looked around. We were the only girls standing in line. 'Doesn't make it right, though, even if there's only a few of us.'

'Yeah.'

'You know, my mother talked about this event the other night at dinner and it was one of the most torturous conversations I've ever had with her.'

'What was it this time?'

'There's a family lunch on today at my Auntie's. I was supposed to go but I refused. Told her that this is the biggest festival we've ever had a chance to be in since we started. Was I wrong to say that!'

Kenari didn't push it when she saw me lighting another cigarette. I blew the smoke into the open sky as my mind wandered back to that evening. The maddening high-pitched complaints of my mother, about how stupid my band was. About what people would think about her daughter running around performing at a rock concert made by men and for men. I had gone insane, she said.

'This, a rock concert, she said. Rock,' I told Kenari.

Kenari laughed, 'Why don't you tell her, Nooo, Mama, this is metal. Metal!'

I giggled when Kenari emphasised last word, complete with the metal hand gesture.

'As if she cares. She doesn't even know we play punk. You remember she stopped me having music lessons.'

'Geez, my mother would have been the same if I asked for that. Most probably a nightmare like yours.'

We both groaned miserably.

'Listen,' said Kenari, patting my shoulder comfortingly, 'We know as a girl band we've had loads of obstacles, and probably still loads more ahead of us.' Her tone changed. 'What are they again?'

'No music education. Unsupportive mothers. Unsupportive musicians, audiences that don't like us. No girls' toilet.'

She smirked as we inched closer in the queue.

'I know what you're saying, Nari.' I threw the butt on the ground. 'We're here, aren't we?'

'Exactly!'

The toilet door in front of us opened.

'Wish me luck,' she said as she squinted, holding her nose, and cautiously entered the toilet.

Waiting my turn, my thoughts back to how my mother treated me. Yet, from her perspective, I was different from her friends' daughters and she must have been frustrated.

We made our way back as fast as we could, pushing once more through the crowd towards the backstage.

'Why are you pouting like that? Are you still thinking about your mother?'

'Yeah,' I said with a sigh. 'Really fucked with my head this time, hasn't she?'

'She has by the look on your face. What would you do if you were a mother, and you have a daughter that's just like you?'

'Nari,' I objected with amusement.

'Right,' she grinned. 'Imagine, you have this daughter and she's a chain smoker like you, loves hardcore music, and disappears at night doing god knows what in the Jakartan underground with older long-haired guys, or even worse, with punks.'

I smiled at her. 'You do have a point.'

'I do, don't I. So, answer my question.'

I took a moment.

'I would be here,' I finally replied. 'I'd be watching my daughter perform. I would bring my camera and take photos of her proudest moments. I wouldn't have an issue paying for her music lessons. And I'd try to understand the music she likes, even if I didn't like it. And all the boys, I'd want to know them.'

'Yeah, sounds amazing, but what if your husband disagreed? And what if he told you that you can't support your daughter with her outrageous passions and behaviour?'

'I wouldn't marry someone like that in the first place.'

'What kind of guy would you marry?'

'I don't know… a guy who wouldn't think that what we are doing was wrong. A guy who believes that a girl can be in a band and he supports her struggles.'

'Yeah, sure. That kind of guy exists in this world,' she chuckled.

'Don't be sarcastic.'

'Really? Come on, just look at this place, Sigi. They don't even have a girls' toilet.'

I laughed and pushed Kenari's shoulder playfully while she giggled.

'Maybe I'm dreaming. Seriously, though, I'll never settle down until I've found a guy who supports me in whatever I want to do, even if I'm a girl.'

'Amen to that,' Kenari nodded.

***

Backstage, Dirga, Danu and Tio were waiting for us with the girls.

'I'm so cold,' said Mirah as she moved next to me and held my palm in hers. Her hands were freezing, despite the warmth of the late Jakarta afternoon.

'Does Dirga know that you're this nervous?'

'He does. He said he would help us onstage.'

'Yes, that's sweet,' I smiled, remembering his comment to Tio.

'I think he feels sorry for us because we don't have a crew.'

What Mirah said stirred something in me. We didn't have a crew, and, yes, we probably should get one. But who would want to be a roadie for an all-girl band?

'Does Lavatory have their own crew?' asked Grace.

'Their boyfriends help them.'

I sighed and threw a sideways look at Danu.

He had never done anything like that.

Danu smiled back. I had to admit that even though I wasn't that happy to see him, his presence did calm me down somewhat. I would soon be on stage with thousands of guys watching. He edged closer to me.

'Hey, babe. You look pale,' he said. 'Are you nervous too?' 'A lot.'

'Don't be. You can do this. I'm here for you if you need anything-'

'Alright, girls,' Tio cut in. 'It's showtime.'

As we climbed up the wooden stairs, I was surprised that Danu was following.

217

Once we were on big stage, the crowd suddenly started laughing, jeering and cat-calling.

'*Hallo ceweek, hai manis, suiiit suiiit duh mau kemana sih*[61]?'

'*Dangdutan nih kayaknya*[62].'

'*Asiiik, buka baju dong*[63].'

I had anticipated this reaction but it was still uncomfortable. I could feel my cheeks blushing as I took the guitar from its stand and wrapped the strap around me. As I adjusted it, the derision intensified. Then in an instant, the heckling and abuse abruptly came to a halt.

Dirga was standing in the centre of the stage. He glared out at the audience with a force that signalled domination.

The fans stared back in silence as they watched Dirga, their superstar metal musician, turn to help Mirah with her bass effect. Then he slowly made his rounds with each of us, making sure our equipment was ready. Danu was at the front of the stage too, standing on the side, making his presence felt with a stern face.

'That shut them up. Why didn't you tell me that Hell Fury's frontman is your boyfriend?' I heard Tio whisper excitedly to Mirah.

'You didn't ask,' replied Mirah, holding back a laugh.

'Alright, girls,' Tio winked. 'It's time. You've got three songs. Good luck!'

The crowd was still silent as Soraya took hold of the microphone stand.

'Hi everyone. We're Wanderlust, and our first song is "Holidays in the Sun" from the Sex Pistols.'

My hands were shaking as I stared at the chords I was trying to play, trying to concentrate on. Out of the corner of my eye, I saw the audience was intense. It seemed like they weren't even blinking.

---

[61]*Hallo ceweek, Hai manis, suiiit suiiit duh mau kemana sih* loosely translates as 'hello girls, hi gorgeous, what are you up to?'

[62]*Dangdutan nih kayaknya* meaning *'probably dangdut eh?'* It is a genre of modern music that draws upon Malaysian, Hindi and traditional Indonesian styles),

[63]*Asiiik, buka baju dong,* meaning *'nice, get your clothes off!' Dong* is an Indonesian particle used in a sentence for emphasis.

Soraya threw that stand about, and her voice was powerful, filling the stadium with her rendition of the rough British punk accent. I could feel her defiance, mocking the crowd with her lyrics, the insolence in her voice.

When the song was over, there were whistles and claps. I dared to look up at the metal fans, some were even excited.

'Thanks, next, another one from the Sex Pistols. This is "God Save the Queen".'

As my guitar roared, the crowd started to do a little jumping of its own. I was proud, knowing it took a lot to make these metal fans move in a different genre. Most of them had never heard the classic punk songs we were playing. To see them opening up was a pleasure. They were cheering and clapping noisily by the end of our second song.

Then Soraya whispered something to Mirah. Behind the drum-kit, Grace's eyes caught mine.

What was going on?

Mirah's eyes grew big, and the shock registered on her face.

'What is it Raya?' I hissed.

People were clapping even louder, cheering us on for the next song.

'I can't do it,' Soraya shook her head emphatically. 'I cannot sing the last song.'

'But we practised, and you were great,' I lied.

I lied because she was right. Our next song was Nirvana and she made Kurt Cobain sound like an angry British nutter.

'Mirah, you sing it,' Soraya insisted. 'Come on.'

'I am not singing today, I told you guys,' said Mirah just as emphatically, clearly in fear. All her idols were there, watching us, including her own boyfriend. With the huge crowd, it was too much for her.

'What's up, girls?' Tio was crouching behind a large speaker so as not to be seen by the fans. His face was worried. 'Still on for the next song? Guys are going crazy out there.'

'All good. Just give us a second,' I said.

I had to make a quick decision.

'I'll do it. I know the song.' I just hoped I had made the right choice.

Soraya's eyes were anxious while Mirah smiled with gratitude. I adjusted my microphone.

'Hey, Hard Wire,' I yelled shakily.

An immense roar from the crowd swirled around me.

Somehow, I mustered the strength to look at the thousands of guys in front of the stage. I closed my eyes for a few seconds and pretended I was at the radio station, broadcasting with Elang.

'The next song is new. Maybe some of you know it. It's our last song, so thanks for your support. We're Wanderlust, and this is Nirvana's "Smells like Teen Spirit".'

I started to play the intro with my quivering fingers. A few seconds later, I stepped on the guitar effect to activate the distortion and, with the full power mode on, the rest of the girls followed suit.

The audience started going mad. I was shocked.

They love this song!

They began pushing each other, falling into a collective slam-dance. I was laughing inside. It was too good to be true. It wasn't my imagination, this was real.

When the intro gave way to the milder tones. I took a deep breath, and prayed. The crowd slowed down somewhat but they were still transfixed by Wanderlust.

I belted out the chorus and watched in awe. My heart jumped, fast and excited as a sea of metal fans began moving again in one giant crashing black wave.

***

Chapter Twenty Six

"No One's Little Girl"
The Raincoats

Backstage in the VIP area, the rock and metal stars from south Jakarta merely gave Wanderlust a bored cursory glance. The girl looking like a boy singing in a fake British accent didn't excite them.

Agam had been carelessly watching the big screen from a few metres away. He was unimpressed when the camera was mainly focused on Soraya. He went back to talking to his friends.

Then vocalist disappeared, to be replaced by one of the guitarists. He recognised Sigi straight away. A smile broke across his face. The close up of her face on the big screen, singing and playing the guitar. He instantly felt it, those lips that had kissed him.

The response of the crowd was massive. It took Agam back to the time when Lavatory first hit the stage and he had also been impressed by those girls and their knowledge of metal.

As he listened to Sigi's raspy voice fill the backstage, he couldn't take his eyes of her. His thoughts drifted along with the lyrics.

Hearing a commotion, Agam looked behind him. Ray had started a chaotic slamdance with the help of Dayan from The Stupid. He had a feeling of pride as his gaze fell back onto the screen, lost in the song.

***

Kenari broke into the lead. It was a simple solo with an infectious melody line yet it further incited the metal fans into some energetic body slamming. My confidence soared. I never felt as high as I did at that moment.

The song hit the softer tones again. With a burst of emotion, I belted out the last chorus, knowing that I had just a minute left.

As I shouted the final lyrics again and again with Grace's drums banging away powerfully in the background, I realised that my short moment of glory was coming to an end.

I decided to articulate the words as passionate as I could. I was proud as my deep, cigarette-smoking voice, mimicking the pain and sorrow of Kurt Cobain, screamed out across the stadium.

Before I knew it, it was over. I shyly looked around and saw a whole lot of guys yelling and whistling. Some threw their t-shirts on stage and others blew kisses.

I bowed to the crowd, waved my hands and retreated as the MC took over.

'Alright, alright. I know it's hard to let go of these fierce girls. Very soon we'll have the ultimate metal girls from Lavatory on this stage,' he shouted.

The crowd was still roaring.

'All the big names are here, Mortus, Vortex, Suckerhead, Hell's Fury, Roxx and more, so don't go anywhere!'

Music began playing over the sound system to keep the mood while the next band came on stage to set up. We headed down to the backstage area and were greeted by Tio.

'That was insane, Sigi, I didn't know you could sing.'

'That wasn't really singing,' I said while trying to slow down my heartbeat. 'It was just screaming.'

'It was awesome,' said Grace, giving me a hug.

Mirah and Kenari hugged me too.

'If I knew you could sing like that, I'd have given the job to you in the first place,' Mirah gushed. 'That was cool.'

'Well done, girls, the stadium went wild. Great job, Sigi,' screeched Kenari. 'You rocked!'

I was beyond happy. It went better than I could ever have imagined. I noticed Soraya standing aside staring at me with her sour expression. I didn't know what to make of it, so I pretended I didn't see her.

As I glanced away, another pair of eyes met mine with a different sort of look. Agam was beaming from the VIP area.

***

The media wanted to do a quick interview with Wanderlust. They took our photos too, although we never saw the result of the discussion published anywhere.

The sports field was packed by the time twilight had set in. Flatlining opened the evening for the famous bands. They played flawless covers from Kreator and Sepultura. Mortus continued the show, followed by Commotion of Resources.

Meanwhile, Danu had clung to my side. It was frustrating. I tried to ditch him a few times, when I left to buy cigarettes and then again when I was having a bite to eat with the girls. I also tried hiding around the corner of the backstage with Mirah, but he always managed to find me.

'God, he annoys me,' I whispered to the girls. 'He keeps wanting to hold my hand, and I don't know how to get rid of him.'

'Put your hands in your pockets,' giggled Kenari.

I gave her a friendly shove.

'He wants to make sure no one else can claim you,' Grace joined in. 'He must love you too much. Maybe you should take him back.'

'I want other boys to claim me,' I groaned. 'He's so lame.'

Just as I finished speaking, he wrapped his arm around my shoulders and leaned in. 'What are you girls whispering about?'

My reaction was to push him away. 'Why do you want to know? It's girl's stuff.'

'Ok,' he said awkwardly.

We ignored him. Grace looked at him sympathetically for a bit, but she soon decided to ignore him as well. We chatted amongst ourselves until he walked away, mumbling something about getting a drink.

'You're mean,' said Kenari laughing.

'Ssssh, I'm glad he's gone,' I said. 'You know he's constantly been trying to hold my hand like I'm still his girlfriend. Funny enough, he never wanted to hold my hand in public when I was his girlfriend.'

'Yeah, I noticed that,' Grace nodded. 'Boys, huh, always want what they can't have.'

The MC announced the next band; it was Lavatory. I had to watch them. This senior girl band had the crowd's support from the moment they stepped on stage. No mocking! No heckling! The audience went absolutely mad for them. I felt a bit of jealousy creeping in as they took over the stadium with their cover of Kreator. The fans were moving, slamming and headbanging.

'How come we decided to play punk instead of metal?' I asked Mirah.

'We still don't have the skills for that,' she laughed.

We stood there, mouths open. They were brilliant.

Razzle followed and, in the growing darkness, the stage lighting created a wilder, more exhilarating mood. The crowd began dancing and headbanging when Robbie sang 'Welcome to the Jungle' with his perfect Axl Rose impersonation.

Next was Hell's Fury. Mirah's eyes were glued to the stage, proudly watching her man rule over the fans. I, on the other hand, was suddenly bored. Yes, the stage was grand, the energy was incredible, but I felt that I had just about had enough of it. My feelings surprised me. I wished I was enjoying the music like everyone was. Well, almost everyone.

'Where's Soraya,' I asked Grace.

'She went home a while ago.'

'I might head off soon too. '

'Don't you want to see Vortex?' asked Kenari. 'They're on after this. Then it's Roxx and that's the end of the festival.'

I looked around to where the Vortex boys had been. They were nowhere in sight. Normally I would do anything to see Agam perform. Somehow, I wasn't in the mood.

'I'm tired of Danu constantly trying to get with me. I'm going to go home.'

'No, let's just hide out in the crowd,' suggested Kenari. She pulled my hand and dragged me away from the VIPs in the backstage and out with the fans. We blended in, well, almost, and looked around for a good spot.

Dirga and his crew were rocking the stage. They were brutal. Dirga looked fantastic with his long curly black hair, singing, or more accurately, growling to Obituary covers. The cheering and screaming increased as Hell's Fury finished their set.

The Vortex crew took over, plugging in their equipment and going through their last soundcheck. The crowd pushed ever closer to the stage as the frenzied atmosphere kept building.

'*Salam Metaaal*[64],' the MC yelled. 'I know you can't wait any longer for this next act, so let's welcome on stage Vor-texxxxx!'

The fans began screaming again as we watched Agam and the boys give an enthusiastic wave. I sighed. His fair skin and long blonde hair were glowing under the stage lights. Ray stood in front of the mike, fair skin and long black hair down past his shoulders, wearing black leather pants and a black singlet.

Ray started to growl and the mass of black in front of the stage began thrashing around as a swirling mosh pit emerged. Kenari and I pushed further back to avoid being crushed.

Vortex had a good start. They played some original songs with style, headbanging together. There was so much energy with the loud distortion and the speedy thrashing on the double pedal drums.

'They're awesome,' gushed Kenari. 'I still can't believe you kissed Agam. I'd die before I could pull a stunt like that.'

'I wasn't thinking.'

'Good you weren't.'

Deep inside, I began to feel numb. The more I listened to the music, the more I realised that I had never really connected with thrash metal. Yes, it was wild and extreme, but, for me, it had little to no rhythm and not much of a melody that could hook me into becoming a real fan.

It hit me.

The only thing I enjoyed about the whole metal scene was the look and the performance of the musicians. These older guys were sexy, powerful, and cool in my eyes and in the eyes of thousands of other girls. That was it.

'I'm tired. I'm going to go home.'

'Don't you want to watch them until the end?'

I shook my head while I tried to think of a good explanation. I couldn't tell her that we were still naïve with stars in our eyes, even

---

[64] *Salam Metal* loosely translates as 'Hail metal fans!'

though we had our own band. We still lusted over these guys like stupid little girls. 'I'm exhausted and not in the mood to face Danu because he'll find me again no matter what. I'm going now while no one knows.'

'Alright, Sigi. You were great. I'll call you tomorrow.'

'Thanks, Nari. Bye.'

I pushed through the wild audience and wove my way past the police security, through the expansive lobby, down the front stairs, and out onto the street. I relished in the newfound sense of freedom.

***

That night before I went to bed, I picked up my diary. After reading the previous entries, I turned the page and picked up my pen.

It seems like forever I've been in the world of underground metal. I began as a fan, and then we formed our own band. But some still called us groupies.

What do they know? Why would they say that? It's like being called a prostitute and a slut because I'm myself. I never heard Agam or any other guys being called that, and they're just themselves.

Then again, who the hell cares? I'm a musician in a band, and we rock. We proved it by what just happened in that stadium. I'm determined to focus on the band, not the boys... or whatever people say about us. Wanderlust is different, so different that it will shake the underground to its core. They'll see it. Of that, I'm sure.

I think I'm now an official misfit in this society, in this culture. I don't belong in my school. I don't belong in my family. Hell, I don't even feel like I belong in my own gender... I should've taken up baking or sewing instead of being in a punk band. Yet I've never felt as elated as I do right now. I've met the Young Offender, a group of fellow misfits just like me. Now I know I am not alone.

I am Sigi, a misfit in society, and that's ok.
Anyone who doesn't like it can just fuck off.
I am going to rule the underground scene.
And that's a promise.

***

226

About the Writer

Meita Kasim began writing in the 1990s as a creative scriptwriter with Hard Rock FM Jakarta, a pioneer lifestyle and entertainment radio station. At the same time, she worked as one of their Music Directors, Radio DJs, and Radio Show Producers.

She has remained the front lady of Wondergel, the most influential all-girl band to emerge from the 90s underground music scene in Jakarta.

In early 2000 Meita moved to Bali and continued her career as a Radio DJ and Program Director at Hard Rock Radio. She maintained her focus on writing by becoming a full-time writer for the magazine *The Beat* and *Let's Eat!*.

By 2008, she had built The Beat United, her international music agency. She also worked part-time as a festival worker for events such as the Ubud Writers and Readers Festival and Earth Day.

After moving to Hong Kong in 2011, Meita worked briefly as a part-time DJ and a language teacher at the Hong Kong Language Learning Center. Upon her return to Bali three years later, she gathered her thoughts on her life as a teenage female rock musician in the 90s and worked on her debut novel with her colleague and editor, Dr Margie Ellery.

Meita is now living in Vienna, Austria.

She can be contacted via email: at mkasimkarner@gmail.com.

About the Editor

Dr Margie Ellery was raised on a farm in Balingup in southwest of Western Australia. She has had a life-long passion for music, reading, languages, travelling, research, and writing. Margie didn't finish high school; instead, she left early, and her first job was working in a library. She soon moved on to other opportunities and was employed in the mining sector throughout the late 1970s and the 1980s. During these years, she travelled widely to Europe and South-East Asia, and she lived for some time in London, Singapore, Malaysia, and Indonesia.

A chance discussion with a friend in the 1990s gave me the enthusiasm to enrol at the University of Western Australia (UWA). She completed her Bachelor's in English in 1996 and graduated with First Class Honours in 1998. The University encouraged her to undertake a Doctorate, and she taught at UWA during this period. Her thesis researched the linkages throughout the Cold War between American politics and international politics, global nationalistic movements, major world religions, and indigenous spiritualities. She was awarded her PhD in 2008.

Since then, she has worked in the Western Australia prison education system and spent several years in Health and Safety in the construction industry.

She has also lived for many years in Bali and worked in Jakarta, teaching English and American literature. She recently divided her time between Australia and Indonesia, mainly in Java, where she was actively involved in numerous music communities. She has worked on several Indonesian music narratives in both print and film. Her favourite past-time was attending major music festivals in West Java.

However, with the current covid restrictions, Margie has returned to Western Australia. She works for the Dyslexia Foundation while running her own private tutoring business for primary, high school, and university students.

She can be contacted via email: at mjellery@gmail.com.